D0272580

THE THIRD DEGREE

A vicious Chinese Triad gang has lost thousands on a racing tip from Mattie Stuart and they want their money back. Mattie, an ex-jockey turned trainer, needs to give them a certain winner—or else. In despair, Mattie turns to old friend Eddie Malloy for help, but his attempt to bail out Mattie lands them both in trouble. A high-tech fraudster is conspiring to bring down the bookmaking industry and Eddie finds himself trapped between this ingenious criminal and the savage Triads. But while Eddie is seeking a way out, someone else is looking for him, to reveal a devastating secret ...

THE THIRD DEGREE

by

Richard Pitman

Magna Large Print Books
Long Preston, North Yorkshire,
England.

British Library Cataloguing in Publication Data.

Pitman, Richard
  The third degree.

  A catalogue record for this book is
  available from the British Library

  ISBN 0-7505-1320-9

First published in Great Britain by Hodder & Stoughton, a
division of Hodder Headline PLC, 1997

Published in Large Print 1998 by arrangement with Hodder
& Stoughton Ltd.

Magna Large Print is an imprint of
Library Magna Books Ltd.
Printed and bound in Great Britain by
T.J. International Ltd., Cornwall, PL28 8RW.

One

At Newbury racecourse on a bleak November day Eddie Malloy was hoisted into the saddle of a 7-1 chance called Chatscombe. Eddie's previous sixty-two mounts had been losers and as his toes in paper-thin boots automatically found the cold stirrup irons he tried to convey to Chatscombe's anxious trainer a composure he didn't feel.

Although most will deny it publicly there has never been an established jockey whose confidence in his own ability has completely withstood a long run of losers. The guys eking out a living by constantly riding poor horses grow accustomed to few visits to the winner's enclosure but riders in Eddie's league were used to several winners a week. When that ratio drops the doubts set in and eat away at confidence and, sometimes, nerve.

There was no way Eddie Malloy could have guessed that the result of this race and the performance of a horse called Carpathian in the next race were to have a devastating effect on his life.

Another man whose future would be put in jeopardy within the following half-hour was Mattie Stuart, a trainer and friend of Eddie Malloy's. Unlike Eddie, Mattie had foreknowledge that trouble was brewing but as it was to turn out, he badly underestimated the size of the cauldron.

While Eddie was on his way to the post Mattie was nervously following his big bay horse, Carpathian, around the pre-parade ring. It would be Carpathian's first ever run and Mattie had told some very dangerous people that the horse would win at a good price. If it lost Mattie thought the main consequence would be to plunge him even deeper into debt with these moneylenders. Violence hadn't really crossed his mind.

As Malloy cantered to the start on Chatscombe he could almost feel the drag of the previous sixty-two losers pulling him back, anchoring him like another sixty-two pounds in his weightcloth. He was nearing his thirtieth birthday now and as the horse moved in steady rhythm Eddie reflected on the past and wondered about the future. He'd begun his career at seventeen and was champion jockey at twenty-one before finding himself warned off for five years for alleged involvement with a doping ring.

At the end of that long ban Eddie

was instrumental in proving he'd been framed and the Jockey Club returned his licence to ride. But in racing a jockey can be forgotten after five months; five years is a lifetime and Eddie had found it impossible to get back into the top division. The failure haunted him; the injustice of his warning off rankled still. He'd spent eighteen months in jail for taking revenge on the man who'd framed him and that sentence had left a residue of shame and bitterness.

As Eddie neared the starting gate a sudden squall of rain, helped by cold gusts of wind, spattered his flimsy yellow silks. Grimacing he lowered his head against it wondering once more why he was still trying to make a living at this stressful, uncomfortable, bone-breaking, dangerous business. He had other talents, potentially much more lucrative.

Since embarrassing the police and the Jockey Club Security Department by single-handedly tracking down the doping culprits five years previously, Eddie's innate sense of justice had got him involved in solving other serious crimes in racing. His success had led to job offers (with long remunerative contracts) from a major insurance company and an Arab Sheikh. He'd turned them down. He'd made his comeback determined to be champion jockey once again and had enough ambition and hope left to give it at least this one more season. Whether those job offers would remain open when he did hang up his boots was another matter.

He gathered Chatscombe's reins, which alerted the horse to the task ahead, and joined the other ten runners falling into place among the circling horses.

He rubbed a badly bruised left knee still painful from yesterday's fall at Ludlow and contemplated the small profit he'd make from the riding fee as there was no chance he'd be up for any winning percentage in this race. Chatscombe needed the sun on his back, not a north-easterly blowing up his tail, before he'd consent to exert himself. No, this was just another day of going through the motions.

The Sheikh had offered him £150,000 a year plus expenses. He managed a wry smile as the starter called them into line and he pulled down his goggles.

Chatscombe had had five runs over hurdles the previous season. This was his first time over fences, which are considerably bigger than hurdles and much more solidly built.

Hurdles are easy to knock over, fences impossible. As he steered Chatscombe towards the first Eddie adopted his normal policy with fencing debutantes.

Jockeys riding first-time chasers often feel a slight apprehension stirred by the unknown or even an excitement because a change to bigger jumps can rejuvenate a jaded horse. Eddie felt neither then and it was probably these relaxed vibes that made Chatscombe feel he was in charge.

While Eddie pondered his future he rode on automatic pilot pivoting as one with his mount who took the stiffish fences in his stride just as a riderless horse seems to do. Drivers often negotiate miles of road when deep in thought or dog tired only to jerk back into the real world with no recollection of the missing miles. This was the case with Eddie and it was only when the blur of colour materialised into a shouting, waving mass of humans that he realised he was only three lengths adrift of the leader with two fences to jump.

Eddie loved coming with a late run and had he been riding winners recently he would have relished timing his challenge to lead yards before the finish. But he was a man out of luck so he went straight for his whip, almost losing it in his haste, and gave a surprised Chatscombe a crack that would have brought a dead horse back to life.

The novice had got to a challenging position without the help of his rider and now, having been so forcefully reminded that he was not in charge after all, downed tools and sulked, getting his stride all wrong going to the last fence and landing in a heap albeit still upright. The leader also took the fence by its roots to land walking which set the race up for a finish between one tired horse and one unwilling one.

The natural rhythm Eddie had unwittingly established with Chatscombe was gone and the jockey realised as he scrubbed and kicked that he and the horse were totally out of synch. But they inched closer to a breathless Bobby Tobin who desperately urged a half-winded Grey Settler to keep his Roman-nosed head just in front and as they crossed the line Eddie knew he'd failed by six inches to end his bad run.

His sixty-third loser. Eddie cursed as he pulled up and turned the horse back towards the exit from the course. Bobby Tobin on the winner cantered up alongside him and said as he loosened his chinstrap a notch, 'Jesus, that was hard work!' He was noticeably breathless.

'Yeah, you're getting past it,' Eddie said.

'And when did you last ride a winner?' the victor teased.

'When the Pope was an altar boy.'

'Want me to remind you what it feels like?'

'No, thanks. I've got some old videos at home. Maybe I'll watch them tonight.'

'Black and white?'

'Ha bloody ha!'

Tobin, smiling, trotted off in front as they headed back behind the stands towards the unsaddling enclosure. In the betting ring Eddie could hear bookies calling odds on the photo finish, trying to squeeze another few pounds out of the race before the official result was called. They were offering 5-1 against Chatscombe and no price against Tobin's. An option to back the loser only. Eddie shook his head slowly; no wonder bookmakers got themselves bad reputations.

As he rode Chatscombe into the bay reserved for the second horse and dismounted to debrief the trainer he couldn't understand why the result had not yet been announced. As he undid the girth and slipped the saddle squeaking off the sweat-stained horse the PA blared: 'In the third race, the judge has called for a further print.'

Eddie and Neil Bradbury, Chatscombe's trainer, looked at each other in puzzlement then Eddie caught Tobin's equally quizzical glance. The judge normally called for a full print of the photo finish only when the result looked desperately close. A murmur went through the crowd around

11

the unsaddling enclosure and the handful of pressmen huddled together mumbled to each other. A minute or so later the announcer's voice silenced everyone: 'Here is the result of the third race: first, number four, Chatscombe; second ...'

Even over the noise of the PA Eddie heard Tobin say, 'You have got to be kidding!'

But there was no mistake. The print of the photo was posted in the public areas and many more people than usual flocked around it to see that Chatscombe had indeed won by a very short head.

In the changing room Tobin sat in shell-shocked silence. Eddie, still mystified, patted him sympathetically on the shoulder as he passed then changed into a set of blue and white hooped colours and went out to ride in the next. His losing sequence broken, he walked into the paddock with more confidence. Halfway across Mattie Stuart fell in beside him, slipping an arm around Eddie's shoulders. 'Eddie, I've seen sleight of hand a few times but that's the first time I've seen sleight of head! Well done.'

'Thanks, Mattie.'

Mattie steered him towards the centre of the lawn then turned him so they were facing each other, close together. Eddie saw immediately that Mattie was over-excited and nervous. He'd seldom seen the trainer completely calm but he was normally ebullient, optimistic. He was starey-eyed today, talking too fast as he gave Eddie instructions on riding Carpathian.

At five feet nine Mattie was the shorter of the two men by an inch. He'd put on less than half a stone since retiring as a jockey ten years previously, the extra weight taking the gauntness from his frame. Mattie was forty-two but his collar-length hair was still thick and dark. His mouth was wide and thin-lipped, his blue eyes deepset and narrow. With his hat low he looked mean and dangerous.

Eddie Malloy's dark hair was mostly hidden under his crash helmet though a few soft curls escaped at the back. The biting winter wind made the short livid scar on his left cheekbone look almost translucent against his pale skin. His deep blue eyes were narrow, his face thinner than normal from recent fasting. Unusually for a veteran jump jockey he had most of his teeth and they were strong and white.

Eddie wore blue and white silks, colours he knew were Mattie's which meant he owned the horse as well as trained it, a fairly unusual combination. The only reason ninety-nine per cent of trainers

13

bought horses was to sell them on. Let someone else take the risk, pay the training fees. None had ever made a fortune training his own horses.

Eddie let Mattie talk himself out, which took a while, then he looked inquisitively at him and said, 'What the hell's wrong with you? You on speed or something?'

Mattie laughed nervously and squeezed Eddie's arm again. 'Nothing like that. I just need a winner. This winner. Be all right then. No problem. Everything'll be fine if ...'

He was off again. Eddie gripped his arm this time. 'Hey, calm down, Mattie! Don't fret so much!' Looking at Eddie, Mattie felt the panic rise and had to fight it. For a second he was tempted to tell him how crucial this was for him but he didn't want to pass the pressure, the nerves, to Eddie. That's when jockeys make mistakes and after that long run of losers the last thing Eddie needed was more pressure.

The tension was broken when they were joined by a blonde woman in a long camel coat and suede boots with three inch heels. The coat was buttoned to the neck and on the right collar was a small diamond brooch. The woman's eyebrows were as fair as her hair which when Eddie saw it close up looked to have some darker

14

tendrils among the soft and luxuriant natural blondeness.

Her eyes were a rich hazel with the odd tiny black speck, her skin pale and smooth. She wore mascara, but no lipstick on her generous mouth. Eddie reckoned she'd be in her mid-twenties and he was sure he knew her.

She leaned forward to allow Mattie to kiss her gently on both cheeks and waited to be introduced to the jockey. Mattie said, 'Eddie, you remember Rebecca ...'

Eddie smiled, holding out his hand. 'I'm sure we've met before, I ...'

Rebecca smiled wide showing brilliant white teeth. 'But you're not sure where,' she teased.

Eddie still held her hand. She didn't pull it away. 'It'll come back to me.'

'In time for you to ride in this race?'

'Hopefully.' Eddie smiled now and it seemed that both of them had completely forgotten that Mattie was there.

Rebecca said, 'I'm Granville Bow's daughter.'

Eddie said, 'Of course. I used to ride for your father years ago! How old would you have been then?'

'Thirteen, fourteen. I remember you much better than you remember me. Had a major crush on you along with half my class at school.'

15

'No doubt your tastes have improved since then,' Eddie said.

'Don't bet on it,' Rebecca said, and finally let go of his hand.

'Well, now that you two are re-acquainted,' interrupted Mattie, 'I can tell you that Rebecca's got a couple of good horses with me and we're going to win lots of races.' He put his arm around her shoulder and pulled her close and Eddie wondered if there was more than a trainer/owner relationship there. Mattie was a bit of a ladies' man and had been married and divorced three times. He was as optimistic about his women as his horses.

Rebecca smiled at Eddie again and said, 'Maybe you'll accept my invitation to ride some time?' and Eddie nodded slowly trying to figure out if the glint in her eye was one of devilment or simple fun.

The mounting-up bell sounded and Carpathian's lad turned the horse in onto the lawn of the parade ring. Eddie saw that Mattie's nervousness had returned as they walked towards the big gelding. He glanced at Rebecca and detected an uneasiness there too. He swung into the saddle wondering what exactly was at stake here.

Within twenty-four hours he found out.

Two

Eddie travelled home to his flat in Shropshire that night with just the one winner under his belt but it was one more than he'd managed for quite a while so he was pleased. He'd been disappointed for Mattie when Carpathian had broken down so badly on the first circuit. Eddie had pulled him up immediately but he knew from experience that it was most unlikely the big horse would ever race again.

After the race Mattie had seemed almost shell-shocked and Rebecca Bow had shared his dazed expression but neither said anything significant to him so Eddie had expressed his sympathy and left to hurry home. He had an important dinner that evening.

Dark curly hair still damp from the shower, Eddie was in his best navy suit and just knotting his blue and yellow tie when the phone rang. He glanced at the clock as he picked up the receiver: 7.50. It was Mattie, he still sounded on edge.

'Eddie, you're riding at Taunton to-morrow?'

'That's right.'

17

'Listen, I've got two runners there.'

Eddie looked anxiously at his watch. 'Sorry, Mattie, I'm already booked in ...'

'No, no, no, I don't want you to ride for me, well not at Taunton. I wondered if you'd like to leave home a bit earlier and drop in here in time for the second lot?'

Eddie held back an impatient sigh. Riding out for Mattie would mean getting up before five. He'd been hoping to have a reasonably relaxed dinner and a couple of drinks. He decided it was worth trying to wriggle out of the offer. 'Mattie, listen, I ...'

'I'd like you to ride work on King Simba.'

King Simba. Mattie's stable star, so precious to the trainer that he'd sweated and worked to regain fitness and re-apply for his jockey's licence so he could ride the horse himself. King Simba had already won two of the biggest races that season and whatever Mattie's reasons were Eddie would have been foolish to refuse this chance to sit on the horse.

'Okay, Mattie, I'll be there.'

'Good. And I thought that maybe we could travel to Taunton together.'

'Sure, why not?'

'Good. Don't be late then, will you?'

'I'll be there around eight.'

'That's fine.'

Although anxious to get off the phone Eddie felt obliged to ask how Carpathian was.

Mattie sighed and said, 'He's in bad shape but who knows, maybe we can do something after a year's rest.'

Eddie smiled. That was more like the old Mattie; never say die. They said their goodbyes and Eddie went to the mirror to finish tying his tie. He looked at himself and wondered what was behind Mattie's invitation to ride King Simba. Why hadn't he mentioned it at Newbury that afternoon?

Eddie slid the knot to the top button of the white Jermyn Street shirt and leant closer to the mirror. His fine-boned face still glowed from the scrubbing in the hot shower, the one inch crescent scar on his cheekbone raised and pink. Eddie couldn't make up his mind whether to be proud of that scar or not. A few jocks had them, mostly from spills on the track. Eddie had got his when a man had bitten him as he lay trussed up in the boot of a car.

A couple of minutes later he was ready for the short walk across the yard to Charles's house. Caterers had been brought in to provide dinner and Eddie imagined he could smell the succulence of the cooking meat floating on the evening air. After a bout of fasting it had been a while since he'd eaten a decent meal.

Just as he was leaving the phone rang again. He was tempted to leave it but was aware it could be a trainer offering an important ride. It wasn't. It was Kenny MacAdam, a jockey Eddie knew well. Eddie cursed himself silently for answering the phone.

Kenny said, 'Eddie, how you doing?'

'Not bad, Kenny, but I'm under pressure for time, I'm afraid, been summoned by the big boss, you know how it is?'

'Yeah, know it well. Old Indian saying: "He who pays retainer has jockey by the bollocks." '

Eddie managed a smile. 'Not quite as bad as that but I've got to put in an appearance in about two minutes.'

'Don't worry. It was just something I thought you'd want to know thinking of your interest in all things mysterious.'

'I'm listening.'

'That winner you rode today, the one you thought you were beat on?'

'Uhuh?'

'Exactly the same thing happened to me at Stratford a couple of weeks ago. I was certain I was beat, a longish short head, I thought. Took the horse into second spot then bugger me if they don't announce me as the winner! I'll tell you summat, Eddie, I make as many mistakes as the next fool riding horses for a living but I wasn't wrong that day. That horse did not win that race. Sure, I took my percentage and I banked my present, you've got to go with the flow, as you know, but I rode a loser and I know it.'

Eddie had been involved in enough scrapes to recognise even the remotest tinkling of alarm bells. Kenny's tale made him uneasy but he hadn't the time right then to discuss things. His final comment was non-committal and Kenny seemed happy that he'd done his duty.

Eddie switched on the answerphone, made a final check of his slim frame in the full length mirror and headed quickly downstairs and across the yard towards the big house, his quick footsteps echoing off the cobbles out into the winter night.

Three

Rising in the darkness of a chilly morning and hurriedly pulling on jodhpurs and a warm sweater was nothing new to Eddie Malloy. He'd been doing it most of his adult life. Even when he'd been warned off he'd worked out of an old caravan breaking rogue horses for a dealer. Five years of that had taught him never to curse the opportunity he had of getting up early every day to do something he loved.

As Eddie made coffee he reflected happily on his dinner last night with Charles Tunney and Gary Rice. Gary was his main employer. He owned the training stables and the surrounding estate. He employed Eddie to ride for him and Charles Tunney to train his string of twenty-two horses. Gary also supplied the flat Eddie lived in which was in a converted barn overlooking the yard.

Last night the multi-millionaire owner had confirmed that he was in the market for another ten horses. He told a surprised and delighted Charles he had a budget of £250,000. Eddie respected Charles's judgement knowing he was now looking at a potential source of some twenty more winners a season.

He sipped black coffee in the small kitchen and reached to touch wood as the thought came to him that maybe yesterday's winner had broken his run of bad luck. Five minutes later he was in his car and heading south for Lambourn to fulfil his promise to Mattie Stuart.

Mattie was a lower ranking trainer whom Eddie had known for more than ten years. To some, Mattie was the most optimistic and enthusiastic man in racing who saw all of his geese as swans and never let any setback get him down for long. To many others Mattie was a clown who proclaimed talent in every animal he handled just in case he ever turned out to be right with one of them. Eddie, quick to recognise a fellow underdog, liked Mattie and rode for him whenever bookings allowed.

At 7.56 that morning Eddie steered his blue Audi into Mattie's driveway and parked in the bow-shaped tarmac area close to Mattie's house. The front door looked freshly painted in a searing lemon gloss which reflected the bright morning sun into Eddie's narrowed eyes as he approached it.

Eddie knocked and turned the handle as he usually did but the door was locked. He took a step back in surprise then hammered hard with the heel of his right hand. 'Come on, Mattie, you lazy sod. Get up!'

In black jodhpurs, ankle length riding boots and a multi-coloured crew-necked sweater, Eddie stood swinging his riding helmet and whip waiting for the door to be opened. If he'd been standing a couple of paces back he'd have seen the edge of the curtain move slightly behind the kitchen window. A few seconds later the door was opened.

Mattie stood there white-faced wiping at

his mouth with a blue-checked tea towel. He too wore jodhpurs, khaki-coloured, and his ankle boots were of blue rubber. A yellow open neck polo shirt showed bushy chest hair, much of it greying. As the tea towel swung it revealed stains down the front of the shirt which looked to Eddie like vomit.

Concerned, Eddie looked up at Mattie. 'What's wrong?'

Dazed and silent Mattie took a few tottering steps backwards opening the door slowly wider. Eddie went up the two stone stairs and into the kitchen. Mattie closed the door and turned the key in the lock.

Out of the sunlight now Eddie saw just how pale Mattie's face was. There was a long pine table in the centre of the room with a bench running either side. Eddie took Mattie gently by the arm and sat him on the bench closest to the sink to which he then turned to get the trainer a drink of water. The stainless steel sink was blocked with vomit. Dishes and cutlery lay askew on the pale blue worktop and at least one mug had shattered on the brown stone floor tiles.

Eddie found a glass and filled it with water. He took it to Mattie and sat silently opposite till Mattie was ready to talk. Eddie watched him. It was the first time for a while he'd seen Mattie without a hat and he noticed the increasing grey in his dark hair, the faraway look in his deepset blue eyes.

The trainer wiped his mouth again and tried to smile. 'Sorry, Eddie. Slight unexpected contretemps with some of my creditors. Was just throwing up in the sink when you knocked. Excuse the mess.'

Eddie said, 'What happened? Did they beat you up?'

'Only mentally. Have ... have a look in the living room.'

Eddie swung his legs clear of the bench and walked through the open door to the living room. Although he lived alone, Mattie was proud of his house. The decor was stylish, the furniture expensive. Eddie surveyed the room. Patches of blood had been daubed on all the pale yellow walls and on the hide-covered sofa and chairs. Three of the four rugs on the stripped polished yew floorboards were bloodstained. The severed head of Mattie's King Charles spaniel, Jinty, lay against the leg of the coffee table, empty eyes staring at the ceiling.

Jinty's body, battered and wrung free of blood, lay draped across the pale blue shade of the standard lamp in the corner by the window. Eddie went back into

25

the kitchen. Mattie looked at him, eyes filling with tears. Eddie went to him, put a hand on his shoulder then sat down once again opposite him. 'Have you called the police?'

Mattie shook his head slowly and dabbed at the first tear which rolled quickly down his left cheek.

'Why not?'

Mattie, head down, shrugged helplessly, like a child, sounding like one too as he stifled the sobs, trying to speak, eventually managing to say that he didn't know what to tell them, the police.

Eddie sighed inwardly and raised his eyes to heaven and wondered why, why, why he always ended up being drawn into other people's troubles. He often wished he'd been born with the ability just to get up and walk out, the will to say, 'Sorry, not my problem. Good luck and goodbye.'

But he'd never been that way and although he wouldn't admit it, it was a certain conceit that drew him in. Sure, he hated injustice, especially against the small guy, but there was also an element of, 'If I don't help them, who will?'

So he stepped free of the bench again, filled the kettle and asked Mattie to tell him the full story and through tears and shame-tinged embarrassment Mattie did.

Four

After telling his story Mattie was very nervous about venturing out onto the gallops. Eddie persuaded him that the fresh air would do him good and that personally he didn't want to miss the chance to sit on King Simba. He promised Mattie he'd stick close by him and that afterwards they could leave for Taunton together—Eddie would drive.

Mattie agreed. He'd sent his second lot of ten horses out in the charge of the head lad so it was just him and Eddie who trotted out of the yard a few minutes after 8.30. They made their way up onto the high downs. Mattie talked more and Eddie listened, though his attention was slightly distracted by his magnificent mount who felt supremely fit and well. Eddie couldn't wait to get him onto the gallops.

The horse was entered at Cheltenham in two days' time in the Murphy's Gold Cup the first really big handicap 'chase of the season. He was a hot ante-post favourite after two scintillating early season victories. Mattie still hadn't said why he'd asked

Eddie to come and sit on him.

On the gallops Eddie immediately sensed the raw power of the big black horse beneath him. Mattie smiled proudly as he saw the glint in Eddie's eye just before he unleashed the horse up the long green swathe.

King Simba had shown enormous promise as a youngster but had broken down so badly at Haydock two years previously that he'd been within a few minutes of being humanely destroyed. King Simba had been insured for £50,000 and his owner would not collect unless the horse was shot under vet's orders. Mattie had pleaded with the owner, promised to find the fifty grand himself to buy the horse off him.

And he had found it. Mattie had begged, borrowed and re-mortgaged then had faced the prospect of having a badly injured horse to feed and care for with nothing but optimism to keep him going. He had nursed that horse through long days and stormy nights and felt closer to him than to any human being.

Now King Simba was forty-eight hours away from landing the biggest prize of Mattie's career as a trainer. But Mattie's pride in King Simba as he watched the bunching, flexing muscles in the quarters of the big horse carry Eddie Malloy further and further clear of his galloping companions was tinged with sadness and now fear.

Buying and keeping the horse for so long through the least successful period in his career had almost finished him financially. He'd been just on the point of declaring himself bankrupt when the Chinese had paid him his first visit. Well dressed in black suits, white shirts and ties, they'd persuaded him they were businessmen who were willing to take a risk that a good trainer like him could pull through and be successful again. Mattie didn't ask how they'd known he was in such trouble. He'd guessed it was fairly common knowledge in racing circles and that they were simply opportunists. Businessmen. He had never liked to think of them as money lenders. Too distasteful. Too desperate.

But he'd agreed their terms: £100,000 to be paid back in monthly instalments. Interest rates would be kept low if he also supplied information resulting in one good priced winner a month. If no information was forthcoming the interest rate tripled until some did. If he tipped them a loser the rate quadrupled.

The pulled-up Carpathian the previous day had been Mattie's third loser in a row. His debt was now £120,000 and they had warned him that morning that the next tip had to win or they would be back to cut him up rather than his dog. Mattie had immediately offered them King Simba in the Murphy's Gold Cup but they'd rejected it—too short a price. They wanted something priced at least 10-1.

As he sat watching his prize animal fade into the distance Mattie felt very alone. He glanced over his shoulder. No one there. He became aware of the beads of sweat on his brow. Why on earth had he been so naïve? Chinese businessmen. Their business was terror, extortion, racketeering. Their company turned out to be a London branch of that well-known international conglomerate, the Triads.

As King Simba powered up the gallop Eddie smiled through the raw acceleration till the cold wind almost closed his eyes. This was a horse and a half right enough and he felt privileged just to have sat on him. When he finally managed to pull the horse up he turned him and headed steadily back towards his trainer.

Mattie watched them come, the image turning into a victorious walk back into the winner's enclosure at Cheltenham then Kempton for the King George VI Steeplechase then maybe, just maybe, Cheltenham again for the Gold Cup.

It was one of those fine crisp frosty

mornings when you can just smell steeple-chasing in the air and the only sound punctuating Eddie's almost babbled admiration for King Simba was that of the metal shod hooves on the road as they walked back to Mattie's yard.

Before leaving for Taunton Eddie offered to remove Jinty's remains and help Mattie try and clean up the living room. Mattie went upstairs and came back with an old blue hat box with a faded yellow ribbon still in place. He held it out to Eddie. 'Not the most appropriate as coffins go but it's better than an old bin bag. If you'd be kind enough to put the poor little bugger in it and put him in the cellar for now I'll bury him later when none of the lads are around.'

Eddie took the box. 'Do any of them know what happened this morning?'

Mattie shook his head. 'I don't think so. I think almost everybody was out with the first lot. In fact those Chinks arrived just after they'd pulled out. Must have been sitting waiting.'

Mattie stayed in the kitchen while Eddie gently laid the little body in the box then placed the head in, trying to arrange it so it didn't look as though it had been severed, then feeling mildly ridiculous for doing so. He took it down to the cold dark cellar and when he returned he and Mattie decided they wouldn't have time to clean up the bloodstains before leaving.

Eddie said, 'I'll come back after racing and help, if you like.'

Mattie brightened considerably. 'Would you? That would be brilliant. You can stay over if you want.' Almost a plea.

Eddie said, 'I'm sorry, Mattie, I can't.'

'Okay. No problem.' Downcast again.

Eddie had a light breakfast. Mattie still couldn't face eating. The trainer was quiet too during the early part of the journey but as Eddie steered them onto the M5 motorway and pushed the Audi quickly up to ninety Mattie said, 'Eddie, I'd like you to take over on King Simba for the rest of the season.'

Eddie was so surprised he inadvertently eased right off the accelerator. He turned to the trainer. 'In his races, you mean?'

Mattie nodded, looking very serious.

Eddie was baffled, almost incredulous, and he half laughed as he said, 'But he's your ride, Mattie! You sweated blood to get your licence back for him!'

Mattie was staring straight ahead now through the windscreen. 'My nerve's gone, Eddie.'

'Bollocks!'

Mattie nodded, as though confirming it quietly to himself. 'I'm afraid not.

This business this morning decided me for certain. My nerve's gone and my concentration's shot. There's no way I can do the horse justice on Saturday in this state.'

Eddie watched him, waiting for the punchline; jockeys were notorious for playing practical jokes and concocting wind-ups. But Mattie's square jaw was set tight, his stare grim and Eddie realised he was serious. And slowly the impact began to dawn on him. Since his comeback more than five years previously, Eddie had prayed for a horse to put him back in the spotlight.

He'd ridden a few good ones but none that came within a stone of this one. If King Simba stayed sound and his stamina held out he had more than enough class to win a Cheltenham Gold Cup—the true champion's race. And between now and the Gold Cup in March there would be other races for the big horse.

Eddie looked again at Mattie. How do you thank a man for providing the launch pad for one final tilt at glory?

Well, Mattie had his own ideas about that.

Five

After the last race at Taunton Eddie Malloy stood soaping himself in the shower trying to damp down the feeling of elation, the surging certainty that his luck had turned at last; Eddie was a strong believer in not tempting fate.

But the evidence was indisputable. Two winners from two rides today. Two more bookings for rides at Cheltenham on Saturday and, the jewel in the crown—the ride on King Simba for the rest of the season. Eyes shut tight against the stinging shampoo, Eddie allowed himself a smile.

The only downside was what had happened to Mattie that morning. The trainer had been hanging around the weighing room most of the day wearing the hunted look Eddie was already becoming familiar with. He'd seemed to seek Eddie out whenever he could, looking less troubled in his company, almost as though he saw the jockey as a bodyguard. And Eddie didn't quite know how to distance himself from it without hurting Mattie.

As he stepped from the shower and began drying himself, Eddie wondered if this was the price of the ride on King Simba—protection. If so, it was one he didn't want to pay. He wasn't afraid of the Chinese but the commitment to Mattie would be too great. Eddie couldn't possibly be at his side twenty-four hours a day. Besides if Mattie didn't conquer his own fear of them, didn't deal with things himself, what sort of life would he have?

Dried, deodorised and dressed in a dark green suit, pale blue shirt and bright multi-coloured tie Eddie checked himself in the mirror. At the beginning of the season he'd taken to wearing a suit and tie to the races every day. There was so much competition now, that anything that made you stick in the memory of an owner or trainer, anything positive at least, was a bonus.

Most jockeys dressed reasonably smartly but casually. Eddie had spent over £2,000 buying three suits plus accessories. The only solid offers it had got him so far were from a mass market mail order catalogue who wanted him as a model and a couple of others from middle-aged male owners (one a Jockey Club member) to spend a night in a hotel. All were declined.

Within fifteen minutes of them leaving Taunton darkness fell and during the trip home Mattie grew more tense. If any particular car was close behind them for more than a mile he began fretting that they were being followed. Eddie was finding it increasingly difficult to reassure him however much he tried taking Mattie's mind off things with some general chat, some teasing.

Lambourn village was quiet in the dark of that Thursday evening. It was raining steadily as they drove through, the lights of the four pubs shimmering yellow on the wet pavements. Mattie's place lay on the outskirts of the village. When they finally reached it Mattie gave Eddie the keys and asked him to go in first while he waited in the car.

Eddie took the keys but held them out in the flat of his hand. He said, 'Mattie, you're just letting them beat you. You can't live like this, constantly looking over your shoulder.'

He saw a spark of anger in Mattie's eyes but it faded quickly and Mattie said, 'I got a hell of a shock this morning, Eddie. Just give me a chance to get over it.'

Eddie nodded, feeling guilty. He went inside the house, checked each room, switched on all the lights then gave Mattie the all clear. As soon as the trainer got through the door he locked it behind him and let out a long sigh of relief.

Eddie told him to sit down at the kitchen table then he went and got him a large whisky from the drinks' cabinet, filled it with water from the tap and handed it to Mattie who drank half in one gulp then sighed again, running long fingers through his hair and visibly relaxing.

Eddie went back to the car and got his kitbag. Changed back into his jods and jumper he got a basin of water and some cleaning stuff and went to make a start on the bloodstains. Mattie said, 'I'll get changed and help you.'

Eddie put a hand on his shoulder, pushing him back down onto the pine bench. 'You stay there and relax. Just holler when you want another drink.'

Mattie smiled wearily. 'Eddie ... thanks.'

Eddie smiled. 'My pleasure. God, what a man's got to do to get rides these days!'

Mattie tried to stand again. 'Eddie, that wasn't why I offered ...'

Eddie laughed. 'I know. I know it wasn't. Just winding you up.'

Mattie sunk back down not looking as amused as Eddie had hoped. He went into the living room to start cleaning but was back in the doorway within five minutes. Mattie looked up at him. 'Sorry, Mattie, I'm just making it an even bigger mess. I think you're going to have to get your rugs and your suite cleaned professionally. The walls look like a redecorating job, I'm afraid.'

Mattie shrugged. 'Should be fun trying to explain what the stains are.'

'Tell them you had a party for abstract painters.'

'Abstract punters.'

They both smiled. Eddie got himself a drink and refilled Mattie's glass then sat down opposite him. 'Mattie, why don't you just go to the police?'

'Because I'm shit scared those Chinks will come back with their swords.'

'The police will give you protection.'

'Night and day?'

'If necessary.'

'For how long?'

'I don't know. Speak to them. Find out.'

'Eddie, I owe these guys over a hundred grand! What are the cops going to say about that?'

'Doesn't matter if you owe them a hundred million, they can't come here and treat the place like the set for some Kung Fu movie. You're entitled to police protection.'

Mattie sighed and massaged his eyes. 'I'll think about it.' He reached for his drink then sat bold upright as he heard a noise outside. 'Someone's coming!'

Eddie strained to listen and heard the engine of a large vehicle. He went to the door and opened it. Mattie was on

38

his feet backing towards the rear door into the yard. Eddie said, 'It's only your horsebox.'

The two inmates of the horsebox had finished unplaced at Taunton but they were entitled to as much care as King Simba and the lads fed them and bedded them down for the night. Mattie checked their legs for signs of heat and finding both okay he and Eddie went back inside.

Mattie sat quietly at the table for a while then said, 'Eddie, I'm going to try and bargain with them to give them one big priced winner and get them off my back for good.'

Eddie shook his head slowly but decided against preaching again. He knew he often made the mistake of expecting everyone to behave the way he did, to react to things in the same manner. He found it hard to understand when they didn't but had taught himself to accept it. He said, 'It's your choice, Mattie. I'll help you if I can.'

Mattie smiled ironically. 'What I really need help with is finding a winner to give them. A certainty at a good price.'

'Not many of those around, Mattie.'

'Don't I know it.'

'Even if you find it and it scoots in at twenties, do you honestly think they'll settle for just one?'

'I'll get their agreement beforehand.'

'And they're real men of honour by the look of things.'

Mattie gave him a look of admonishment and Eddie apologised for preaching again. Mattie drank and said, 'If you get to hear of anything promising will you let me know?'

'As long as you don't hold me responsible if it gets stuffed.'

'I won't. But I don't want just general gossip. I need something very very solid.'

'I know you do, Mattie. I know you do.'

Mattie nodded slowly and stared at his drink. Eddie felt deep sympathy for him. 'Have they given you a time limit for this next tip?'

'No, but they won't wait long and the longer it takes the more interest piles onto the loan.'

Eddie reached across and squeezed Mattie's forearm. 'I'll do what I can.'

Mattie looked at him warmly. 'Thanks, Eddie.'

Eddie got up. 'Mattie, I'd better go.'

They walked to the door in silence and went outside. Mattie looked at Eddie as he stepped under the outside light. 'Looking forward to Saturday?'

Eddie smiled. 'Never more so. Thanks for the chance to ride him.'

'You deserve it.'

Eddie nodded, his instinct nosing around the unspoken bargain that Mattie was proposing: I'm offering you the ride on King Simba, now for God's sake help me out of this hole.

They looked at each other, white faces suspended in the dark, bodiless. Mattie lowered his eyes and mumbled, 'Think I'll have an early night. Have a safe trip home and I'll see you at Cheltenham.'

Eddie said, 'Call me if you need me.'

Eddie heard the key turn in the lock and again felt a strong surge of sympathy for Mattie as he went to his car.

As Mattie climbed the stairs towards his bedroom his despair deepened. When he finally fell asleep, he was wakened within twenty minutes by the ringing of the phone on the bedside table. The luminous hands of the small alarm clock read eight minutes past two when he dazedly scrambled the receiver from its perch. The shrill menacing Chinese voice demanded, 'You gimme horse now!'

Mattie banged the receiver down almost in terror then scooped it off the hook. Tense and wide-eyed he sank back slowly onto the pillow in the darkness, his only company a disembodied female voice repeating, 'Please hang up and try again ...'

Mattie wept.

41

Six

As Eddie Malloy set off on the Saturday morning for the short journey south from Shropshire he jabbed the radio on, swung right at a junction, flipped the sun visor down against the morning glare and accelerated towards Cheltenham and the dream of three winners.

Eddie thought of the legions of people from all over the country who'd be making their way to Cheltenham that day for the Murphy's Gold Cup, to the purist, the first 'big' race of the season and one that meant the new National Hunt campaign was truly launched. Among those thousands there would be few travelling without some thrill of expectation, anticipation, be they gamblers, owners, trainers, jockeys or stable staff. Organised racing has survived for hundreds of years and Eddie knew it did so not because of the tangibles like money, improved facilities, fine thoroughbreds or inspirational personalities, but because of hope and optimism, the main attributes of most of those involved in the sport.

Hope for most of the punters meant wishing that luck would send at least one winner their way. Two casually dressed middle-aged men on the 9.40 from Paddington to Cheltenham Spa railway station hoped simply for a fairly close photo finish. One, heavily bearded, sat by the window. In the leather holdall at his feet were two very expensive miniature radio communications units and fifty thousand pounds sterling.

Eddie arrived at the course two hours before the first race but several thousand racegoers were already there drinking in the atmosphere of what many considered to be the best National Hunt racecourse in the world. Eddie always felt a sense of pride coming racing at one of the major tracks. It was an ego thing which he admitted only to himself although anyone watching him stride confidently, chin raised, through the milling crowds could have guessed that he felt special.

He was one of the men these people had come to see although few would have recognised him in the navy suit, brilliant white Italian shirt and blue and yellow diamond silk tie, freshly shaven, hair groomed, black shoes gleaming. Once he was in a set of racing silks staring out from beneath his skullcap his face would start to ring a few bells with racegoers. But they would always be the audience. Eddie may not have been a star any more but he was a prominent member of the cast. And that was one of the things that kept him going season after season.

Eddie always got a buzz just being at Cheltenham; riding a winner there was a bonus and on that Saturday he rode two. He won the Murphy's Gold Cup as expected on the evens favourite, King Simba, and won easily. He swore he'd remember for the rest of his life the smile on Mattie Stuart's face as he greeted them after the race. The man's troubles were forgotten, for a while at least.

But it was Eddie's second winner that brought him the most personal pleasure because he rode one of the finest races of his life on a handicap hurdler whose challenge had to be timed to the last possible second. As Eddie brought him coolly to lead a few yards before the winning post he felt a stab of nervous tension as he glanced across to see that he'd won by a longish head, maybe a neck. At that moment he recalled the photo at Newbury and Kenny MacAdam's one at Stratford and, dwelling on those, he was reluctant to take his horse straight into the winner's berth till the result of the photo finish was called.

By the time he'd turned the horse to enter the bottom end of the parade ring going towards the winner's enclosure the PA announcer called the result. He'd won it all right. He smiled and reached down to accept the handshakes and congratulations. After he'd weighed in and changed into his colours for his final ride of the day Eddie came back outside to stand on the weighing room steps and bask in the satisfaction of not just a second winner but a job well done. The praise from his peers for a masterly ride meant more to him than the appreciation of the owner or his share of the prize money.

He stood on the steps smiling stupidly, vaguely aware of the darkening sky and the cold wind rising. The misery and frustration of the past winnerless weeks seemed a long way back. He felt deeply happy, powerful, supremely confident.

He became aware of someone standing by his left shoulder and turned, slightly embarrassed that she may have been there all the time he'd been inwardly congratulating himself. She was about five five and very plump, maybe twelve stone plus, most of it covered by a tent-like brown wool coat. The fine hairs of grey fur on her pillbox hat constantly changed patterns as the wind stirred them. She had greyish, blue eyes and a very smooth complexion. Eddie would have found it hard to guess her age, but his memory banks searched all vaults for a name for he felt he should know her.

Before he could recall it she introduced herself. 'Mister Malloy, my name is Laura Gilpin, I'm a permit trainer.' Eddie placed the accent as North East. She said, 'I hope you don't mind me approaching you like this ...'

Eddie smiled warmly. 'Of course not. I've seen you around when I've been racing and I'm glad to meet you at last.'

She blushed slightly and let go of his hand. 'I thought you rode a brilliant race on Seminole. I think it's about the best ride I've ever seen a horse given.'

Eddie's smile widened and Miss Gilpin felt slightly patronised. She blushed again and said, 'That's not to say I count myself as having great experience, I mean I didn't mean ...'

'Talk about a back-handed compliment,' he teased.

She squirmed slightly, raising her eyes, realising she was digging a hole for herself. Eddie reached to touch her arm. 'I know what you mean, I'm kidding you. Thank you for the compliment.'

She nodded and hesitated as she gathered her thoughts. 'Would it be terribly cheeky of me to ask you to ride for me at Aintree next Saturday?'

Eddie hesitated but could think of no

other commitments. 'Which race?'

'The novice hurdle.'

'Fine. I'd be delighted to.'

'Brilliant!'

Eddie watched her smile with genuine pleasure, something he seldom saw, and he liked her for that. Her enthusiasm started bubbling and she got excited as she told him about the horse which was to have its first run at Aintree. She said she thought it might be very useful but was convinced from its work at home that it needed holding up till the last strides, like Seminole. And would there be any way at all he could come up and have a sit on the horse before Saturday?

'Remind me again where you train?' Eddie asked.

Miss Gilpin looked slightly sheepish. 'Alnwick,' she said quietly.

'The Alnwick, Northumberland?'

She nodded, slightly tense in case he'd change his mind. Eddie said, 'Do they still check your passport at the border?'

She smiled again, knowing now he'd accept, and said, 'Yes, same place as they issue the oxygen mask and ice axe.'

'Okay, when?'

'Well Sedgefield's on on Thursday. I thought maybe if you had a couple of rides there you could have come to me in the morning.'

'I don't know what the northern jocks'll think of a stranger in the camp but I'll see what I can do.'

'Brilliant!'

Eddie reached to shake her hand again. 'See you Thursday,' he said.

'Okay.' She walked away across the parade ring lawn, smiling. Eddie called after her. 'What's the horse called?'

She turned. 'Samson's Curls.'

Eddie's puzzled look said, 'Odd name.'

Miss Gilpin said, 'By Sharpen Up out of Delilah's Dilemma.'

He smiled. 'Nice one, Laura.'

She raised a hand in a small goodbye wave and set off again, the spring in her step belying her bulk. Eddie shook his head and said to himself, 'I must be crazy.' Then he went inside to get ready for the next race.

As Eddie's head popped through the neck of the green and gold silks he found the slight figure of Kenny MacAdam beside him. Kenny wore his usual wide smile as though he knew something nobody else did. Mid-thirties, he had red hair, a big nose and ill-fitting dentures. And Kenny could talk non-stop; he was the weighing room gossip. Eddie's heart sank a bit when he saw him but he tried not to show it.

'How you doing?' Kenny asked.

'All right at the moment. How are you?'

'Well *I've* not rode two winners today so make your own mind up!'

Eddie smiled and tucked his top into his breeches. Kenny said, 'Had any more thoughts on what I told you the other night?'

'Not really. Should I?'

'Well something's not right, is it? I got a race I know I didn't win and so did you.'

'Maybe we should be keeping quiet then rather than talking about it,' Eddie said, running out of patience already.

'You wouldn't be saying that if it was the other way round!'

'I suppose not but you know what they say, "The camera never lies". We both thought we'd lost but I've made mistakes before.'

'I have too but I didn't this time. I lost that race at Stratford, Eddie.'

Eddie lifted his helmet. 'Who rode the second?'

'Julian Cross. He agrees with me. He won that race.'

Eddie looked at him as he buckled the chinstrap. 'I just don't know what you want me to do about it, Kenny?'

'Well nothing really, I just wanted you to know what I thought.'

'Okay. Thanks.'

'No problem. No problem at all.' And he turned and left.

Eddie rode a loser in the last and as he came back into the weighing room a blonde woman dashed up and took him by the arm. It was Rebecca Bow, Mattie's new owner. Her eyes shone and she smelt of booze but Eddie thought she looked very alive, very attractive. 'Eddie, Mattie asked me to come and find you. He wants you to come up to our box and help celebrate.'

'I'll be glad to. I'll just get showered and changed.'

Rebecca held onto his arm and walked into the weighing room with him close enough for him to feel her hips swing. Rebecca wore a long fake fur coat over a figure-hugging charcoal dress. Her black hat was round with a big brim with a broad cream ribbon. Eddie drew in a long silent sniff of her perfume then left her in the main body of the weighing room while he went into the jockeys' changing room.

While she waited for him Rebecca Bow opened her handbag and took out a small compact mirror. She wanted to look her best for Eddie. The thing that Mattie had let slip to her when he'd drunk too much made it imperative she get Eddie Malloy into bed as soon as was decently possible.

Apart from the erotic angle, the potential

50

orgasmic benefits which she'd considered with increasing moistness for the past hour, she thought and hoped that the subsequent pillow talk may well save her life.

Seven

It was dark, frosty and very early when Eddie Malloy left for Alnwick on the Thursday morning and as he scraped ice from the windscreen of the blue Audi he wasn't relishing the prospect of riding out so close to the North Sea.

Three hours later with coffee and one slice of toast inside him he was legged up onto Samson's Curls, a smallish, light framed gelding who was nothing to look at. When she'd brought the horse out of his box Laura Gilpin had seen the disappointment on Eddie's face. She smiled, 'Don't worry, he's got an engine.'

Eddie nodded thinking it was likely to be a lawnmower engine though he said nothing. It seldom paid to criticise people's horses but he was convinced he'd had a wasted journey. Laura introduced him to two other riders, two girls, whose horses were going to help put Samson's Curls through his paces. Eddie smiled warmly and said hello. Stepping onto a concrete mounting block Laura Gilpin got aboard a big Cleveland Bay and urged him forward. Eddie turned his horse to let her come alongside and all four set off towards the gallops.

Samson's Curls moved easily and athletically under him and Eddie warmed to him at once. Horses give off signs even at a walk and before the newly acquainted pair had broken into a trot Eddie knew that at the very least Samson's Curls had more about him than his chunky body, short neck and loppy ears gave off at first glance. The horse looked a bit ponyish yet once Eddie had settled in his saddle it felt as if he'd grown several inches. The horse's movement was like a coiled spring and Eddie could not wait to see if his faster paces measured up.

Laura at the head of the four-horse string urged her mount into a trot as the winding lane took them above the village towards the cliffs where she worked them among the sheep and occasional rocky outcrop. Even though Samson's Curls was plainly the runt of this litter his lengthy stride kept taking him too close to the bigger Cleveland Bay who put his ears back in threat several times. Eddie liked the feel.

Once out onto the age old turf that had never felt a plough the horses wanted to be off but Laura shouted to her two girls and Eddie to give her five minutes to get to her vantage point first. They followed at a good half speed then let the three quicken over the last two furlongs of the winding uphill mile and a half gallop.

Not knowing the terrain, Eddie let the other two set the pace and decided if he was to find anything out he'd need to give them a ten length start. Samson's Curls pulled hard for his head, wanting to get to his fleeing stable companions but Eddie needed to know if he had speed, as many hard pullers stop going forward the moment they're asked to quicken.

He was not disappointed as the easy moving bay ate into the deficit and joined the leaders just at the point where they really started to move into top gear. Samson's Curls made the others look pedestrian as he passed them just where the young trainer sat motionless on her hack, a wide grin showing her excitement at what she'd seen.

Once in front, Eddie distinctly felt the little horse lose his enthusiasm which indicated Laura had been right in telling him the horse needed holding up till the last moment.

Laura sat watching Eddie come back

between the other two, chatting, smiling, shaking his head. Eddie trotted Samson's Curls back to a red-cheeked smiling trainer, hard hat making her look like an oversized pony club kid on her fat gelding who was interested in nothing now but chewing grass.

'Well?' Laura asked nervously.

'He's good.' Eddie stroked the horse's neck.

'How good?' she asked proudly.

'I've won races on a lot worse.'

'Do you think he can win at Aintree on Saturday?'

'From what I've seen of the rest of them he'll win all right if I don't mess it up.'

'He's a thinker, isn't he?'

Eddie patted the horse's neck. 'Makes Einstein look like the village idiot though maybe it's just immaturity, that can make young horses stop when they hit the front. We'll find out on Saturday.'

Laura looked triumphantly at the other two. 'Let's give them a paddle before we go back. Have you got time, Eddie?'

'Sure. I'm not due at Sedgefield till the second. Bags of time.'

They turned the horses and Laura led them down towards the wide empty beach where the fine golden sand, chased in little flurries by the wind, stuck to the horses' legs. Gentle white breakers rode a turning tide as they took the horses in to a depth of six inches and turned their backs to the wind.

Laura looked fulfilled as though she'd just had a baby. Eddie was thoughtful, narrow-eyed, a bit troubled looking, wondering if he could ask the favour that had just occurred to him. He urged his horse through the surf alongside Laura, the wind sufficient to muffle his words so the other two couldn't hear. 'Laura, this is going to sound pretty damn cheeky of me and I feel awkward asking but ... well, are you a gambling stable? I mean, do you plan to have a decent bet on Saturday? I hope you don't mind me asking.'

'As George Washington once said, gambling is the child of avarice, the brother of iniquity and the father of mischief. So we won't be having more than ten grand on him.'

Eddie stared at her, unsure. Amused by his bafflement Laura laughed heartily showing perfect teeth and Eddie thought that if she lost a few stone she would be an attractive woman. 'No, I don't bet, Eddie, I'm in it for days like these. For horses like the one you're sitting on and the only thing that scares me is that he might be so good I'll become addicted and want another just like him. After seven years hoping and settling for moderate horses I'm scared of what he'll do to me.'

Eddie nodded, wondering if she'd finished. Launa undid her chinstrap and eased her helmet off, shaking out sandy coloured hair to be blown from behind matching the pattern of the mane and tail of her mount. 'That's better.' She looked downwards towards the water. 'Soft landing for a hard head.' Her smile widened. 'So I hope that answers your question, Eddie. I don't know what you've got in mind but I'm happy for you to make some money on Saturday, if you can.'

Eddie looked anxious. 'No, that wasn't what I meant. I'm not a betting man either but there's a friend of mine who's in pretty deep trouble ... he badly needs something like Samson's Curls, it would ...'

'Fine. Go ahead. I appreciate you asking, Eddie, a lot of jockeys would just have mouthed off without saying anything to me. Help your friend out.'

'You're sure?'

'Absolutely.'

'What about the owner?'

She smiled across at him, the wind pushing tendrils of hair across her face. 'The owner's happy as well. No problem.'

'You own him, too?'

56

'Lock, stock and barrel or should that be bloodstock and barrel? Anyway he's all mine. Tell your friend to fill his boots on Saturday.'

Eight

That evening in a plush London penthouse apartment, three men were seated around a coffee table drinking cappuccinos and stacking bundles of banknotes like tower blocks, competing with each other to see whose would topple first. The lights of the city were visible through the big window. The buzz of commuters and traffic rose from the street. A high tech computer system sat on a large black desk in the centre of the room.

Two of the men had been at Cheltenham. They had travelled on the train with the leather holdall and radio system. Their names were Walter and Magnus. The other man, Ben Turco, was in his early thirties and the game they were playing had been suggested, as ever, by Turco whose mind was never still.

If he wasn't messing around with his computers (with which he'd robotised half the stuff in his flat including an expensive music system), he was inventing childish games like the one they were now playing.

And to make things worse for his long-suffering companions, Turco always won, as he did with this money tower game. Magnus and Walter were relieved when he tired of it and packed away the thousands in cash into a leather holdall.

Turco spoke. He was American. 'We haven't had a tickle for a while so let's go for it Saturday. That's over a hundred grand all in.'

Magnus said, 'It's too much, Ben, we'll never get it on. Even if we did we'd blow everything wide open. It would have to be our last tilt.'

'So let's make it the last tilt, who cares? I'm getting bored with it anyway, we'll find something else. Let's check with Phil and book the hotel.'

Turco went to the PC screen, put on a tiny headset with a mouth microphone attached and clicked his mouse a few times. A telephone ringing tone sounded though there was no phone obvious anywhere. A man answered. 'Hello?'

'Phil?'

'Ben.'

'You okay for Saturday?'

'No reported hazards.'

'Good news! Magnus will call you tomorrow night with the frequency.'

'A1.'

'Where are you staying?'

'The Atlantic Tower.'

'Best avoid that then.'

'I'd say so.'

'Fine. Good luck.'

'Over and out.'

Turco clicked again. Walter and Magnus stood either side watching the screen. Turco talked as he scrolled through. 'What are we looking for, the usual stuff: heated pool, gym, sauna, hot and cold running chambermaids? Atlantic Tower's out ... The Moat House, how's that?'

Both men shrugged and nodded knowing that Turco'd already hit the dial button. A receptionist answered. 'Good evening, thank you for calling The Moat House Hotel, my name is Belinda, how can I help you?'

'You could cut about three paragraphs from the greeting, Belinda, that's how you could help! Jeez, my phone bill will be higher than my room bill!'

'Sorry?'

'Only kidding. I'd like to book two rooms for tomorrow night and could you organise a taxi for Aintree racecourse for noon?'

'Certainly, sir. May I take the names the rooms are to be booked in?'

'Sure you can. Johnny Hooker and Henry Gondorif,' Turco said, smiling at the other two like a mischievous schoolboy.

Nine

At Aintree bright sunshine alternated with heavy showers. In the parade ring, a nervous Laura Gilpin spoke to Eddie as the twelve runners circled. 'Did you pass the information to your friend in need?'

Eddie smiled. 'He was very grateful.'

'He's welcome to join us to watch the race, you know. Is he here?'

'He had to go to Ascot but I'm sure he'll be watching on TV.'

'Let's hope he'll be watching a winner.'

'Fingers crossed.'

Eddie mounted and Samson's Curls trotted lightly out of the parade ring and down the horsewalk, spooking mildly as the TV camera came into view.

At Ascot racecourse Mattie Stuart, too nervous to watch the race in the Owners' & Trainers' Bar, hurried out through the crowd into the betting shop. Following him at a distance of ten paces were two Chinese men. They also entered the shop and watched Stuart closely as he stared, tense and unblinking, at the TV screen showing the runners in the 1.35 at Aintree lining up to start. A caption

60

showed Samson's Curls' price at 16-1.

In a dark room in a London nightclub a TV showed the same picture. A Chinese man speaking on the phone was noting figures. He hung up and turned smiling to his colleague. 'All money on. One hundred thirty-five thousand.' The smaller man nodded and fixed his eyes on the runners as the tapes went up.

At Aintree the crowd concentrated on the race. The bookies' betting cries died away as they totted up bets and organised the money they'd taken. Moving among them was Magnus, the bearded man from the flat. A tiny speaker was lodged deep in his right ear. Concealed in the inside of his coat was an equally small microphone. His colleague, Walter, was positioned on the tarmac at the winning post wearing the same communications kit as Magnus.

At the start Eddie eyed up the others and thought the favourite, Surrealist, the only one who could spoil the party. He felt a heavy responsibility. Mattie had no say in his own destiny now.

Eddie knew that Aintree's hurdle circuit was fast and furious and suited to nippy front runners who could fly around the tight bends halfway to victory while those coming from behind had to fight to get free from the dross.

All was going to plan for Eddie who

decided to settle Samson's Curls in last place. The little horse was keen to race but Eddie was aware that if he started to get him buzzing too soon there'd be nothing left for the finish where it mattered. By dropping behind the others Eddie managed to kid Samson's Curls that it was no more than a routine bit of work, a morning canter. The horse responded by relaxing into a regular stride pattern and popped the first four hurdles as he did when schooling at home.

With less than a circuit to go Eddie decided to ease past several stragglers to remain in sight of the serious contenders without asking for any real effort. Now there was just the long last bend and the final two jumps before the sprint to the finish. At this point he was faced with a dilemma: to go up the inside rail, saving ground but running the risk of finding his way blocked, or to go around the bunch and be forced to travel much further to get onto the heels of the three horses that looked as if they would fight out the finish.

He went by instinct, easing through a gap next to the rails where only the bravest horse and rider would have ventured. The unwritten law among jockeys is that you don't make your rivals look silly by stealing up their inside. In reality most took great satisfaction in doing just that and many a youngster made trainers sit up and take note when regularly running this gauntlet.

Eddie crept stealthily up the inner as the bulk of those under pressure ran wide off the last bend and without expending much energy had placed Samson's Curls in fourth place approaching the second last hurdle. Now with daylight in front and his touch paper lit by passing so many horses Samson's Curls launched himself at the obstacle fully a stride too soon. But his natural flair for jumping saw him pass the three leaders in the air as none jumped it nearly as well as he.

'Jesus!' Eddie heard himself cry as much from the thrill of such an extravagant leap as from realising he had now hit the front much sooner than planned. Teeth gritted he rode for the last jump knowing that once the surprise of being in front registered with Samson's Curls it would be an agonising run to the line. The last hurdle kept the horse's mind occupied until he flew over it then he downed tools at once.

When a horse cries enough no amount of brute force will change his mind so Eddie bit the bullet and played him at his own game by shortening the reins and sitting relatively still compared to Surrealist's jockey who now saw he'd been given a second chance.

Experienced punters in the stands murmured that Eddie was bent, trying blatantly to let the favourite pass him. And even though Laura and Mattie knew the horse needed holding up they thought Eddie had badly misjudged things. They watched in helpless desperation as Surrealist's head came upsides Eddie's thigh then drew ahead with just fifty yards to go.

But Eddie knew that being headed again was the only thing that might rekindle his mount's racing instincts. It did but the winning post closed quickly as Samson's Curls surged again. Eddie's blood was up too and crouching low on his mount's neck he rode in rhythm, his trunk pushing forward as his legs kicked back to encourage his partner to lengthen a little more.

With the red and white circular disk almost close enough to touch Eddie played his last trump by letting out a scream that could be plainly heard in the stands. Samson's Curls lunged forward to get away from the noise and in doing so popped his head in front of Surrealist again a few yards from the line.

'Photograph, photograph,' the course announcer's voice rang out although both the jockeys involved and the spectators opposite the finish knew the result was a foregone conclusion. Eddie had snatched victory.

As they crossed the line, Walter, positioned on the winning post and staring as though trying to look through it, straightened suddenly and spoke into the concealed microphone. 'Okay, Phil, let's go for this one. Magnus, Surrealist.'

A few bookmakers chalked up betting on the photo finish: 1-6 Samson's Curls, 9-2 Surrealist. Walter moved calmly among them with sheaves of notes betting on Surrealist. The first three or four took his money with a knowing, slightly sympathetic, 'there's one born every minute' look but as he piled on more and more they got nervous and started asking for their tic tac man to check his judgement. Walter continued betting.

Eddie walked the horse towards the winner's enclosure seeing the wide smile of Laura Gilpin as the heavy figure hurried to meet him. Eddie was smiling too, relieved, his thoughts with Mattie Stuart.

At Ascot Mattie looked much more relaxed as he waited for the result and price to be confirmed. The two Chinese stood stern faced. On the TV they were replaying the finish in slow motion. The commentator was saying, 'Although the judge has called for a print of the photo there's no doubt that Samson's Curls under a superlative ride from Eddie Malloy has got up to win. It's as cool a ride as I've seen. We'll confirm the result to you as soon as we get it but in the meantime back to Steve in the studio.'

Wearing a wide smile Mattie left the betting shop and returned to the Owners' & Trainers' Bar to order champagne. As he entered the bar he heard the voice of the BBC front man say, 'We now have the result of the photo finish in the one thirty-five at Aintree and I'm afraid to say our lads at the course called it wrongly. Surrealist just held on to beat Samson's Curls by a short head.'

Mattie stood stunned, waiting for some sort of action replay of those words.. Waiting to be told it wasn't true, couldn't be true. He'd seen the race with his own eyes.

Outside, the two Chinese had been walking towards the carpark when one had received a call on his mobile phone. He listened briefly then grabbed the other man by the sleeve and returned to the Owners' & Trainers' Bar where they waited for Mattie Stuart to come out.

Ten

At Aintree Walter moved among sour resentful bookmakers, collecting wads of notes. In the unsaddling enclosure, as her horse was led away, Laura Gilpin stood silently in tears. Eddie put a hand on her shoulder. 'Laura, I don't know what happened after we passed the post but we passed it first, I don't care what the photo finish camera says. Let's go and see the print because if it shows Surrealist finishing in front of us I'm going to speak to the stewards. There must be something wrong with the camera equipment.' They both set off towards the course noticeboard.

At Ascot a bewildered Mattie Stuart wandered through the carpark looking for his car, a blue Rover 820. He found it, got in and sat in the driver's seat looking completely dazed. He put the key in the ignition but when he turned it there was just a click. Then another click as the driver's door opened and Mattie looked up to see a Chinese man.

Another walked past the front of the car to the passenger side. The one who opened the door had a short broadbladed sword in his left hand. He said, 'Come with us now, Mistah Stuart.' Mattie went, white-faced.

The Chinese bundled Mattie into a black Merc and headed for London. They took him to the backroom of a nightclub to be confronted by another Chinese man called Lee Sung who Mattie judged to be in his late fifties. He was small, mean looking and obviously very angry. The two escorts left Mattie in the centre of the room and backed away. Lee Sung stared at him. Mattie was very frightened and confused, unsure whether to start pleading his case or wait for the man to talk.

The room was gloomy, windowless. What looked like vertical blue strip lights had been partly concealed in two corners giving off a dull tropical light. A makeshift bench top ran from wall to wall towards the rear of the room at about hip height. Things lay on top of it but Mattie could not make out what they were. Lee Sung moved slowly towards the bench, leant forward and clicked the switch of a small table lamp. A soft white beam shone down onto an empty wooden chessboard. The man stooped and brought something from below the bench. He laid it across the chess board. It was a short sword. Mattie saw the tiny flaws on what looked like a newly sharpened blade twinkle in the lamplight.

Eddie was driving down Melling Road heading for the motorway. He was trying to figure out what was going on with these photo finishes. He smiled wryly as he pictured Kenny MacAdam telling everyone how he'd warned Eddie, he'd warned him! But he hadn't seemed interested.

Laura had demanded to see the stewards and they'd agreed that although the video 'deceptively showed her horse as the likely winner' the photo finish print was infallible and the judge's decision had to be final.

Something was badly wrong. Somebody, somehow was fiddling with the photo finish equipment. But how? The camera took a picture and within a minute the result was announced. How could anyone have the time to mess around with the print? How had this passed the Jockey Club Security guys by? He knew one of the officers well, a guy called Peter McCarthy. Eddie reached for his mobile. As he did so it rang.

'Eddie Malloy.'

'Eddie! It's Becky Bow. Mattie's in bad trouble!'

Rebecca. A picture of her pretty face came immediately to Eddie's mind.

'What's wrong.' Eddie asked.

'The Chinese got him! They—they kidnapped him! From Ascot!'

'When?'

'Today! Before the end of racing! I saw them get him in the carpark and push him into a car. I followed them!'

'Okay. Okay. Do you know where Mattie is now?'

'He's in a nightclub in Wardour Street in London.'

'Where are you?'

'Outside the club.'

'Have you called the police?'

'I called them first. They've been here and they've been into the club and said there's nobody in there who's in any trouble at all. They talked to me like I'm some kind of crank. They just wouldn't listen!'

'So where are they now?'

'They've gone. They said they've got enough to do without drunken women making malicious calls.'

'You don't sound drunk.'

'I'm not for Christ's sake! I had a couple of glasses of bubbly at the races, that's all. Now I don't know what to do!'

'Could they have taken Mattie out through a back door or something?'

'I suppose they could. I don't know.'

Eddie looked at the dashboard clock. 'Rebecca, it's going to take me around three hours to get to you. Can you stay there that long, keep watch?'

'Of course I can! Of course!'

'How big a street is Wardour Street?'

'Don't know. I haven't been to the end of it.'

'I'll call you when I'm closer. You can tell me exactly where you are.'

Rebecca gave him her number. He said, 'If anything changes call me.'

'Okay. I will. Drive safely, Eddie.'

'Be a first.'

He swung into the fast lane of the motorway and pushed the Audi up to 100 mph. Why had she called him? How much had Mattie told her in the last week or so and what exactly was their relationship?

Eddie chided himself for thinking about incidentals when Mattie was obviously in deep trouble. He should have thought of him earlier, tried to ring him. But Laura Gilpin had been pretty distraught about Samson's Curls losing the photo and that had taken his mind off Mattie and his problems with the Triad. Eddie tried to look at it from their angle: killing Mattie would be pointless, they'd never get their money then. But how much more terror could they fill him with?

Eddie shook his head and tightened his jaw in anger. 'Bastards!' he said and pushed the accelerator flat to the floor.

On a wooden chessboard on the tabletop Mattie Stuart's hand, fingers spread across the squares, leaked blood from a number of small cuts. The point of a short sword rose and fell sticking into the board in die spaces between his fingers. Blood had congealed on the nail of his index finger and his hand trembled.

Lee Sung said, 'Rememba, if your hand leave board your hand leave body.'

Stuart's face in the periphery of the lamplight was sweat soaked, darkening the ridge of his shirt collar. He looked impossibly strained, on the verge of breakdown, concentrating hard almost as though he was the one wielding the sword.

Lee Sung said, 'Tell me how you gonna pay back the money? One hundred thirty-five thousand at fourteen to one is ovah two million pounds. You owe me two million pounds, Mistah Stuart, how you gonna pay?'

At junction 10 on the M6 Eddie was brought to a halt by a long tailback of vehicles. He cursed.

Halfway down Wardour Street Rebecca Bow's yellow Mercedes was parked partly on the pavement outside the narrow entrance of the nightclub. Inside the car, Rebecca, looking relaxed, smoked and listened to rock music on the radio.

Eleven

In that darkened room Mattie Stuart's fingers were caked in blood. He was unable to flinch any more as the dried blood had stuck his fingers to the chessboard. Some of his wounds were an inch long though many were small but deep nicks. In some of these holes Lee Sung had pushed splinters from the now badly damaged wooden board, arranging the splinters in order of black and yellow paint which still clung to them.

Mattie had passed out a couple of times to be brought round by frantic slapping of his face. He was cold in just his shirtsleeves; the sweat had dried on his face though moist tear tracks could be seen. He felt he'd been there for days. The muscles in his left shoulder and arm burned and ached with the effort of constantly keeping his hand on the board. It had been a long time since he'd looked at the hand itself.

Lee Sung said, 'You not go home till you say how you pay me back.'

'I've told you I cannot pay you what you want. I gave you the information on that horse in good faith. I have no way of paying you that kind of money. Maybe I can give you another horse soon and we can hope for better luck. That's all I can keep telling you. That's all.'

The effort of speaking seemed to exhaust Mattie and drive him close to tears again. This appeared to please Lee Sung who was enjoying Mattie's suffering. He said, 'Maybe you jockey frien', Mistah Malloy, can help. Maybe he ride some races the way I tell him.'

'He won't. He's an honest man.'

'No honest men in this world.'

Lee Sung brought the sword down taking an aspirin sized piece of flesh from Mattie's index finger and raising it on the tip of the sword to glisten gruesomely under the lamplight. Mattie tensed and grunted and another single tear squeezed from his clenched right eyelid and ran down his cheek. Lee Sung smiled. The two others watched impassively.

When he reached the city boundaries Eddie called Rebecca Bow. She told him she'd be waiting on the pavement opposite the club and that there were spaces close by to park his car if he didn't mind risking a ticket. Eddie thought that the least of his worries.

When Eddie hung up, Rebecca started

the car and drove about 300 metres before turning into a side street and parking again half on the pavement. She switched off the engine killing the radio and the heater fan. Then she opened the glovebox and took out a handgun. She got out of the car dragging her fake fur coat from the passenger seat. She slipped it on and put the gun in the right-hand pocket then locked the car and walked back towards the club.

Eddie's first thought when he saw her under the street light, the yellow rays catching her blonde hair, was of a prostitute touting for business. Their eyes met and she smiled. Looked quite calm. Eddie wasn't but he forced himself to park slowly and to get out of the car without drawing too much attention to himself. It was almost eight o'clock. The street was becoming quite busy with pedestrians.

Rebecca crossed the street and automatically offered her cheek for a kiss as she reached his side. Hardly the time for niceties, Eddie thought, but he kissed her lightly then said, 'Is there another way in?'

At the rear of the club were steps leading to a concreted basement level. Eddie led Rebecca down. The building was narrow here with just a double fire door and a small upper window with wired opaque glass. Four metal beer barrels stood under the window. Eddie looked up at it but knew there was no way he or Rebecca would get through even if they could force it open.

'Eddie!' Rebecca whispered harshly.

He turned to see her pushing gently at the fire door which gave and opened silently.

Mattie's hand was a bloody mess on the chessboard and Lee Sung was about to prise it away and start on the other hand when he heard the doorlatch click. He looked round at the same time as his two henchmen to see the door being pushed slowly open.

Mattie looked up and cried out, 'Eddie!' and immediately began sobbing with relief.

Lee Sung smiled wider saying, 'Ah, Mistah Malloy! You come rescue you frien'?' He brought the sword down again neatly taking off Mattie's little finger which Lee Sung picked up with his left hand and threw towards Eddie. 'Here, rescue finga instead!'

Eddie shouted, 'You bastard!' and lunged towards the Chinaman. Eddie was no trained fighter but he was exceptionally fit and hard muscled and with danger an everyday threat for him his reactions in critical situations were fine-tuned. He was also enraged.

His speed and tenacity took Lee Sung by surprise. The Chinaman tried to raise his sword but it had barely cleared shoulder height when Eddie, like an Olympic sprinter desperate to breast the tape, head butted him full in the face pulping the small yellow nose and sending him crashing to the floor. As Eddie followed him down he bent both knees and parted them to land with one grinding deep into Lee Sung's groin and the other smashing into the left side of his ribcage.

This happened within seconds of Mattie losing his finger and Lee Sung's henchmen seemed rooted but they moved quickly now to try and take Eddie while he was still on the floor. That was when Rebecca stepped forward pulling the gun from her coat pocket and holding it at shoulder height in both hands. 'Back off, fellas! Never heard of a fair fight?'

Fear in their eyes, both men retreated immediately. Rebecca smiled wide and said, 'Get down on the floor, face first.'

They did and she moved behind them to where she could see how Eddie was doing. The jockey stood over the prostrate, groaning man threatening the man with his own sword. Rebecca saw that Eddie had the Chinaman's left wrist pinned under his right foot, the sword raised in his right hand. Eddie looked down at him and saw that his split nose and wrecked mouth were causing him breathing problems. Each exhalation sent small bubbles erupting through the mass of blood like geysers on a mud flat. Eddie was shouting at him. 'Which finger would you like to lose, you bastard! Spread them or I'll take your whole hand off! Spread them!'

Lee Sung's fingers, pale from the circulation block caused by Eddie's foot, spread slowly almost as if they had a life of their own. Eddie stared down and raised the sword, holding it there for what seemed a long time. Rebecca moved to the side, better to see his face, his eyes. And she saw immediately that he wouldn't do it, couldn't do it.

Eddie stepped off the man's wrist and went down on one knee taking a hank of the Chinaman's hair and twisting it till his head came up. 'Look at me,' Eddie said. 'Look at me!' The man opened his watery, pain-filled eyes. Eddie put the sword point to his neck. 'If you ever come near this man again, or this woman or any other person I know or have known I will take this sword and shove it so far up your arse it'll take your head off from the inside. And that goes for any other crawling yellow rats you might know. Do you hear me?'

Lee Sung grunted what seemed like a yes. Eddie said, 'And listen, I do not give a toss how many are in your Triad or how big and bad they are. If any of them cause my friends and me any trouble of any kind I'm coming for you. Do you hear and understand that?'

Lee Sung grunted again and Eddie turned the sword and swung it towards the Chinaman's head embedding it in the floor by his ear so he could hear the blade vibrate as it settled in the wood.

Eddie stood up and seemed to become aware again of the others in the room. He looked at Rebecca who smiled very slowly at him. His nerves were tingling now as the impact of what had happened got through. He knew he couldn't have found a smile the way she had and he admired her cool. Turning, he realised that she must have dealt with Lee Sung's henchmen who lay face down at his feet. Puzzled, he looked again at Rebecca and she held the gun up so he could see it and winked.

Eddie raised his eyes to heaven. Where the hell had she got that? He turned to Mattie who seemed transfixed. He had watched wide-eyed throughout becoming increasingly convinced he'd stumbled into a movie set. Eddie said, 'You okay, Mattie?'

The trainer nodded slowly, looking up at him. Eddie took his good arm and said, 'Can you stand up?' Mattie got slowly to his feet and took a step away from the chair. As his mutilated hand came off the table the splintered chessboard came with it stuck fast with congealed blood. Eddie put an arm around him. 'Let's get you to hospital.'

Like a child Mattie rested his head on Eddie's shoulder and, clutching the chessboard to his chest, shuffled forward.

Eddie said, 'Wait a minute,' and started looking around on the floor. Rebecca opened a cotton handkerchief exposing Mattie's bloody severed finger. 'Got it,' she said, smiling again. Eddie managed to return the smile this time and, one either side of Mattie now, they left grinning.

A surgeon at Bart's tried unsuccessfully to sew Mattie's finger back on but he did manage, with delicate stitch work, to repair the rest of his hand. While the surgeon worked Eddie and Rebecca sat in the waiting room talking about what had happened.

Rebecca told Eddie the gun was only a replica and she'd been bluffing, that's why she hadn't gone in with it before he had got there.

'Well, you're pretty damn cool,' Eddie said.

'And you're pretty damn fiery.'

'Not normally. I just lost it completely when that bastard cut Mattie's finger off. Jeez, how can you do that in cold blood?'

'You couldn't. I watched you. You were thinking about it.'

Eddie sighed, rubbing the bristly beard shadow he had now. 'I know. I should've. Just couldn't do it.'

Rebecca smiled and nudged him playfully. 'I'm glad.'

'I bet he is too, the bastard.'

Rebecca shifted in her seat as she felt herself growing moister, warmer low in her belly, that slow tingle caressing her spine. She'd never experienced such strength of libido outside of intense lovemaking and she could only put it down to the after-effects of being at the heart of such a dangerous situation. She said, 'Were you afraid in there this evening?'

Eddie hesitated. 'I don't know. I suppose so. Didn't really have time to think about it.'

'How do you feel now?' she asked, trying hard not to sound seductive.

Eddie smiled. 'Pretty chuffed, I suppose. Pretty bloody chuffed!' Just then a nurse brought Mattie back out and Rebecca and Eddie got up to greet him. The nurse was anxious that Mattie stay and wait for the police to come and interview him but he said he had to get home and would she please ask them to contact him there. Reluctantly she agreed and a groggy Mattie was led slowly out towards the carpark, Eddie on one side and Rebecca on the other.

They got him into the back of Eddie's car. Eddie shut the door and turned to Rebecca. 'Are you coming back with us? I'll stay the night at Mattie's place.'

She smiled in the darkness as the cold wind caught her hair and blew wisps across her face. 'I've got to get home, I'm afraid.'

'Where's that?'

'Normally, St John's Wood but my flat's being decorated so I'm at the Dorchester at the moment.'

'Nice place.'

She pushed tendrils of hair away from her smiling mouth. 'It's okay.'

Eddie looked around awkwardly then said, 'Can I call you?'

'I'll come looking for you if you don't.'

They smiled and looked at each other, knowing this was the beginning of something. Eddie didn't know where it would lead and that was the way he wanted it. Rebecca had a blueprint in mind and she knew she'd just laid the foundations.

Twelve

Deep snow put paid to Monday's three racemeetings and two of Tuesday's looked doubtful. Only Huntingdon seemed hopeful of racing on Tuesday and Eddie managed to get himself one ride booked there. He planned to drive over to Newmarket on Monday evening and stay with his mother and sister leaving himself just a short trip to Huntingdon in the morning.

Eddie had been reunited with his family eighteen months previously after a long acrimonious rift caused by his father's treatment of him. His father had died last December since when his sister, Louise, had moved in with his mother to help her run the small stud she owned in Newmarket. For the first few months after his father's death, Eddie's mother had seemed to be getting over the trauma of losing a husband, albeit a tyrannical one, after over forty years of marriage.

But in the autumn she'd taken ill and since then her condition had fluctuated without the doctor being able to pin down anything specific. They'd decided it was delayed reaction to the death of her husband and said time was likely to prove the healer. Eddie and his sister had kept in close touch since the illness came on and Eddie visited whenever he could.

He rang Louise now to make sure it was okay to stay over that night. She said he'd be welcome and that their mother would be glad to see him as she had been deteriorating again over recent days.

He put the phone down but stayed sitting at the table by the window in his flat looking out on the snow-covered roofs of the stables below. The yard had been swept clear early that morning by a shivering group of stable-lads working under the moon.

The acres of surrounding Shropshire fields and hedgerows lay under a thick white blanket, which was nice for Christmas card artists but useless to racehorse trainers. Fresh snow tends to ball up the hooves of horses causing them to lose their grip and the trainer Eddie worked for, Charles Tunney, had decided that morning that even the all-weather gallop was unusable.

So, horses too bored to give more than the occasional whinny gazed out at each other over stable doors, half a dozen lads played card games in the warmth of the tack room and Eddie Malloy wondered how to fill the rest of the day. He decided to ring the Jockey Club Security Officer, Peter McCarthy.

He tracked McCarthy down to his office in Portman Square, London. 'Mac, Eddie Malloy. How are you this snowcovered morning?'

'Glad I'm not driving to a racetrack, that's how I am. Long time no hear.'

'Well, Mac, I've been behaving myself. No need to call you to bail me out of trouble.'

'Sounds ominous. Makes me wonder why you're calling now.'

'To tell you something that'll interest you and maybe add to your brownie point collection.'

'I'm all ears.'

'Saturday, Aintree. I rode the winner in the second race and the photo finish camera decided I hadn't.'

'Biased things, these cameras. Maybe you should have smiled as you passed it.'

'Mac, listen, you've got a problem with them.'

'*I've* got a problem? How do you work that out?'

'I think somebody's fiddling with the camera.'

'Come on, Eddie, a camera is a camera! A button gets pressed, the shutter opens and whatever image is in front of it gets printed on the film. That can't be fiddled with, it's impossible.'

'Mac, you know I wouldn't bullshit you on this, you know my record. I'm telling you that somewhere between horses passing the post and the judge calling the result somebody is fiddling something. Watch Saturday's race on video then have a look at the photo finish print. Do the same with the novice 'chase at Newbury a couple of weeks ago when the result went in my favour, and Kenny MacAdam was involved in a race, at Stratford I think it was, where the same thing happened. Have a word with Kenny.'

McCarthy went quiet then said, 'You're serious about this, aren't you?'

'Never more so. Get hold of those tapes and let me know what you think.'

'Leave it with me.'

Eddie hung up and sat at the window in the snowbound silence. Turning in his chair he looked around the small flat; there wasn't much furniture: a three-seater couch, a big easy chair by the gas fire, a variety of rugs on the hardwood flooring, a few racing trophies, some pictures on the walls and one mirror, three tall lamps, a combined TV and video recorder and a small but powerful music centre. Only the trophies were his. The rest of the stuff came with the flat, which came with the job.

As did the retainer of ten grand a year which wasn't a fortune but at least it gave him something at times like this. Not that he needed much. No dependants. Life had taught him that the only person he could really depend on was himself. Others, like Mattie, depended on him which was a burden sometimes but he'd rather carry a burden than be one.

Poor Mattie. Eddie had worked hard to reassure him that the Chinese would be well and truly frightened off after Saturday night but Mattie had kept ringing him at home asking him to come and stay awhile. Eddie had promised he'd be there at the first fresh sign of trouble.

And Rebecca. They'd spoken a few times since Saturday. She was cool and laid back, pretty and sexy, and they'd agreed to go for dinner after racing one day. If this weather ever let up. Eddie was beginning to think that Rebecca might just be a bit different from the other women he'd known, might last a bit longer. Living in hope. Of a normal life. Something he'd never really known.

Looking around the silent lonely flat now and seeing his bedroom door open he wished briefly for a woman to take back to bed to while away this empty day with lovemaking until dusk.

Rebecca?

He went into the bedroom, packed an overnight bag and set off for Newmarket. He'd arrive much earlier than he'd told Louise but he didn't think she, or his mother, would mind. Downstairs he cleared the Audi's windscreen, the engine turned and the exhaust pipe blew a grey trail across a small drift banked against the side of the building as the tyres crunched through virgin snow.

Thirteen

The further Eddie Malloy drove across country the more convinced he became that there'd be no racing in Britain for a few days let alone at Huntingdon in less than twenty-four hours. The countryside was white; snow and ice narrowed many of the B roads to single tracks and the temperature didn't lift all morning.

Eddie was still an hour from Newmarket when his phone rang.

It was McCarthy. 'I've just pressed stop on the VCR. I've seen all three races.'

'And?'

'And if I'd had to bet on the outcome of

the photos I'd have lost all three. It is very difficult to believe that the still photo of the finish didn't match the video evidence.'

'Would you agree that something's going on?'

'It's too early to say, Eddie, I'm waiting for copies of the prints themselves.'

'Well do yourself a favour, Mac, don't get copies get the originals.'

'What's the difference?'

'Well, something's going on with these photos, you may as well keep your suspicions as quiet as possible just now. If you start asking the technical guys for copies you might alert whoever's behind it. Why don't you just quietly ask the racecourse managers to let you have the original prints?'

'I'm not certain they always keep them.'

'It's worth a phone call to find out.'

'Okay, leave it with me.'

The weather worsened. Eddie really wanted to see his mother and sister or he would have turned back by noon. More than four hours after setting off he finally reached the house.

Louise greeted him as he walked to the door and he thought how much she resembled their mother as Eddie remembered her from childhood: dark shoulder length hair, bright blue eyes, wide mouth, slightly upturned nose peppered with faint freckles which Eddie knew would spread and darken come summer. The whole family had been apart for almost fourteen years and Eddie had not yet grown used to seeing his sister as a woman—she'd been barely fifteen when he'd left home all those years ago.

Approaching her now he returned her warm smile and they hugged closely and kissed lightly. 'It's good to see you, Eddie.'

'And you.'

She stepped inside and ushered him in with a hand on his lower back. In the kitchen they waited for the kettle to boil and Louise told Eddie how worried she was becoming about their mother. Eddie got up. 'Where is she now?'

'She's upstairs but she's only just managed to get to sleep. Been awake half the night. Maybe it's best if you wait till she wakes.'

Eddie sat down again. 'Sure.'

They sat in silence for a few seconds then Eddie said quietly, 'She's not in dad's old room, is she?'

'No, don't worry. She's in the big room at the front. Plenty of daylight and fresh flowers.'

Eddie was relieved. He hated the dull dingy back room his father had insisted on spending the final months of his life in. It was almost as if the room itself had crushed the breath from him. He told Louise this and they had a long discussion about their father whom neither had loved. They drank tea, then went outside to check on the four stallions owned by the stud. It was early afternoon but gathering snow clouds darkened the sky and the density of their twin breaths in the air told Eddie the temperature had dropped again.

Eddie's mobile phone rang. It was McCarthy again.

'Hi, Mac, what news?'

'You told me that Kenny MacAdam was one of the jocks involved in the Stratford photo?'

'That's right. That's what he told me.'

'Well I've just had a very interesting conversation with Kenny. *Very* interesting.'

Fourteen

Two hundred and fifty miles to the north-west among the hills of the northern Lake District the snow was much deeper. At times it touched the belly of the strong fell pony which carried Kim Oliver in the search for his parents. Kim had not seen them since the previous day when they'd set out to rescue their sheep from deep drifts. The boy had been left at home to study, as roads to his school in Penrith were impassable.

Kim had sat up through the night waiting for them, falling asleep from time to time in front of the fire he kept banked up to warm them on their return which he was certain could be any time. But come dawn there was no sign. The boy was worried now. His parents were experienced hill farmers and he'd known them to spend a night out there in the past when conditions were bad but never both at the same time. Just after 7 a.m. he'd picked up the telephone to call the police but the line was dead, another victim of the weather. Kim decided to saddle Crystal, his pony who had carried him since he was three years old, and set out to look for them.

Kim was twelve now, Crystal two years older and the pony knew these hills better than her rider did. So they set off westwards towards the many snow-topped fells east of Kirkstone Pass, the land ahead of them a white untrod desert of humps and hollows and padded ridges which they both knew to be dry-stone walls. Yesterday's terrifying winds, which had sculpted these strange soft shapes, had moved on leaving a silent windless morning. Only the crunch of Crystal's hooves could be heard and a worried but optimistic Kim imagined the sound carrying way out over the hills to where his parents would hear it and know he was coming to find them.

It seemed to young Kim that he and Crystal had wandered for miles through the deep snow. Despite his warm jumpers and fleece and his long wax coat, the extra socks and thick leather boots, the cold had eaten into his bones draining optimism and hope. He knew if he were this cold when constantly on the move and with the heat from Crystal's body to sustain him that his parents, unless they'd found warm shelter, would be freezing by now. But he urged Crystal on to check one more gully. He looked anxiously at the pale sun as it settled ever lower, knowing he had to be back home before dark.

Crystal's step hadn't faltered even though she'd never been less than hock deep in snow. Small stalactites of ice hung from her belly but she kept her head down and pushed forward, often ploughing a trail with her barrel chest when it had been impossible to lift her feet high enough. As he always did, Kim had spoken to her frequently, encouraging her, sharing his troubles, wondering aloud where his parents were and asking the pony if she thought they'd find them soon.

Crystal was everything to him. Although he loved his parents they showed him little real affection. He was an only child and had no proper friends as all his classmates lived too far away to let him form any out-of-school friendships. Adults too were strangers to Kim. Apart from his teacher, his parents were the only grown-ups he had contact with. He had never met an aunt or uncle and as far as he knew neither of his parents had any family. His friends and companions all his life had been Crystal, the sheep, the numerous sheepdogs they'd had and the wild birds and creatures of the Lake District hills.

He rubbed Crystal's right ear with his gloved hand. 'Come on, Crys, we'll check Buckbarrow Gully then head for home, I promise.' The little black pony flicked her left ear back as though acknowledging and agreeing the deal and Kim steered her north to the ridge where the land fell away towards Buckbarrow Crag. At the foot of the crag in a shallow cave Kim found the frozen bodies of his father and mother.

Fifteen

Three days later, on Thursday, racing resumed at Uttoxeter and Eddie Malloy went there for two rides. Also at Uttoxeter that day were Kenny MacAdam and Bobby Tobin, who'd suffered the same fate at Newbury that Eddie had at Aintree. All three sat on the slatted bench in the corner of the weighing room sipping hot black sugarless coffee, saddles resting on metal racks above them and colours sharing hanging space with their daily clothes on hooks around the walls. Portable calor gas heaters warmed the place, cooking up stale smells of sweat and damp, old socks and tobacco smoke, saddle soap and boot polish.

Kenny MacAdam's lined, weather-beaten face was as intense as always as he told a tale. 'Couldn't figure it for days till I spoke to Kingsley who'd had ten times as much paid exactly the same way; Jiffy bag through the door, cash, no note, no questions asked, two thousand four hundred and sixty-five pounds. Nice as ninepence.'

'Nicer than ninepence I would say,' said

Bobby Tobin. 'And did the trainer get his percentage?'

'To the penny!' said MacAdam, slapping his knee by way of confirmation.

Eddie asked, 'Was that the same with you, Bobby?'

'Identical. All three of us about a week after the race. The exact amounts we would have won if the photo had come out the way it should have done.'

'All cash? No letter?'

'Nothing. Money. Right there. In a Jiffy. End of story.' Tobin drew on a thin roll-up cigarette and crossed his legs.

'No postmarks?' asked Eddie.

Tobin and MacAdam shook their heads. Tobin said, 'Hand delivered. Late at night or very early in the morning.'

'Weird,' Eddie said.

'Expect yours any day,' MacAdam told him.

Eddie said, 'I'd better call Laura Gilpin. She was the trainer and owner. Wonder if she'll get all hers in one package?'

'I wonder who's sending them?' said Tobin.

MacAdam said, 'Probably some crank who's seen the photos and feels sorry for us.'

Eddie smiled. 'Some crank!'

'Rich crank!' Tobin said.

Eddie pondered. 'How about it being

the guy who's fiddling the photos. Doesn't mind skinning the bookies but gets a guilty conscience over the innocent dupes?'

'In that case,' said Tobin, 'how does he get to pay the thousands of innocent punters who've done their money?'

'And more to the point,' said MacAdam, 'how's he fiddling the photos?'

'And what are Jockey Club Security planning to do about it?' asked Tobin.

'What indeed?' asked Eddie and went outside to ring McCarthy then Laura Gilpin.

In Ben Turco's London penthouse flat what he'd hoped would be a celebratory farewell meeting, where winnings would be split and champagne swilled, had quickly turned sour. Turco, Magnus and Walter who'd worked closely together throughout the project had been at the flat more than an hour waiting for Phil Grimond, the man who'd been central to the whole operation. They'd passed the time playing a new game invented by Turco on his PC.

Phil Grimond finally turned up just after eight o'clock. Turco registered his entrance from the corner of his eye and called a warm welcome asking him to make himself comfortable for a minute, 'while I finish off Captain Fantastic and the Brown Dirt Cowboy here!'

'Make it fast,' Grimond said, grumpily. 'I've got better things to do than piss around here.'

Turco finished his game quickly while Grimond fixed a whisky and ice from the bar in the corner and settled himself on the enormous black leather couch. Grimond was around five nine, three stone overweight, early thirties but balding significantly. He had a thick black moustache and a heavy beard shadow. The blue shirt under a tan suit had the top button undone although the navy blue knitted tie was pushed tight to his throat. A sheen of sweat glinted on his forehead and six of his fingers bore gold rings. The thick gold bracelet on his right wrist clinked against his watch as he raised the glass to drink.

Turco hurried across to shake hands and welcome him properly although Grimond showed much less eagerness for hand-shaking than his host did.

'How you doin', Phil?' Turco asked.

'Fine.' Grimond drank. 'Couldn't you just have posted the cash like you normally do? Why drag me down here?'

'For a final team drink.' Turco smiled showing perfect white expensive teeth. He turned to the others. 'Come on, guys, bring the bubbly and the glasses!'

Neither Walter nor Magnus had much time for Grimond but they nodded to him.

98

He acknowledged them with a dismissive look and stared at Turco as the other two brought the ice bucket and trays of glasses.

'Final?' Grimond asked.

'That's right,' Turco said. 'End of the old trail ride. Saturday was the last round-up.' He pulled the magnum dripping from the bucket and filled four glasses.

'Says who?' Grimond asked, anger brewing.

Turco offered the glass and his smile faded as he realised that Grimond wasn't happy. 'Well all three of us think we've gone as far as we can go with this. We've pulled it off three times now and the bookies are getting wise. Aren't they, boys?'

Magnus nodded his big head, looking serious. 'They're onto us now, it's too risky to carry on.'

'And what risks have you been taking?' Grimond asked sourly. 'I've been the one taking the risks. I've been the guy at the sharp end.'

'And you've been paid well,' Turco said. 'And now we're all getting out before we get caught. We've taken the best part of £350,000 off the bookies inside a month and it's time to say thank you and goodnight, applaud the fat lady, lock up the theatre and find a new show

99

somewhere else. The word on the course is that the jockeys are getting suspicious. These guys know when they've won a race, doesn't matter what the photo finish tells them. It's time to get out, Phil.'

Grimond said, 'We can do at least two more.' It was almost like an order.

'No, we can't,' Walter said.

Grimond sat forward menacingly. 'Who rattled your cage?'

Magnus said, 'Listen, Phil, we're not doing any more.'

'You listen to me, we're doing two more!'

Turco said, 'You might be doing two more but not with us. You'll get your cash now and we're finished.' Turco got up and went to get the big leather holdall.

Phil said, 'Listen, Turco, you do two more with me or I tell the police everything.'

Turco kept walking away from him speaking as he went. 'And land yourself in the shit too?'

'I'll turn Queen's Evidence, probably get probation. You three are looking at five years each.'

Turco stopped and turned, looked at Grimond then at the others. 'You're serious, aren't you?'

'As always.'

Turco got the bag and came back,

undoing the straps as he walked. He knelt on the rug by the couch and emptied out banded wads of notes. He said, 'Let's split this then talk.'

Walter left London later that evening with three Jiffy bags filled with cash and two addresses. The thought of the journey to Shropshire didn't faze him but the prospect of reaching Northumberland well before dawn made him shiver and he wished it had been Magnus's turn for the delivery. He'd promised himself and Hannah, his wife, a month in Spain and she was already packed. Now he'd have to roll home next morning and tell her that Grimond had not only messed up their plans but was putting them all in grave danger of a long spell in prison. Pulling off the M25 onto the M40 Walter said to no one in particular, 'For every decent bloke you meet there's an arsehole waiting round the corner.'

On the way home from Uttoxeter Eddie had a call from McCarthy, the Jockey Club Security man he'd rung earlier. McCarthy said, 'The photo finish operator on all three occasions was a man called Phil Grimond. He's worked on the technical side for almost five years. Not the most likeable human being in the world apparently but he has

101

a clean history apart from his personal life.'

'Meaning?'

'Got a taste for young boys.'

'Paedophile?'

'Not as far as I know but I'm told he uses rent boys.'

'So if he's involved in some scam a third party could be blackmailing him.'

'Everything's possible. Anyway, he could stand an interview. I plan to go and see him tomorrow.'

'Is that wise, Mac? Even if Grimond is involved he might not be the man behind the whole thing. How this thing is being worked is, well, it seems almost impossible. Whoever's running it must be pretty smart.'

'Well he'd have to be ultra smart Eddie because I've just been reminded that as from around three months ago we don't even use photo prints any more. Everything's done from the video. There's no developing involved. The horses are freeze framed on video as they cross the line and a printout of the screen image produced within about a minute. And the operator sits right there in the same box as the judge.'

Eddie whistled through his teeth. 'How the hell are they doing it, then?'

McCarthy said, 'That's what we'll have

to find out and that's why I think we need to speak to Grimond sooner rather than later.'

'Mac, do me a favour and give me a couple of days on this before you do anything. I've a feeling I might be able to pin something down.'

'Eddie, we can't risk it happening again.'

'Well it's pointless confronting Grimond when you haven't any evidence. A simple denial from him and it leaves you nowhere, gives him a get-out and if someone else is running it he simply finds another stooge to replace Grimond.'

'I suppose you could be right,' McCarthy said thoughtfully.

'Mac, give me forty-eight hours.'

'Okay, but keep me in touch.'

alter reached Eddie's place just before midnight. It was his experience that the more dedicated jockeys would be in bed by ten or half past ready for an early jump next morning either to ride out or make a long trip to the races. He'd discovered that Eddie lived in a flat at this yard and that there were a number of flats in the building.

He'd been told that Eddie's was the first one, the one on the end with a ground floor entrance door, which led up a steep flight of internal stairs. He parked the car in the trees about half a mile from the yard and walked stealthily down the track.

In his right coat pocket were a dozen dog biscuits, which he'd found would keep farm dogs quiet enough, most times, to let him get in and out. Most of the snow had gone and he made the minimum of noise as he walked. The sky was clear with a moon just more than half full but bright and silvery, giving good light. He saw the dark hulk of the barn conversion against the sky as he approached and he knew that was where he'd find Eddie's door. He pulled the Jiffy from his pocket. Just a small bag, should be no problem with the letterbox.

And there was none. The metal plaque below the letterbox said E. Malloy and the bag slipped through almost silently. Walter eased the box flap back gently on its spring. Not a sound. Neither a bark nor a whinny from the animals. He smiled and headed towards the car. Just as he passed the back of the building, someone stepped from the shadows and placed a cold metal tube just below his right ear. The shock made Walter draw such a huge involuntary breath he almost choked and went into a heavy coughing fit, which bent him double.

Eddie Malloy, holding the weapon at his neck from behind, said, 'Nasty cough.

Still, you will work these long hours. I hope the Royal Mail pays you guys good overtime. Unfortunately, your next delivery's going to be badly delayed.'

Sixteen

It had been a week since he'd found his parents dead and the images of that day and night had haunted Kim since: pictures of them as they lay huddled in their bright mountain clothing, dusted with ice crystals, stuck frozen together like candy dolls in some ice-box compartment; the hardness of their flesh; Kim imagined he could have rapped his knuckles on his mother's cheeks and heard the sound echo up the valley; the long trek then through the gathering dusk looking for a farm with a telephone, and the sound of the RAF helicopter coming over the fields, the bright beam of its searchlight raking Buckbarrow Gully then picking out those sparkling bodies so starkly as though highlighting the final act in the darkest of theatres ...

Kim tried to push the rest from his mind. The post-mortem had shown his mother had a broken back and his father a broken leg. Near the top of the gully a dead sheep was found trapped in a small crevasse. The police concluded that Kim's parents had been trying to reach the sheep from the top, probably in a joint effort, and had fallen together and frozen to death as they lay injured.

The local Social Services had come for Kim next day and taken him away to this horrible children's home on the outskirts of Carlisle. This square grey concrete prison. This small room. This strange smelling single bed against the grimy wall. Apart from the numbing grief he had worrried constantly about Crystal and the dogs and two cats. And the sheep, the lifeblood of the hill farm, the reason the farm existed.

Mr Young of the Social Services had assured him 'provision would be made'. Mr Young had seemed very annoyed when Kim had insisted on knowing exactly what he intended doing about the animals.

Mr Young finally told him that the animals had been dispersed among Kim's three 'neighbours' (the closest farm was seven miles away). They had agreed to 'collectively assume the burden until more permanent arrangements can be made'. Kim had heard some of the adults in the home discussing the fact that no relatives of the Olivers could be traced.

As each day dragged past Kim felt increasingly isolated and terribly homesick.

106

Even though he knew there would be nobody at the farm, not even Crystal (who'd been taken in temporarily, Mr Young said, by Mr Durkan at Clent Fell). How he longed for the warmth of his pony's breath, the feel of her long winter coat, the sound of her hooves, the smell of her, the smell of his old saddle ... The tears came again as he lay in the darkness but he brushed them away, made himself sit up, propped on his elbow feeling the tug of these strange pyjamas.

Kim decided there and then that he wouldn't spend another night in this place. He'd run away the next day, go back to the farm. He could fend for himself there, hide away from the Social Services when they came searching. He knew the hills like he knew his own bedroom, he and Crystal did. He'd walk to Mr Durkan's tomorrow night and get Crystal back, slip away with her in the darkness. Excited now and determined he pushed the covers back and swung his legs out of bed. Picking up the pillows he decided he'd take the pillowslips with him to wrap around Crystal's hooves so Mr Durkan wouldn't hear them leaving.

No. Bad idea. That would be stealing and he didn't want to give them any more reason for wanting to come after him. Besides, he needed nothing from this place, wanted nothing, no memory of it. He'd build a new life, his own life on the farm and make it the biggest and best farm in the hills. He'd breed more stock, maybe get some cattle. What about some ponies? Yes! A few top class fell ponies, he could breed them too as a sideline! And when he was twenty he'd marry someone beautiful, someone who loved ponies and sheep. And Kim.

That was it. Come dark tomorrow evening he was going.

Seventeen

Inside Eddie's flat a subdued Walter sat facing the jockey, who was feeling quite pleased with himself. After his conversation with the other jockeys at Uttoxeter he'd decided to stake his own place out at night, knowing that he'd stand a good chance of nailing whoever was delivering the 'guilt' money. That was why he'd asked McCarthy to be patient.

He'd promised himself he'd do it every night for a week and couldn't believe his luck when Walter had turned up on the very first night.

Looking at Walter, Eddie could see why

they'd chosen him. He was your everyday man in the street: difficult to guess his age, medium height and build, mouse brown hair, no striking features, seemingly bland personality—just the type. Potential victims of the scam like bookmakers would be hard pressed to compile a photo-fit of this man. He sat there very subdued in his brown raincoat, cloth cap on his lap.

Eddie had expected him to be angry when he discovered he'd been captured by a man armed with nothing more than a narrow piece of copper pipe but Walter seemed simply to be resigned to his fate.

Eddie made them both a cup of tea. Walter thanked him politely and sipped it. Eddie said, 'Do you have another envelope for Laura Gilpin?'

Walter nodded.

'Were you supposed to deliver it tonight?'

Another nod. Another sip of tea.

'Long way to Alnwick.'

Walter spoke for the first time. 'I drew the short straw.'

Eddie smiled. 'Tough break.'

'I was supposed to be going to Spain with the missus.' Doleful now.

Eddie decided he liked this man. The least likely criminal he'd ever seen. He resisted the smile of amusement he felt coming on lest Walter was offended. 'Be nice this time of year, Spain,' Eddie said.

Walter perked up a bit. 'We go every year. We're planning to retire there if we can get enough money.'

'I'd've thought this little scam would have set you up with the price of a medium sized villa?'

'Well we wanted one with a bigger pool.'

Eddie watched him closely, sure that he must be taking the piss now but Walter looked deadly serious, almost as though he was chatting to a neighbour over the garden fence. 'That's a shame,' Eddie said.

Walter nodded. 'Yes.' And sipped tea again, adjusting his cap on his lap.

'Did Grimond get the same share as you and the others?'

'We all got ...' He stopped and looked at Eddie. 'How did you know about Grimond?'

'Oh, Jockey Club Security have been onto him for a while. I think they plan to pick him up tomorrow.'

Knees together, cradling his mug of tea, Walter began to rock very slightly in the chair and stare at the carpet. He said, 'What's going to happen to me?'

'That depends. Will you tell me who's behind the whole thing?'

Walter shook his head. 'That wouldn't be fair.'

'No more than it would be fair for you and Grimond to take the full flak on this. It's a major fraud, you know. You could be looking at five to seven years inside.'

'And what difference will it make if I tell you who organised it all?'

'I don't know if it'll make any difference at all but you never know, we may be able to reach some agreement.'

Walter looked straight at him. 'I respect the fact that you're not promising me anything falsely.'

Eddie nodded, resisting a smile again.

Walter said, 'Would you mind if I used your phone?'

'Feel free.'

'Will you promise not to note the number I dial?'

'Promise.' Eddie was beginning to think he was involved in some weird children's game. He watched Walter put his tea down carefully and walk to the phone at the window. With his back to Eddie he punched in a number. He spoke. 'Hello, it's Walter. I'm afraid I'm in a little bit of trouble.'

Eddie listened to him explain what had happened. Walter made quiet apologies to whoever was on the other end but he dressed nothing up, telling it exactly as it had happened. After a couple of minutes he hung up and turned to Eddie. 'I think you can expect a call back in a short while,' Walter said then returned to his seat and his tea.

Eddie asked no further questions and they both sat staring at the telephone. It rang within ten minutes. Eddie answered. The voice on the other end said, 'Eddie?'

'That's right.'

'You're a wily old fox.' American accent, amusement in the voice. 'I should have told them not to pull one where you were involved.'

Eddie knew he should know that voice and so did the owner of it who kept talking. 'A victimless crime, Eddie. Bear that in mind. The only losers were the bookies.'

'What about the punters?' Eddie asked.

'As many won as lost as always.'

'That's not the way to look at it.'

'Lighten up, Ed, you were never this serious when we rode together.'

'Ben Turco.'

'Eddie Malloy. I wondered how long it would take you.'

'I think we'd better meet, Ben.'

'I think you're right, Ed. Come to London tomorrow, I'll buy you dinner.'

'No, thanks. Last time I was there a little

112

yellow guy tried to trim a few pounds off me which I'd sooner have lost in the sauna. You come here.'

'Aw shit, Eddie! When? I'm busy!'

'Too bad. You'd better come and bail your pal out.'

'Now?'

'No. I need some sleep. Make it tomorrow night. Buy me dinner here.'

'You're in the middle of nowhere, man! Do they know how to cook up there? Has fire been invented?'

'I'll tell them now to start rubbing the sticks together.'

When he'd hung up Eddie let a surprised and relieved Walter go home then made himself coffee and sat at his table by the window marvelling over Turco's change of career. He'd last seen the American around three years ago when Turco had retired from riding after a year as an amateur. He'd been a talented jockey but lacked the necessary nerve. They'd had a few drinks together. Eddie had always found him amusing.

How the hell had the Yank got involved in this? The guy had pots of money, he knew that. His father, a New York industrialist, was a billionaire who'd financed his son's riding career before Ben had chucked racing at the age of twenty-five to 'make his own fortune'. Well he'd

113

certainly tried to do that.

Eddie smiled as he thought back. If the police were to be involved now he would find it tough to hand Turco over. He decided he'd best phone McCarthy.

But then again, nice guy Turco had caused Mattie Stuart one hell of a lot of grief and cost him a finger and a few hours of torture that Mattie would probably never forget. Eddie had spoken to Mattie almost daily just to see how he was and he was still a frightened man, terrified the Chinese would come back again and take more than his finger. Eddie was caught between reassuring Mattie and not giving him the impression that he wanted to stay deeply involved. He saw the rescue as a one off, he wanted Mattie to understand that he'd have to look after himself from now on but couldn't quite bring himself to say that outright.

Then there was Rebecca Bow. Sexy Becky Bow. He wondered how she was. He'd rung her at the Dorchester a couple of times but she'd been out. Not wanting to appear desperate he hadn't left any message.

Rebecca had his number. Why didn't she ring him? He decided that if he didn't hear from her over the weekend he'd give her another call. Ask her out. You never knew where it might lead.

Eighteen

Turco turned up at Eddie's flat on the Saturday evening as arranged, still complaining about having to leave London and come out 'to the sticks'. He followed Eddie upstairs making shivering noises as he walked quickly towards the gas fire and stood with his back to it staring through round, steamed-up specs. He wore a long thick dark green overcoat and a fawn scarf. Although it had been three years plus since he'd seen him, Eddie thought the Yank hadn't changed.

He stood five six, slim with the square jaw, thickish lips and prominent cheekbones looks that Eddie associated with East Europeans. His hair was the colour and texture of coconut hair. He had a constantly intense look in his brown eyes. The full iris was always exposed making him look starey, frightened at times.

Reaching under his still buttoned coat he dug into the waistband of his trousers and pulled out a section of denim shirt to wipe his glasses on.

'Can't you afford a hankie?' Eddie asked.

Without looking up Turco said, 'I can afford a whole damn cotton plantation but I like to wipe my glasses on my shirt.'

'I won't ask where you wipe your nose,' Eddie said, sitting down in the easy chair.

Turco put his glasses on and, smiling, drew his coat sleeve across under his nose then said, 'You look pretty fresh for somebody who had four rides today.'

Eddie had ridden at Warwick, less than half an hour from home, and had been back in time to shower and change into clean blue jeans and a maroon sweatshirt. Beside him on the small table by the fire was a glass of whisky and ice. He sipped it and watched Turco, marvelling at the guy's attitude. You'd think he'd been caught after a game of hide and seek rather than a major scam. He waited till Turco took off his coat then poured him a whisky and soda and asked him to sit down.

Turco finished the drink in three swallows, asked for a beer, which Eddie got for him, then he settled back into the corner of the soft dark blue couch, eased off his loafers, lifted his right leg till he was lying half stretched out.

Eddie said, 'Well?'

'You wanna hear the full story?'

Eddie knew how the guy could talk. 'I'll settle for the highlights.'

Turco smiled, settled deeper, swigged

some beer and started talking. 'When I came over here four years ago from Westchester County to ride in England for a season it wasn't for the sport, sport. I was convinced that good money could be made from betting on horses over jumps. Now racing over jumps back home takes place about as often as an orgy in a convent as you probably know and I needed to play regularly. The beauty of betting on jump racing here is that you can get to know the horses so well. The same ones appear season after season giving you the chance to learn all about their true abilities, their characters, which courses they like, what ground suits them and, well, you know, I don't have to tell you.

'Anyway, I had developed this computer system for analysing everything about a horse, not just its current form but everything from its breeding to whether or not the lad who looked after it loved it or didn't give a toss. I was convinced the system would work and that it would make me heaps of money and that it would help me show my dad that you didn't have to be in industry or big business to make a million.

'The one thing I didn't know, one thing vital to the success of my system, was whether jump racing in England was straight. You know the stories you hear 'cause you've heard them yourself. You know what I'm saying, Eddie?'

Eddie nodded and watched him, studied this intense little dynamo of a man who slugged his beer and sat up straight now, sliding forward to sit on the edge of the couch as he warmed to his mission.

'Now, I could have paid for information, I could have mixed it with the bookies and the tough guys, the hard-bitten regulars at the races every day, schmoozed with the touts and the sharpies at night, but I didn't. Know why? Because I had to get the knowledge from the inside. I had to get it by doing it, by taking part, by mixing with you guys in the weighing rooms up and down the country, by going out there and riding round with you, against you, competing, watching, listening, finding out exactly how it was, how straight it was, who was taking bribes to pull them, who was fixing races, who the bullies were, who the guys with the influence were and watching how they used it.

'And I don't have to tell you what I found, Eddie. You already know. I found that the game was about as straight as a guy like me could pray for. Straighter! Ninety-five per cent straight when the best I'd thought I'd find it would have been seventy-five and even at that I'd have made money, let me tell you. So when I found it was ninety-five per cent reliable you can imagine the hurry I was in to hang up the boots and saddles.

'I was tempted to go after six months and just steam into those bookies but I made myself see the full year out, knew I had to be totally professional about it. And, Eddie, can I tell you something?' He drank more beer, the gas from it seeming to pop his eyes open even wider. He put the can on the carpet and as he sat up again he burped loudly. 'Pardon me! Listen, I thought you guys were crazy. I used to drive to Plumpton and Kelso and Southwell and all those other godforsaken places for just one ride knowing lots of you guys were doing exactly the same. I'd watch you go out to ride a bad novice in the cold and the rain and the mud with nothing in your stomachs but black coffee and butterflies and I'd sit there waiting to see who'd come back in the ambulance.

'And I'll tell you something, Eddie, I never was so glad I was born into money!' He stretched out an explanatory hand lest Eddie misunderstand. 'Don't get me wrong! I'm not being boastful or trying to bring up a class thing or anything, Christ knows there's enough of that over here already. What I'm saying is I felt genuine relief and not a little humility, I can tell you, that I was doing it through choice.'

'We all do it through choice,' Eddie said, leaning forward to lower the heat on the fire.

'Okay, accepted, but you know what I mean. I could quit when I wanted. Most of you guys can't. Most of you are addicted. You don't know anything else.' Turco opened both hands now, almost pleading for his point of view to be accepted. 'It's a slow form of Russian roulette, Eddie, several games each day, a spin of the barrel every time you swing up into that saddle. And you guys can't get away! You won't stop till you find one in the chamber then it'll be too late.'

'Maybe.' His preaching was beginning to irritate Eddie now. 'Go on. We haven't got all night.'

'Okay, fine, sorry, Eddie. I was just trying to get across how important it all was to me.'

'You're doing just that now, cut to the chase.'

'Okay, long story short. I knew I could trust you guys and that was the final ingredient. I quit riding, took a flat in London, set up my system and started taking money off bookmakers for a living. Within eighteen months I'd made almost two and a half million dollars. Trouble was I couldn't get bets on any more. Every bookie closed my account. I moved the operation on course for a while but they limited my stakes so much it wasn't worth going on. Tried a few agents then around the country and got almost another six months and another half million dollars out of that before the bookies got wise and closed the agents down.

'I could have taken a break, looked for a few more agents, started the treadmill running again, but I thought, why? Why keep going through it all? It was becoming just like an everyday nine till five job again and I thought the hell with it! I'll figure out a way to get those guys back for closing my accounts.' He raised the beer can again, pressing it so hard to his mouth this time that it left a pink exclamation mark on his top lip. Eddie watched the mark fade quickly as Turco shuffled his feet and rearranged his thin body into a comfortable position for the next burst.

Elbows on knees and hands clasped he went on. 'I messed around with a few things which didn't really work out when, just as I thought I was going to have to quit, the authorities go and introduce something that they may as well have delivered to me first in a gift box the size of the Ritz.' His curiously round brown eyes sparkled now and Eddie noticed in them the reflection of the gas fire's two burning columns.

Turco smiled widely, wildly. 'They brought in the still photo finish picture. On screen. Immediate. No print. No developing. Just a frozen image from video as the horses passed the post. Know what I said to that, Eddie? Wanna know what I said? Apart from thank you very much me lords I said, dim. I said, dim, Eddie, D-I-M. An acronym, which belies the name, misleads the innocent listener. For dim read smart, read very smart!'

Eddie waited patiently, wondering if Turco's ancestors had ever run those travelling medicine shows in the Old West.

'Dim stands for Digital Image Manipulator. It was an idea I'd been messing round with for a while based on the sophisticated technology in movie making. It's all technical so I won't bore you.'

Too late, Eddie thought, swilling ice through what remained of his whisky.

'But what it means in essence is that the operator of the photo finish freeze frame can, with DIM software installed, change the finishing positions on screen almost instantly so that the judge, by the time he's watched the others pass the post live as it were and turned to the screen to check the photo, sees exactly what we want him to see so he's got no choice but to call the result as he sees it on screen.'

Eddie said, 'By which time you've made a killing among the bookies betting on the outcome of the photo finish.'

'Correct!' said Turco proudly and drained the last of his beer.

'And you felt sorry for the poor mugs who were connected with the real winners so you decided to pay them, anonymously, what they would have won in prize money.'

'Only fair!' beamed Turco.

'And did you ever allow for disappointment, or for bets lost, or for the poor punters who keep the show going every day?'

'They'd put it down to luck, Eddie. These guys have photos going against them every day.'

'So you didn't think beyond that? All that high tech brain power and you couldn't think beyond that? Not even about how simple it would be for someone like me to spot the routine of compensation and draw the obvious conclusion that one of your henchmen was delivering the cash by hand?'

Turco looked puzzled and slightly hurt. Shaking his head slowly Eddie got up and went to the fridge. Bringing back another beer he handed it to Turco saying, 'Settle back because I'm going to tell *you* a little story now, about a trainer called Mattie Stuart and the trouble you got him into.'

Nineteen

Accustomed all his life to the fresh air of
the open fields and the hills Kim Oliver
found the atmosphere in the breakfast
room like a hothouse. The refectory they
called it, this place with the long tables, the
hard shiny floor and white walls; with its
cloying fatty cooking smells, dismal adults
and pale children who seemed to be either
unruly or silent and still as dummies. No
happy medium. No normality.

Kim chewed toast and drank tea from
a white mug resisting the temptation to
dip the toast in the tea as he would
have done at home, not really wanting
to do anything here he would normally
do at home, anxious to leave no part of
his personality here after he'd gone.

He looked at the windows; ten in this
high-walled room, the lower sill of each
more than six feet off the floor. Easily
reachable by dragging a chair or table
over but he couldn't see if they were
locked. Once morning classes broke for
lunch he'd try to wander around as much
of the building as possible to look for the
best way out. That thought set Kim off

dreaming again of the farm and how big it was going to be, and for what seemed a long time he was off to the hills again.

Slowly he became aware of an adult standing close by him at the table. Kim looked up to see the tall, thin, grey-haired, stern-faced Mr Young staring down at him. 'Come with me, Kim, please,' he said and walked towards the door. The other children watched in silence as Kim slid the bench back and stepped out to follow Mr Young out of the refectory.

They were in the same office Kim had been brought to on the first day: small, dingy, soulless and, like the refectory, overheated. Seated by a desk was a man around the same age as Kim's father. He had the same hair colour too and a similar nose. Different coloured eyes and more of a forehead but the first sight of him gave Kim's heart a curious lift and the boy watched him get up and come smiling towards him to offer his hand.

'Kim, my name is Campbell Ogilvie, I'm a solicitor who did some work for your father.'

Shaking Mr Ogilvie's hand Kim felt suddenly grown up and responsible, ready to discuss the business of the farm as his father would have done. Then just as suddenly he felt awkward and stupid for thinking like that and his face reddened as he lowered his eyes and sat down in the hard upright chair Mr Young had slid towards him.

'Kim?'

Slowly Kim looked up again to see Mr Ogilvie gazing even more kindly at him. He seemed a nice man, the first decent one he'd met since the helicopter crew. Mr Ogilvie went on, 'Kim, I was very very sorry to hear about your tragic news ...'

Kim was confused for a second. Had some terrible thing happened? News is something that's much less than a week old. '... I knew your parents well. They were good people and I know they were very proud of you and had big plans for you. I've come here today to tell you about those plans and the provisions your parents made for the future.'

Provisions. Future. Maybe he wouldn't have to run away after all. His attention was now riveted on Mr Ogilvie who was leaning forward on his chair, elbows on knees, fingertips touching. 'Once the insurance policy payments come through there will be enough money to let you complete your education at a very good boarding school and then go on to university.' Mr Ogilvie watched for Kim's reaction but the dark haired boy sat staring intently, knowing there was more.

Ogilvie cleared his throat. 'I'm afraid that the farm is to be sold, Kim.'

The farm is to be sold.

The words reverberated inside his skull as though a church bell had been rung in there. He could find nothing to say but the words came out unbidden, instinctively. 'You can't sell the farm.'

Mr Ogilvie reddened slightly, not relishing the prospect of the boy breaking down. He knew from discussions with Kim's father how much the place meant to him. 'Kim, I'm sorry, but there is nobody to run the place, nothing to ...'

'I'll run it, sir! I'll look after it.' Kim was off the chair now, feet splayed, hands apart, pleading.

Mr Ogilvie shook his head slightly. 'Kim, you can't. I'm sorry, you're too young.'

'But I can do it! Please, I can do it! I've done it before.'

'I know how capable you are, Kim, but I'm afraid the law simply wouldn't allow it. Look, the money from the sale will be put in trust for you until you are twenty-one. Maybe then you can buy the farm back. Interest will have accrued, you could well be in a position to buy it back if you still wanted to.'

Kim fought back tears of frustration and clenched his fists in anguish and Mr

Ogilvie glanced at Mr Young and was disgusted to see a smirk of enjoyment on the man's face. Ogilvie stood up. 'Please leave us alone for a few minutes, Mr Young.'

Young looked surprised and half rose from his chair. 'But I'm supposed to ...'

'Please give us some privacy. I have some more personal news for Kim.'

Young scowled and left the room. Kim stood, shoulders drooping, head down, resolved not to raise it till his eyes had cleared, determined not to let them think he was beaten. Mr Ogilvie reached forward and put his right hand softly on Kim's left shoulder. 'Believe me, Kim, and believe in yourself. The next nine years will pass much more quickly than you think and you will be able to buy the farm back if you want it badly enough.'

Kim edged away slowly and sat back down on the seat. What had remained of his world was in fragments. Campbell Ogilvie watched the boy with a wretchedness of his own as he tried to decide whether to tell Kim the other piece of news he'd brought. Information that would either give the boy renewed hope or finish him off completely. It had been the most harrowing week Kim was ever likely to face and Ogilvie was now finding the whole situation equally distressing.

The solicitor knew he had a professional duty to complete his task by telling Kim everything before leaving that office but he simply did not know if he had it in him as a human being to test the boy's spirit any further on this day. What he had to tell him would only have helped prepare Kim for the ultimate news which Ogilvie himself still awaited. He wouldn't know the final outcome for a few days so it was probably best, he convinced himself, to leave it; that would give Kim time to recover from the misery of this morning.

The thought of returning within a week bearing even worse news for the boy was something Ogilvie could not even bring himself to contemplate. He would go home and pray that the result he needed would materialise. If it didn't and Kim chose to blame the messenger then the boy would undoubtedly hate the sight of this particular solicitor as long as he lived.

Ogilvie called Young back in and said his goodbyes to both of them. While Kim walked along the corridor to his maths class, head held high and tears beaten for now, outside in the cold northern air Mr Ogilvie wept quietly as he walked to his car.

Twenty

Being caught by Eddie was, in some ways, a relief to Ben Turco. He was bored with the photo finish scam and eager to find some other way of fleecing his old enemies. Eddie had called yesterday to discuss how to arrange a compensation payment to Mattie Stuart. Turco had agreed to pay Mattie £25,000 if Eddie agreed not to hand him over to the authorities.

Eddie added another condition: Turco had to agree to stop the photo finish scam immediately and never to get involved in fraud in racing again. Turco promised he'd comply and Eddie had promised he'd make things right with Jockey Club Security.

Turco was happy with the deal. What the hell, it had been good fun while it lasted but it was time to move on. Turco was never happier than when there was a problem to solve, preferably a fiendishly difficult one like coming up with a new foolproof scheme. He already had one or two ideas.

And this time he'd leave Phil Grimond out of things. He'd had Grimond checked out before inviting him to be at the sharp end of the photo finish plot but the guy had turned on them in the end with that stupid demand to go for two more. Well now he didn't have a choice. Eddie had made sure of that. Turco was on his way to meet Grimond at a service station on the M1 in Northamptonshire.

The American swung into the carpark through the dirty slush of early December. The clouds looked as though they might be ready to snow some more. Turco had never known so much of it before January and began to wonder if he should be betting on a white Christmas. This set him wondering further on the possible creation of a snow machine which could stimulate an inch of snow to fall on the roof of the London Weather Centre—the bookies' yardstick for paying out. What a coup that would be! Imagine if he could put snow there and not a flake of it anywhere else in London.

He resolved to give it some serious thought.

Grimond was slurping soup as he waited for Turco. The fat man wore the clothes he'd had on at their last meeting: tan suit, blue shirt, navy-blue knitted tie. As he slid into the seat across from Grimond, Turco noticed a ragged ridge of red along the bottom of the fat man's moustache and wondered how long it would be before he'd get around to washing out the caked tomato soup.

Turco was irritated at having to drive up to meet him but Grimond had insisted he wasn't coming to London again. Anyway, Turco didn't mind letting him think he still had the upper hand. He'd soon put that right.

Turco eased off his brown cord jacket with the broad fake fur lapels then rolled up the sleeves of his crimson rugby shirt and undid two buttons at the neck. He smiled at Grimond. 'Hot in here.'

Grimond scowled and grunted as he spooned the last of the soup under his moustache. He slid the empty bowl away from him and splashed tea into a mug. He added milk and three sachets of sugar, stirred it with the handle of the dirty soup spoon and took a drink. He washed the tea round his mouth before swallowing then put the mug down and looked at the thin figure smiling falsely at him. 'What dates have you got?' Grimond asked.

'For what?'

'For the next two hits.'

So it was 'next' now, not 'last'.

'None.'

'None?'

'No dates. Nothing. It's all over. We've been rumbled as they say.' Turco was finding it tough to keep the spark of mischief from his eyes. He was enjoying watching Grimond's face. He told him all about Eddie.

When he finished Grimond stared at him for a while as though he despised the American for trying to fool him. 'You're a liar,' he said flatly.

'Oh no I'm not!' Turco said, suddenly remembering they were close to the pantomime season. Grimond didn't catch the seasonal mood. He said, 'You made this up to try and make me back off.'

Turco reached into his jacket pocket and pulled out a mobile phone. He pressed two buttons then held the phone up so Grimond could see the small screen. It read, 'Eddie' and gave the jockey's mobile number. Turco slid it across the grey tabletop. 'Why don't you just press send and ask him yourself?'

Grimond, unsure now, looked at the phone then stared unblinking at Turco who met his gaze. After what seemed a long time Grimond pushed the phone back across and said, 'I'll handle Malloy, you just sort out the next dates.'

Turco half laughed. 'What do you mean handle him? You're kidding! Eddie is smart and he's tough and you'd be better doing what we've done and call it quits. Be thankful he's offered us the easy way out.'

'Too easy. Eddie might know but you must have told him. Just to try and get me out of the picture.'

Turco raised his eyes and sighed in frustration. 'Look, Phil, there's no picture left, which doesn't mean we stuck the frame around you! Eddie found out because he was smarter than us. He's keeping quiet because I've agreed to recompense some of the people who suffered. Now can we just drop the whole thing and roll on home?'

'You roll on home, cowboy, and work out the next date with your two partners. Leave Malloy to me. He won't interfere.'

Twenty-one

Over the previous weekend the condition of Eddie's mother had improved so much that she was now up and out of bed for the first time in weeks. Her daughter, Louise, sat sipping tea and guiltily eating a warm Danish pastry in the bright kitchen of their Newmarket home. She could hear her mother moving around upstairs and at one point she stopped chewing and sat still, listening keenly. Her mother was humming a tune, a song Louise remembered her singing as she'd worked around the house

134

and farm all those years ago, when she'd been a child.

And her bright blue eyes filled slowly as she relived it. The few happy days the family had had were back then, back on that little stud farm in Cumbria. As the pleasant sound from upstairs faded Louise strained harder to catch the final bars, her wide mouth breaking slowly into a melancholy smile.

When the humming stopped Louise realised she was sitting with the sweet pastry poised close to her lips. She became aware of a chewed mouthful waiting to be swallowed but when she tried to get it down the lump in her throat wouldn't let it past. And she laughed at that. And the plaintive childlike sound of that laugh caught her by surprise and finally triggered the tears.

The riflecrack sound of the big letterbox being pushed roughly open snapped her back to the present and, still seated in the kitchen, Louise watched two sheaves of mail falling into the wire basket behind the door.

'Various shades of brown,' she muttered to herself as she went to collect the day's bills. And most of them were bills but there was one yellow envelope with a Carlisle postmark. It was addressed to her parents. Dad had been dead a year. The label on it was neatly typed and the heavy franking mark read 'Ogilvie, Speed and Minto, Solicitors'. Louise normally opened and dealt with all the mail but she thought that it might be best if Mum opened this one herself. She took it upstairs.

Her mother was by the window in her bedroom, fully dressed, grey hair fixed in a tight bun. She even wore a touch of make-up, the first time since the funeral that she'd taken the trouble. The sun highlighted the older woman's right profile as Louise approached and the resemblance between mother and daughter was noticeable even though half a lifetime of worry and misery had made Mrs Malloy look at least a decade older than her fifty-eight years. Louise touched her arm and smiled widely making the point of her upturned nose dip slightly. 'Mum, you look brilliant!'

Mrs Malloy turned. 'I feel much better. As well as I've felt in the past year.'

'And you look it. The kettle's on, come down and have some tea and a Danish. Make me feel less guilty. I've had mine!' They linked arms and went downstairs, Louise becoming aware in the narrow hall of the smell of talc from her mother. The relief of seeing her mother almost fully recovered so quickly had made Louise forget about the letter she carried in her left hand. Her mind raced as she saw the world opening up again.

She had pictured herself being stuck here for years looking after an increasingly dependent mother, nursing her alone till she herself was grey and wrinkled and sour. Till her bright eyes had been dulled, her dark hair become grey and wiry, all semblance of attractiveness gone, taking with it the chances of finally finding the man she'd been waiting for all her life.

The man she'd thought she'd found seven years ago. Stephen. Stephen of the dark eyes and even darker soul. The marriage had lasted five years, patched and mended over the final two till it was little more than a ramshackle vehicle slowly dragging two reluctant passengers along a road they no longer wanted to travel. With undisguised irony it had finally lurched into the scrapyard on St Valentine's Day and she hadn't seen Stephen since.

But she'd been reunited with her mother. She'd made peace with Father before he died. And she was rebuilding her relationship with Eddie. Things were getting better and the rapid recovery of her mother brought a renewed certainty in her heart that she was close to finding the man she would love for the rest of her life.

Her thirtieth birthday was sixteen months away. He would come before that. Surely he would.

Her mother sat at the big pine table slowly stirring her tea. The warm Danish sat temptingly inside the delicate flowered border of the fine china plate that Louise pushed towards her. Mrs Malloy smiled slowly. She still had all her teeth but Louise noticed narrow gaps between them now in the bottom row and they grew increasingly discoloured.

She'd put the yellow envelope on the table and forgotten about it. Her mother noticed it and asked what it was. Louise said, 'Oh, that was what I originally came upstairs to tell you about. It's from some solicitor's office in Carlisle.' She handed it to her mother who looked suddenly wary. She stared at the front of it for some time and her frown grew deeper as she pushed a wrinkled, workworn finger under the flap and slowly peeled it open. Louise watched as she eased the matching yellow page out and carefully unfolded it. Sunlight through the window showed the swirling watermark in the expensive paper.

Louise watched her mother's face drain of colour. The letter dropped from her hands, hit the edge of the table and somersaulted gracefully to the floor. Louise gasped in panic and surprise as she lunged forward to try and catch her mother as she collapsed unconscious.

Twenty-two

His one thumb, three still-scabbed fingers and scarred hand held a morbid fascination for Mattie Stuart and on the trip home from Lambourn that Tuesday, Eddie chuckled at the memory of Mattie regularly spreading the remaining fingers on any flat surface and admiring the handiwork of the Chinaman.

The drunker they'd both got the more they'd laughed about it. When Eddie had told the trainer about the twenty-five grand, Mattie had almost done a dance and then gone on to quiz Eddie intensely but good-naturedly as to how he'd managed to organise that. Despite the booze, Eddie had remained discreet and steered Mattie off the subject. When they were both on their way to becoming completely drunk Eddie asked Mattie if he'd seen Rebecca Bow lately.

Mattie leered at him over his whisky glass. 'Fancy her, do you?'

'Not if I'm tramping on anybody's toes, if you know what I mean.'

'Meaning my toes, you bugger! Well you've got no worries about that. Becky and me are just business partners.'

Eddie looked at him. 'I didn't know.'

'I don't have to tell you everything, do I?' Mattie teased.

'Business partners in the stable, you mean?' Eddie asked.

'Well, not strictly. Becky sent me two horses and I'm training them for nothing till her twenty-fifth birthday when she gets another million from daddy's trust fund.'

'So when's the birthday?'

'March 17th, Gold Cup day.' Mattie drew on his forehead with a scarred middle finger. 'Etched in my brain. King Simba wins the Gold Cup and Becky Bow gets her million.'

Eddie swirled whisky and ice. 'And then what? If you don't mind me asking.'

Mattie smiled. Quite drunk now, Eddie thought. 'Then Miss Bow buys another half-dozen horses and a half share in the yard.'

Eddie was tempted to ask if that meant a half share in the debt to the Chinese but he didn't want to raise that particular spectre right then. He thought about Rebecca Bow. The more he learned about her the more interesting she became. He wondered if she ever would ring him.

It was mid-afternoon next day when Eddie got home. The yard was quiet. Horses dozed in their boxes. Some of the lads would be grabbing a nap too before evening stables. The others would be in the local bookie's shop. Eddie unlocked the door and hauled his kitbag upstairs.

Just inside the door he stopped, as he always did, and looked around. He'd had his share of intruders over the past years and he liked to reassure himself that nothing had been disturbed.

All seemed fine.

He dumped the bag by the couch, switched the radio onto 5 Live and clicked the switch on the kettle. The light on his answerphone was flashing: he had seven messages. Two were from an impatient Peter McCarthy of Jockey Club Security, and four were from trainers unable to reach him on his mobile in the last forty-eight hours. The final one was timed at 9.42 that morning. He played it and Louise's tearful voice begged him to call quickly, to come quick, as Mum was in hospital, very seriously ill.

Twenty-three

Campbell Ogilvie had left the children's home trying to convince himself he'd done the right thing in not telling Kim Oliver what he knew would have to be told.

He'd excused his actions to himself on the grounds that he was only acting humanely but deep down he knew he'd neglected his professional duty. In the end his agonising over it lasted less than twenty-four hours. A telephone message on the Wednesday morning, confirmed by fax a few minutes later, saw him pulling on his long dark brown coat and trudging reluctantly out into the freezing east wind to head back to the children's home.

Since hearing the farm was to be sold Kim had calmed himself, made himself try to think rationally about what he could do to save it. If he accepted the course mapped out by his parents of boarding school then university, he knew he'd have little chance of getting the farm back even if he did have the cash. The new owners would be too well settled in, too much in love with the place to ever want to leave.

He wondered if Mr Ogilvie could be persuaded to let him have the insurance money that was to be set aside for his education. He could start up his own business with that and maybe make enough in a year to buy back the farm. Okay, they'd say he was only twelve, but he knew how to run a farm. He could employ older people to help out with accounts and stuff.

Maybe the farm wouldn't be sold for

years, anyway. He'd heard his father say often enough how tough things were for farmers so it had to be possible they wouldn't manage to find a buyer quickly. Lying awake on the Tuesday night he'd resolved to ask Mr Young if he could see Mr Ogilvie again as soon as possible.

On the Wednesday morning Kim rose early and ironed the only white shirt he had and pressed his dark trousers. He showered and combed back the thick dark hair still damp from washing. Kim looked at himself in the oval plastic-framed mirror in his room. It was important to look as mature as possible. He wanted the adults to start taking him seriously. In the mid-morning break he made his way along the corridor towards Mr Young's office.

Ten paces from it Kim heard the outside door close and a few seconds later Mr Ogilvie walked into view. They both stopped and looked at each other. Mr Ogilvie smiled and said, 'Kim, good morning.'

'Good morning, sir. I was just going to ask Mr Young if I could see you.'

Ogilvie's mind raced as he wondered if someone had called the home that morning. But Kim looked reasonably untroubled, his fresh clean freckled face open and honest. Ogilvie said, 'Well that's a coincidence, Kim, because I've come to

143

see you again anyway. If you don't mind waiting a second I'll just let Mr Young know I've arrived.'

Kim nodded, gazing at Ogilvie as he knocked on the office door and obeyed the instruction to enter. The solicitor had seemed on edge. Kim wondered if something had happened. Maybe the insurance company wasn't going to pay out after all. Maybe they'd already found a buyer for the farm. His mind raced looking for other potential disasters and he leaned back against the cream coloured walls, resting his bottom on his hands, head down in deep thought.

The office door opened and Mr Young came out smiling. He said to Kim, 'Mr Ogilvie wishes to speak to you again.' He stepped to the side holding an arm outstretched to usher Kim inside. Kim was relieved when Mr Young pulled the door closed leaving him alone in the room with Mr Ogilvie who'd removed his coat to reveal a well-cut tweed suit over a mustard coloured shirt and brown tie. He crossed his legs and Kim noticed the heavy brown brogues. Mr Ogilvie had big feet. He asked Kim to sit down. Kim chose the same chair as yesterday but tried to sit straighter in it, taller.

Ogilvie's smile faded and his voice sounded tense. 'Kim, I have some more news for you which I've just received this morning.' He picked up the soft leather briefcase, undid the buckle then thought better of it. What was the point of pulling out the fax? He'd only be using it as a prop, a piece of paper to try and push the blame onto.

He put the case down again and said, 'Kim, I know that there could be no bigger shock to you than the dreadful thing that happened to your parents but I have something to tell you that you may find distressing. That ... that you will find distressing.'

Kim swallowed involuntarily and felt his mouth go suddenly dry.

Ogilvie tried to relax a bit, leaning forward to place his elbows on his knees. He was tempted to look away, to hang his head and spend some more time winding himself up for this but he knew that would only be torturing Kim more. He looked directly at the now pale-faced boy and said, 'Kim, I've got to tell you that your mum and dad were not your natural parents.'

Kim stared at him, not really taking it in. Ogilvie continued, 'Your mum and dad adopted you at birth. They couldn't have children of their own and this made you extra special to them. I know this. I've known them both from before you were born.'

Kim was forcing himself to replay these words in his head trying to make them sink in but something was making him think that Ogilvie had the wrong person, that he'd gone to the wrong children's home this morning. Kim had had his share of bad luck, surely this was someone else's mistakenly delivered to him.

Ogilvie watched him. 'Kim, do you understand what I'm saying?'

Kim nodded vaguely. His mouth had dropped open an inch.

Ogilvie said, 'I know it must be desperately difficult for you to take in and perhaps I should have pre-warned you yesterday but I was waiting for one more link in the chain and I received that, so to speak, this morning.' He paused to draw a long breath then interlocked his fingers and leaned further forward. Kim watched now as if hypnotised. Ogilvie couldn't tell if he was taking this in but he had to continue.

'Your mother and father made separate Wills, Kim, and both of them specifically requested that should something like this happen, this terrible tragedy, that I was to act on their behalf and contact your natural parents to offer them the chance to, to renew ... to take over ...'

'To have me back?' Kim offered quietly as the reality of it began to sweep over him.

'Yes, in effect.' Ogilvie felt his scalp prickle with sweat.

Kim said, 'And they don't want me.'

Ogilvie cleared his throat. 'The family circumstances there are very very difficult, Kim. I spoke to them this morning. If there was any possible way I'm certain they would have you back.' Ogilvie hated the expression, felt as though he was trying to shunt damaged goods around.

Kim sat half stooped now, staring at his shoes. 'What're their names?'

'I'm sorry, Kim, I can't tell you.'

'Why?'

'It wouldn't be ethical and it wouldn't help you in the long run. I'm sorry.'

'Where do they live, then, can you tell me that?'

'No, I'm afraid I can tell you absolutely nothing about them. It was an agreement your mum and dad had with them when you were born and that cannot be broken.'

'But Mum and Dad are dead, do my real parents know that?'

Another deep breath. 'Yes, they do.'

Kim stared at the floor. Ogilvie writhed inside as he watched the boy swallow lumps in his throat, watched him desperately trying to come to terms with this.

'And they still don't want me. Won't they even see me, just for an hour or something or half an hour?'

'I'm sure the family would want to, I'm certain, but many things have happened in the past fifteen years and those things mean ... they have brought about circumstances which make it impossible now for them to see you no matter how much they may want to.'

Kim sat in silence for a minute, downcast and angry. Angry that everything had happened to *him*. Angry that his mum and dad had never told him the truth, never explained. Angry that his real mum and dad had simply given him away. And angry, sad, desolate now that twice his natural parents had rejected him.

Ogilvie watched him, feeling a deep sorrow for this good, pleasant, well-mannered, fine-looking boy. He wished for a moment his own circumstances would permit an adoption but he quashed that instinct quickly, knowing himself to be prone to outlandish notions.

Kim said, 'You said about family, Mr Ogilvie, you mentioned the family. Does that mean I have brothers and sisters?'

'Kim, look, I'm sorry, I ...' Ogilvie raised his cupped hands and massaged his face and eyes. 'You have a brother and a sister and please do not tell anyone I told you that.'

Despite his misery, Kim's heart leapt for a moment. He'd always wanted a brother.

In his younger days he'd invented one who'd gone everywhere around the farm with him, slept in the same room, loved the same things. Kim managed a smile as he remembered and Ogilvie, seeing it, relaxed a notch or two.

'Can you tell me how old my brother is?'

'I can't. I don't know. I'm sorry, Kim, I can't tell you any more. You realise that this changes nothing about the plans we discussed yesterday? You'll still get to go to boarding school and university and you'll still have the chance to buy back the farm some day. And who knows, maybe your real family will find that their circumstances will change sufficiently in the coming years to seek a reunion with you. Stranger things have happened.'

Kim nodded slowly, not really listening, his thoughts miles away. Maybe nobody else wanted him but Kim would bet they hadn't asked his brother. Kim *knew* his brother would want him. Absent-mindedly he shook hands with Mr Ogilvie who was rambling on about how he'd already chosen a wonderful boarding school. As Kim made his way back along the corridor he knew he wasn't going to any boarding school and he knew he wasn't staying in this place one more night. Kim Oliver was going to find his brother.

Twenty-four

Louise sat in the waiting room of Cambridge General Hospital cursing the invention of answerphones. She knew she'd been too hasty in calling Eddie's number, she'd panicked and left that message about Mum, and Eddie would come rushing to the hospital as soon as he got it. If she'd had his mobile number she'd have stopped him.

Mrs Malloy had regained consciousness shortly after being admitted and she'd clutched Louise's hand grimly and made her promise to call the solicitors and say that on no account did she ever want to see the boy and that he was not to try and make contact under any circumstances. And she made her promise too that she would never mention it to Eddie.

Although she'd been estranged from him for many years Mrs Malloy understood her son well enough to know he would champion the boy's cause. Eddie's own experiences in life would ensure he'd come down strongly on the boy's side. If Eddie were to find out then the result would be further family misery and God knows they'd all had enough of that. The past was done with and it should have been buried last December along with her husband. Now, a year on, it loomed again, more threatening than ever.

Weak and shocked as her mother was, Louise could see from the passionate way she spoke from the hospital bed that it was pointless arguing. Louise had some curiosity about this brother she'd never known, about the reasons he'd been sent for adoption. She recalled now the lie her parents had told her when her pregnant mother had returned sad and weeping from hospital on that hot July day twelve years ago saying that the child had been stillborn.

A boy child. How painful for her mother to lose him too after all that had happened before. The adoption would have been her father's decision, his command, another example of his tyranny. Of this she was certain. That tyranny had so scarred her mother that Louise was not surprised that she had totally rejected the chance to meet the boy, terrified by the prospect.

Ten years ago, or maybe even five, Louise would have tried to persuade her. But with things as they were Louise was unwilling to chance driving her mother back into a long-term sick bed. She felt deep sympathy for the boy having lost both his adoptive parents but who could tell how that would affect him? Who could know what he was like as a person? And if he turned out difficult Louise knew it would be she who'd be left to try and straighten him out, to bring him up properly, and Louise was just not willing to give up any more of her life for anybody else, brother or no brother, orphan or not. Jesus Christ, she was almost thirty years old and she had her own life to worry about, her own comfort and security to search for. Why feel guilty? Nobody in her position should be made to feel guilty!

When Eddie arrived she'd just tell him Mum had had a relapse but she was going to be fine and she was sorry she'd panicked and rung him like that. And when Eddie got there almost running down the corridor, that's exactly what she told him and as he went to get them both a drink from the vending machine she crossed the waiting room floor, entered the ladies' toilet, locked herself in a cubicle and tore the lawyer's letter into tiny yellow pieces. Although she emptied the cistern three times trying to flush the shreds away one tiny determined piece refused to disappear. She shrugged and, feeling very much better, returned to join Eddie.

Eddie spent an hour with Louise and

half an hour with his mother before driving back through the darkness to Shropshire. He'd had to refuse Louise's invitation to stay overnight at the stud as he was riding at Catterick in North Yorkshire the next day. Besides, he was satisfied that his mother was going to be okay and saw no real need to stay close to the hospital. They'd said they'd let her out the next morning if nothing untoward happened overnight.

Back at the flat there was a message from Ben Turco asking Eddie to ring him right away. Eddie did.

Turco answered but his voice boomed and echoed down the line. Eddie said, 'You sound like you're in a cathedral.'

'The cathedral of dreams, Eddie, the cathedral of high technology. Would you believe I am two rooms away from where the telephone is?'

'I'd believe you're two rooms short of a full apartment.'

'Excuse me?'

'Forget it. You wanted to speak to me.'

'Yes.' Still the big echo.

'Ben, do me a favour? Get to the phone and pick it up. I feel like I'm talking to God.'

'You almost are! Only kidding! Jesus, that's blasphemy.'

A few seconds later Turco's voice sounded normal. 'I called you to warn you about Phil Grimond—you know, the guy who was in with us?'

'The photo finish operator?'

'That's him. I spoke to him this morning, told him you knew so we didn't have any choice but to pack up but he was having none of it. He said I was to let him deal with you and I was just to sort out the next date.'

Eddie thought for a few seconds then said, 'Why does Grimond actually need you? If he's got the computer chip or whatever it is why doesn't he just get himself another partner to help him run the scam?'

'Ah, well now ...!' Eddie could hear that Turco was smiling. 'There was no way Ben Turco was letting go control of that little baby. The system won't authorise until I send it a signal via satellite. No one can run it without my co-operation.'

'Okay. What did Grimond mean when he said he'd deal with me?'

'He didn't elaborate but I don't think his intentions are honourable.'

'So how did you leave it? Is he expecting you to carry on, to give him another date?'

'I told him what I'd already told him ten times before, that I was finished, but

I don't think he's gonna leave it at that. He's a greedy man, Eddie, and he looks and sounds a bit desperate. It wouldn't surprise me if he's got himself in with some people he can't handle, some guys out of his league. Maybe it's them who're putting the pressure on him to set up another one.'

'But how could he have tied anyone else in to the photo finish con? He never knew what race it would be, if any. There's obviously no way of predicting whether or not a race will end in a photo.'

'But if it did and we were operating on it he'd only have to tell his confederates to keep an eye on Magnus and see if he started betting on the outcome then they'd just follow him in.'

'True. I hadn't thought of that.'

'So, Edward, the problem remains. What do we do about Grimond?'

'I don't know. McCarthy's away for a few days. He's promised to meet me as soon as he gets back which I think is on Friday. I can easily tell him about Grimond and still keep you out of it. You've given the guy a chance to pull out and get clear and if Grimond chooses not to then I wouldn't feel any obligation to him. Let the Jockey Club Security guys get him if they can though they're not the brightest bunch around.'

'So why don't we help them along a little bit?'

'How?'

'Set him up. Tell him there's another job on, authorise the chip then have those security guys bust in on him.'

'Wouldn't he try to drop you in it, then?'

'He could try all he wanted but there's no way he'd be able to prove it.'

'You're sure?'

'Positive. I'd take my chances for the sake of getting him off my back once and for all.'

'Okay, how do we play it?'

'The way I said, we just need to work out the details.'

'Fine. Just bear in mind McCarthy will need about a week's notice to get his team in gear.'

'Okay. See you soon.'

'Ben, when you get off the phone, can you arrange another transfer into my bank account. Five grand should do.'

'Operating expenses?'

'Payment of a debt from you to Laura Gilpin, the girl who trains Samson's Curls.'

'She got her money! Walter delivered it!'

'Walter tried to, remember? Trouble was he dropped into my place first and never got any further.'

156

'Oh! ... I forgot about that. Okay, no problem. When are you seeing Miss Gilpin?'

'She's got a horse entered at Catterick tomorrow. She'll be there.'

'Fine.'

'Right. See you.'

'Eddie!'

'Uhuh?'

'Tell Miss Gilpin I'm sorry, will you? Anonymously?'

'I will.'

Twenty-five

Yorkshire's December winds were as cold as ever though the day was bright and clear as Eddie parked and hauled his kitbag out of the back seat. The first race was two hours away but the newspaper sellers, bookmakers, police and catering staff were making their way in, setting things up for what would be a crowd of no more than a couple of thousand. Still, Eddie knew they loved their jump racing up here and the small crowd would keep the atmosphere charged up.

As Eddie approached the exit from the carpark he heard a shout from behind him.

He turned to see the unmistakable figure of Tiny Delaware lumbering towards him. Tiny was six feet seven inches tall and must have weighed thirty stone. Although fat-bellied he had huge broad shoulders and a barrel chest. Eddie thought he looked like a modern version of a fairy-tale giant.

Tiny always wore a long tan canvas-type coat, the many stains on it looking like small maps on a wide parchment. Then there was the big white Stetson and the tartan kipper tie. He had been around racing for as long as Eddie could remember and was one of the more colourful characters. Likeable but with a history of shady deals behind him.

Eddie smiled, waiting to feel the ground shake, as Tiny hurried towards him. He started slowing down about ten yards away and pulled himself to a halt right in front of Eddie who said, 'How you doing, Tiny?'

'Brilliant, Eddie! Great! The past week has been the best of my life ...' He was panting. Eddie waited. Tiny, red-cheeked under the shade of the Stetson, went on, '... came at just the right time too with Christmas just round the corner.'

'Good. Good for you,' Eddie said, knowing that whatever money Tiny had he would lose by the weekend never mind by Christmas. 'What can I do for you, Tiny?'

Looking perplexed, the big man was pushing his hands deep into his trouser pockets. 'Eddie, I'm sorry, I didn't mean to delay you. Won't keep you a few seconds actually, if I can just ...' He dug deeper in his pockets. 'Tell you what it is, I just bought my little nephew an autograph book for Christmas and he's racing mad, racing bonkers ... where is the bloody thing? I thought I'd ask you to sign it, Eddie, if you don't mind. I want to get a few jockeys and trainers in it for him. Be a lovely surprise.'

'Of course I will. No problem.'

'Great. You'll be the first in it. If I can find it. Bloody typical, i'n't it?' Tiny felt the outside of his coat below the pocket, squeezing with his right hand. His face lit up in satisfaction and he opened the coat to reach inside a big poacher's pocket. Eddie watched him pull out banded bundles of ten and twenty pound notes which he tried to balance in the crook of his arm.

Eddie said, 'You have had a good week. You weren't kidding.'

Tiny smiled wide. 'Small change!' Still pulling out wads of cash he handed three bundles to Eddie. 'Here, hold this a minute, I'm near the bottom now!' Eddie held the cash and took two more before Tiny found the autograph book and handed it to him, taking the money and stuffing it back into the deep pocket.

Eddie reached into his jacket pocket for a pen. 'What's the boy's name?'

'Matthew, it is. That would be great, Eddie, if you could put, to Matthew with best wishes.'

Eddie wrote on the first page of the thick leather-bound book and handed it back to Tiny with a smile.

'Brilliant, Eddie, thanks a lot! Now what do you know today?'

'I know you'll probably lose that money unless you keep it in your pocket.'

Tiny smiled. 'No chance. I'll be putting half of it on the hotpot you ride in the second.'

'It'll be odds-on, Tiny, you should never bet odds on when they've got eight obstacles to jump.'

'Nah, he's different class. See you in the winner's enclosure.'

'Well, I hope so.' Eddie turned to head through the entrance.

Tiny said, 'Come on, I'll walk in with you.' And they ambled into the racecourse, Tiny slipping an arm round Eddie's shoulder and leaning low to pump him for more information.

With no ride in the first Eddie sat in the

weighing room catching up on the gossip among the northern jockeys. He wondered if anything had filtered out about Turco's racket. He knew Ben wouldn't have said anything but he didn't know enough about his sidekicks, Walter and Magnus. Nothing was mentioned in the warm fug of the Catterick changing room and Eddie was in a relaxed mood when he went out to ride the favourite in the second race.

The horse was called Keelhaul and it was going for its fourth win in a row. An unbeaten novice hurdler, Eddie had ridden it in all three victories and today it was three to one on to beat much inferior opposition. But Eddie wasn't complacent. He knew that Catterick was the only course in the country where the record of winning favourites over jumps was worse than that on its flat racing track.

When Keelhaul's trainer legged him up into the saddle Eddie was prepared for the usual jinking and jogging. The narrow, almost black horse was an edgy type, all nervous energy, a natural front-runner who couldn't wait to get on with things. But this time the horse stood still as Eddie slipped his toes into the stirrups and gathered the reins. Pleasantly surprised Eddie smiled down at Keelhaul's lad. 'You been sending him to transcendental meditation classes?' The lad looked slightly puzzled then gave a slightly embarrassed half-smile and tugged on the bridle leading Keelhaul back round the parade ring as the trainer gripped the half-folded blanket letting his horse walk away from under it.

The lad unclipped his lead rein and let Keelhaul go. Just as he reached the course to canter down, Eddie gave an encouraging clicking sound by curling his tongue, a noise some jockeys make when they want a horse to sharpen up a bit Eddie recalled that it had never been necessary to gee Keelhaul up before.

The canter down was uneventful for Eddie while the normal selection of antics could be seen from several others. A huge chestnut with a head like a blacksmith's anvil had almost got the better of his young jockey who wisely pulled the horse's head over the running rail and ran him into the back of a steeplechase fence which for one heart-stopping moment he looked like jumping. 'I'll give that one a miss,' Eddie thought to himself then decided to take out some insurance by adding, 'Hey kid, do yourself and the rest of us a favour. Drop that wooden-mouthed brute out at the back on the outside. If you lose the battle then kick him in the belly. He won't run away for long.'

Eddie smiled remembering his own early riding days when, like this boy, he'd only been offered rides that top jockeys would not partner for treble the fee. It was literally 'shit or bust' when you started out and in this kid's case it looked ominously like the former.

Eddie could not make his mind up if Keelhaul was just growing up a bit or was in fact off colour. He had cantered down to the start a bit lethargic but not enough to consider asking the starter to look at him, he was definitely sound and anyway he'd only need to be half-right to beat this lot.

He lined up next to the inside rail, Keelhaul's white blazed head just inches from the starting tape, which was rattling, vibrating in the strong wind. The horse never flinched at the noise even though the grey beside him objected and spun around barging into three others as he tried to get away.

Again it crossed Eddie's mind that perhaps all was not well with his mount. The horse's reactions were gentler without being too alarming. But when the starter let them go Keelhaul led for the first three hurdles although more on sufferance than due to his own speed, and despite getting a few sharp cracks from Eddie's whip he slowly lost ground to drop back among the tail-end Charlies.

Eddie's thoughts naturally turned to the

best course of action, any percentage of the prize money had long disappeared. It just remained to decide if he should pull the horse up and walk back to unsaddle. Had he been on a horse with no obvious chance perhaps he'd be happy enough to be toiling among the also rans but Keelhaul had started the odds-on favourite.

It was probably the fact that Eddie had a ride in the next race and needed to get back as quickly as possible that stopped him pulling up and as it turned out the breather seemed to do the trick. Keelhaul passed several horses that had been going nowhere, like himself.

The leaders had flown leaving a twenty length gap to the next bunch with Keelhaul now rapidly closing on them but too far off the real action to give Eddie any hope of being involved with the leaders. Not wanting to give his mount a hard race for nothing, Eddie let him ease through the tired and plain backward horses to run on into fifth place some twelve lengths behind the winner. Keelhaul pulled up fresher than when the race had started and Eddie knew only too well there would be questions asked as to why he had ridden such a peculiar race. The Stewards' Inquiry was announced even before he had dismounted beside an angry looking trainer and dejected owners.

None of the connections seemed convinced by his explanation and Eddie walked away shaking his head slowly. He tried to ignore the inevitable gibes from losing punters. He understood how they felt but there was nothing he could tell them that would make things better. Some of the name-calling was particularly crude and he was tempted to turn on the crowd but forced himself to walk on towards the weighing room.

Quite simply the horse had just not felt his normal perky self and that was the only explanation. Perhaps he'd cough on the way home or when having a bite of grass. Maybe later his lad would see the tell-tale signs of blood in Keelhaul's nostrils that would indicate he'd broken a blood vessel.

That was exactly what Eddie then told the stewards, the explanation was that there was no explanation. They heard from the starter who corroborated Eddie's assertion that the gelding had been unusually subdued before the race. The trainer was also baffled and the Inquiry ended with a dissatisfied taste in everyone's mouth.

The stewards 'noted' Eddie's explanation, which meant that they didn't quite believe it but, for the moment, couldn't prove anything else. Eddie marched out with mixed feelings. He knew the stewards, all unpaid volunteers, had a job to do but he knew too that what had happened to him over ten years ago, when he'd lost his licence after being falsely accused of involvement with dopers, had tarred him for life in the eyes of some officials.

Since his comeback he'd never walked into a Stewards' Inquiry with any real confidence in the outcome. Angry now, he went straight outside in the perverse hope that some of those punters who'd barracked him so viciously might still be around. Though he could risk nothing more than a verbal onslaught he felt like taking out his frustration on someone.

He stood leaning on the fence glowering at the few passers-by, looking for a potential protagonist. A voice from behind and off to his right cried out, 'Hey, you, Malloy!'

Teeth clenched, eyes blazing, he spun round to see the large figure of Laura Gilpin walking towards him. She was smiling warmly and when she saw the anger in his face her eyes opened wide and she held out her flat palm at arm's length as though warding him off though she kept coming towards him. She laughed, slightly nervously, and said, 'Calm down! I was only joking! Jeez, if looks could kill. I'm sorry,' she said as she reached and placed an elbow on the wall to stand comfortably beside him.

The anger in his eyes cooled quickly as he saw the funny side. 'You almost got a real mouthful then, Laura,' he said.

'As the Bishop said to the actress.' Her cheeks were rosy, her eyes bright and happy. 'Did they give you a tough time in there?'

'You just know they don't believe you, know what I mean?'

She nodded, impressed by Eddie's anger. Face animated and hands expressive he went on, 'They don't even try to hide it. They just sit staring and their eyes are saying, "We know you're bent, Malloy, we only wish we could prove it." It makes you feel like getting in close to them, making them stand up face to face so you can try and get your point across more forcibly, but you're made to stand there like a naughty schoolboy; "Yes sir, I understand; no, sir, I agree it doesn't look good." Jeez if they'd only treat you like a human being! They don't seem to realise ...'

Laura watched him, fascinated, attracted by his fiery attitude, amused by the hurt, almost childlike look, curious about what he was really like inside, wondering what sort of lover he would be. She became aware of him looking at her as though expecting an answer, but she hadn't heard the last few things he'd said. She smiled wider and guessed. 'Don't worry, tomorrow's another day,' she said.

Eddie frowned in puzzlement. 'What?'

Laura owned up. 'I'm sorry, I wasn't listening. Too caught up in watching you be Mr Angry. What did you say?'

'I said I've got something for you.'

Laura wondered if he could read the immediate glint in her eye, which said silently, 'I know you have.' She said, 'Animal, vegetable or mineral?'

'Collateral.'

She smiled. So did Eddie. She said, 'In the form of?'

'That rare modern day commodity, cash.'

'I'm all ears. And pockets.'

'Well, as good as cash. A very solid cheque.'

'From whom?'

'From the man who made you cry at Aintree.'

It was Laura's turn to look puzzled. Eddie said, 'Can you meet me after the last and I'll tell you all about it?'

'Oh come on, Eddie, that's hours away! You can't tell me something like that then just walk off.'

He smiled. 'Sorry, I'm riding in the next. See you later.'

Laura clenched her fists and stamped in mock frustration. Eddie laughed and went back inside the weighing room.

They met again as arranged. Eddie had ridden a winner in the third and Laura Gilpin's one runner at the meeting had finished second so both were happy with the day's work. They went to a small half-full bar at the end of the stand and Eddie was pleased that Laura came up to the bar with him rather than staying at the table they'd found. He also felt an odd satisfaction when he discovered she liked the same drink as he did, whisky on ice: same brand, too.

Someone had taken their table. They found another by the window, which was heavily steamed up. Eddie smiled as he watched Laura make baby footprints in the condensation with the side of her clenched fist and her fingertip. He could see she was being determined about not begging to be told what he had for her and the story behind it and he played on it, making small talk about the day's racing until she finally banged theatrically on the table and said, 'Oh, come on, tell me! Tell me!'

He laughed. She smiled and he reached to the floor and opened his kitbag to take out his cheque book. He wrote her a cheque for £5,000 and told her it was from a racing enthusiast who thought she should be compensated for the defeat of Samson's Curls at Aintree.

She placed the cheque on the tabletop and looked at it. 'You said earlier it was from the man who made me cry at Aintree.'

Eddie shrugged. 'A figure of speech.'

She shook her head in disbelief. 'A figure of five grand. It's either conscience money or some sort of payoff.'

Eddie leaned across the table. 'Laura, all I can say is that the cheque is clean and above board. You can take it without a worry. I wish I could tell you more about it but I can't. Not at the moment.'

She pushed the corner of the cheque under a beer mat. 'How did he fiddle the photo?'

'I can't tell you any more.'

'How did you catch him?'

'Laura, just take the money, honestly ...'

'Don't worry, I'm taking it. I just want to know the story behind it. I'm a Gemini. Curiosity's my driving force.'

'Well I'm a Taurus and obstinacy's mine.'

She sat back in her chair, drank some whisky and stared at Eddie over the glass. 'Oh well, I'll just have to ask around on the racecourse, I'm sure the grapevine will be carrying it soon.'

'Please don't do that.'

'Why?' She smiled mischievously.

'As a favour to me. It's not finished yet.

All the ends need to he tied up.'

'Then you'll tell me?'

'I promise.'

She reached a hand across the table silently offering to seal the agreement. Eddie smiled and shook her hand then watched as she undid the top two buttons on her pale green blouse. 'I've always wanted to do this,' she said, picking up the cheque. She folded it and pushed it slowly down her cleavage. Still smiling, Eddie shook his head slowly and finished his drink.

Through the fading light they walked together to the carpark, Laura's thirteen stone bulk under the long brown coat exaggerating Eddie's slimness in the dark tailored suit. She asked if he thought she should enter Samson's Curls at Cheltenham in ten days. He said she should and agreed to ride it.

They stopped beside Eddie's car to say goodbye before Laura headed off to the horsebox park to drive her sole runner back home. There weren't many vehicles left around them but standing beside a silver estate car about two hundred yards away Eddie could see for the second time that day the huge figure of Tiny Delaware.

Eddie didn't recognise the man he was with but he could see that Tiny seemed to be handing the guy the bundles of cash he'd had this morning. Eddie reckoned the man must be a bookie and he wondered what Tiny was planning to use now to buy his Christmas presents. He told Laura about Tiny and, getting into his car, said, 'Let that be a lesson to you to keep that five grand in your cleavage. The bookies always win.'

'I told you, I'm a non-gambler.'

'Good. See you at Cheltenham.'

'See you.' Laura pushed his door closed and watched him pull away. She waddled off to find her horsebox, thinking for the first time in years of going on a diet.

Neither Tiny nor his companion noticed Laura passing close by. Nor had they seen Eddie leave. The smaller man peeled £200 from one of the sheaves Tiny had given him and handed it back to the giant. Then the man got in his car feeling very happy with the day's work. In a bag in the back seat of his estate was a roll of film, every frame on which showed shots of Eddie taking wads of money from Tiny Delaware. There was also a video recording of the 1.30 in which Eddie had appeared to ride such an ill-judged race on the odds-on favourite.

The man started his engine and, still smiling, eased the car quietly forward towards the exit. His name was Phil Grimond.

Twenty-six

Though he'd often cursed it for shortening a working day in the hills, Kim was glad of the early darkness of December. He hadn't wanted to escape in daylight, too risky. And had it been summer, leaving after dark would have meant trying to hitch lifts at midnight.

At 6.30 Kim finished a game of table tennis and told the others he was going to his room to read. What few clothes he had, along with a spare pair of shoes, his toothbrush and shampoo had been fitted into two plastic carriers which Kim found easy to push through the upper window in the bathroom at the end of the hall. Climbing up to stand on the sink he got a knee onto the white-tiled sill and wriggled through, pale blue paint flakes from the window edge sticking to his thick black woollen sweater.

Kim dropped silently to the ground, rose to a half crouch and stayed perfectly still, his senses fully alert. No shouts. No footsteps coming after him. He gathered his bags and, still stooped, hurried away through the sparse trees in the acre of grounds that surrounded the home. No fence to negotiate, just a low stone wall fronting a thick hedge. Kim found a gap and a few broken twigs joined the paint flakes on his sweater.

On the pavement underneath the orange street lamps his breath mingled with the cold mist. Still no noise. No traffic. Down the hill to his right he could hear a stream burbling over rocks. He decided to find the stream and follow it for half an hour or so before coming back onto the streets.

By eight o'clock he'd been waiting by a slip road on the M6 for almost half an hour and the cold was beginning to get into his bones. Underneath the black sweater he wore a hooded light grey sweatshirt which he now tucked into his blue jeans to try and keep some warmth. He'd been optimistic about getting a lift to Penrith, certain that a friendly lorry driver would stop for him, but they'd all gone whizzing past as though they didn't care or hadn't even seen him.

Hadn't seen him.

Kim wondered if that was the problem. He was dressed in very dark clothes. Shivering violently he stripped off his tops and reversed the order, pulling the light grey sweatshirt on over the black jumper. Within ten minutes he sat in the warmth of a big lorry cab telling the driver he was planning to pay his mum a surprise visit.

Two and a half hours and two more lifts later Kim found himself on the closest main road to the farm, which meant a walk of almost six miles. But he smiled in the darkness of the hills. His hills, the smells familiar again for the first time, it seemed, in ages ... the feel of the place ... even close to midnight.

Swinging his bags and whistling, Kim set off along the narrow track leading west knowing now that he was nearly home. He knew he couldn't stay but he had to see Crystal before he set off to look for his brother. He didn't know how that search would end or how long it would take but he'd missed his pony almost as much as Mum and Dad, which made him feel guilty. He tried to push that comparison from his mind when it came, sometimes having to sing stupid songs louder and louder in an effort to blank out those guilty thoughts.

He couldn't see Mum and Dad again but he could see Crystal. He would stop at the farm and collect the money he'd saved in the old milk churn in the hayloft and maybe he'd rest a while and try and find something to eat. Then he'd set off to walk across the fields to Mr Durkan's place. That's where they'd said Crystal was. He'd spend an hour with her and be away before dawn. Before they came after him.

As he came to the end of the tarmac section of the road his feet crunched across the loose stones, which he knew surfaced the remainder of the track to the farm. The noise of it became almost hypnotic and he began to hear it echo back from the hills. He knew the peaks of the fells were all around him but he couldn't see them. Then, after a while, the heavy clouds suddenly parted showing a full moon shining like polished silver, lighting the twisting road ahead and revealing the hulking silhouettes of the hills. Kim smiled. Nearly home.

On his return from Catterick, Eddie had a light dinner with Charles Tunney, his trainer, and afterwards, nursing whiskies by the fire, they spread some paperwork on the yew-topped coffee table and made plans for stable runners over the coming month. Many of Charles's horses had been out of sorts but they were now showing signs of returning to form. This meant that Eddie wouldn't have to graft so hard for rides elsewhere as he'd be guaranteed a reasonably regular supply from Charles.

Charles also told him he was leaving next week for Ireland to have a look at four new horses.

They had three runners at Leicester the next day and Eddie would be up extra early to school four over fences before breakfast. Charles was on his third whisky and his tenth daydream when Eddie left him to it and headed back across the yard to his flat. There was a message on the answerphone from Ben Turco. Eddie called him back.

'What can I do for you?'

'Cheltenham, a week Saturday. How does that sound for setting up Grimond?'

Eddie hesitated, wondering if there was any reason to say no. 'It sounds okay to me. It'll depend on McCarthy.'

'Is that time enough to get his boys moving?'

'Should be. I'll try and reach him tomorrow.'

'Good. I'll start finalising arrangements my end.'

'What about me? Is there anything I have to do?'

'Nope. Leave it all to me.'

'Okay.'

'Eddie, you know that stuff you do for The Racing Channel?'

'The studio guest thing?'

'Yeah, where you go in for a day and spout comments on runners, give tips and stuff. Do you have full access to the studio where the live broadcast goes out from?'

'Why are you asking?'

'Because I've an idea which is probably the most brilliant thing I've ever come up with.'

'If you say so yourself.'

'If I say so myself! It would make both of us a very serious amount of money. I'm talking millions here.'

'And just how crooked is it to have that sort of potential?'

'That depends on where you're standing.'

'Well let's say I'm standing outside the dock and want to remain outside it.'

Turco cleared his throat. 'The main victims would be the bookies and they deserve everything life throws their way. They deserve no mercy.'

'And who would the other victims be?'

'A few punters might lose but the same number would probably win and even the ones who lost would applaud the audacity of the whole thing when the news broke.'

'I doubt it somehow.'

'Don't judge till I've told you more about it.'

'Save it. I don't want to know.' Eddie ran a weary hand through his hair and glanced at the window as heavy blobs of rain splatted against the pane.

'Eddie, gimme a chance to explain it properly. Come down and see me. We'll

178

have dinner. Take in a show.'

Eddie sighed, 'It'd have to be some show to beat you for entertainment. I'm not interested in any of your scams, Ben, let's get Grimond tied up and out of our hair so I can get on with riding.'

'We could pull this off easily providing your access to The Racing Channel studio also gets us in to the full SIS bag. I'm telling you, you'd never have to ride again in your life. Just think, no more rainy Hexhams, no more long trips to Plumpton, the end of swinging your leg over raw novices and hoping you don't come back paralysed, no more ...'

'Goodnight, Ben.'

'Eddie! Just hear me out, please, you owe it to yourself.'

'Oh don't give me that bullshit for God's sake. Look, I'm tired. I'll speak to McCarthy in the morning about Cheltenham. I'll be in touch. Goodnight.' He hung up and stood for a minute by the phone listening to the rain on the window. He undressed by the light of the lamp then brushed his teeth, scouring out the remaining morsels of the fillet steak dinner.

The bedroom was warm and comforting though the sheets were cool against his naked body. He lay thinking, wondering what Turco was cooking up now, marvelling at the guy's non-stop imagination, his inventiveness. He smiled. Turco had set him thinking about SIS. Eddie hadn't done a stint there for weeks.

SIS, Satellite Information Services, is a broadcasting company who cover all of the race-meetings in the UK, sending live pictures or, on busy days, an audio coverage back to almost 10,000 betting shops. They run quite a sophisticated operation and occasionally, if he wasn't riding, Eddie would appear as a studio guest just chatting about racing and offering what wisdom he could inside the libel laws and the unwritten ones that ruled out offending any trainer or owner on air. An art in its own right. Eddie smiled again and drew the now warm duvet up around his shoulders.

Eddie's last thought before sleep was of his mother and sister. He'd been ringing regularly to make sure his mother was recovering but Louise always seemed distant, anxious to get off the phone. Maybe he should get himself back over there.

Far away, in another double bed, Laura Gilpin lay awake listening to the vicious wind screaming in off the North Sea to rattle the roof tiles and howl in the eaves. Her feelings were a strange mixture of the melancholy of loneliness and the thrill of an unrealisable crush that took her back to her schooldays.

The arm of the long cotton nightdress tightened as she turned onto her right side feeling her heavy breasts rolling to settle softly in her new position. Drawing her knees up she felt her belly touch her thighs and, a picture of Eddie Malloy still clear in her mind, she whispered sadly to herself, 'Dream on, Laura.'

Away to the west of Laura Gilpin, Kim Oliver was spending a second night sleeping at the farm, his home. He'd meant to leave that morning but a combination of fear and sadness had kept him in the only place he'd ever felt secure. He'd gone to bed knowing that if he didn't leave at first light they'd probably find him there, recapture him. He had intended to sleep in his own room but he lay in his parents' bed. Their smell was still there and the effort of breathing it, of trying to take long last draughts of it into his lungs, had caused a heavy coughing fit followed by racking sobs and tears of desperate grief.

Kim forced himself to sit up in bed. If he fell asleep and they came for him tonight he'd be caught. But he was tired, desperately tired.

That morning, when Kim's disappearance had been reported to the head of the children's home, Mr Kenneth B. Young, he had decided to do nothing. Young hadn't liked Kim since the day he'd first seen him. He thought the boy arrogant, haughty, too aware of his good looks, his thick dark hair, his fine bones, his youth. And it wouldn't bother him in the least if Kim were never found.

Young knew that the earlier he alerted the police the more chance they'd have of finding the boy and bringing him back so he decided to wait until later that evening before reporting it. If anything came of it in future he'd claim he'd been following internal leads in the belief that the boy was still somewhere in the grounds. Young supposed he'd better let that idiot lawyer, Ogilvie, know as well.

Young's statement was taken by an enthusiastic detective called Plimpton who looked to Young to be no more than twenty-five, making him wonder grudgingly how Plimpton had got into the CID at that age. Plimpton looked at the window Kim had left by and instinctively pulled a strand of black wool from the frame. Young had a sarcastic comment ready but Plimpton said nothing. The detective told him he'd alert the city guys to keep an eye out on the streets and he'd ask the Penrith cops to go out and have a look at the Oliver place.

When he called it in from the station, a sergeant at Penrith told Plimpton that it would have to be tomorrow morning before they could get a man out there.

'Get somebody there tonight.'

Twenty-seven

Ogilvie got the news as a message on his answerphone next morning and called Young immediately. The home head played on the obvious worry Ogilvie had over Kim's possible plans. 'Yes, I think he did mention something to one of the other boys about trying to find his natural parents,' he lied.

'Did he say where he might begin looking?'

'Eh ... don't think he did but I got the impression he was pretty determined about it.'

'Probably try the national register ...' Ogilvie mumbled.

'Pardon?'

'Nothing. I'd ... I'd better warn the natural parents.'

'Yes, you'd better.'

Louise lowered the telephone handset and

as it slipped back into its cradle she felt the weight of the world once again settle on her shoulders. The boy was loose, careering around like some deadly weapon, some heat seeking, mother seeking missile that would kill its target as surely as if a warhead were attached.

Mother was back home but had isolated herself again, bedridden with the shock of it all. She'd discussed nothing with Louise, said nothing about the boy other than to extract repeated promises from Louise that she would never acknowledge the boy's existence no matter what. And Louise had promised and with that had strapped yet another millstone around her own neck and she hated all this now, wished she'd never responded to Eddie's call last winter, wished she'd never come back.

And suddenly she envied Kim, envied his strength in running away, breaking free, and she wished she could do that now.

She sat on the long bench and rested her elbows on the big table.

There was complete silence.

Louise buried her head in her hands. What about Eddie? Why didn't he come and take his share? It was Eddie who'd got her back into all this. Then he goes back to his boy's life. Playing at jockeys. No wife, no children of his own, no worries, no responsibilities. What about bloody Eddie!

When was he going to do his share?

And how was she going to keep this from Mother? What if the boy just turned up on the doorstep? Resourceful, Mr Ogilvie had called him, resourceful and determined. And all Louise had managed to say to him was thanks for letting us know, I'm sure everything will be all right. And she knew it would be far from all right. She knew the sight of her youngest son would all but kill her mother. But she knew too that if she told Eddie what was happening he would fall on the boy's side. That was the way he was.

Louise made a low moaning noise and pushed her fingernails hard into the skin on her forehead trying to kill the turmoil in her brain.

The last horse Eddie schooled next morning completely misjudged the third jump and, soft as the fence was, took a heavy fall. Eddie baled out and suffered nothing more than the discomfort of wet clothes after rolling through the thick dew-soaked grass.

Changed and with a light breakfast inside him, Eddie sipped black coffee and made two phone calls. The first was to Peter McCarthy and the second to Rebecca Bow. McCarthy couldn't meet him till Monday but Rebecca readily agreed to have dinner with him on the Saturday night. Tentatively, he asked her to come racing at Sandown on Saturday afternoon where he had two booked rides. He wasn't sure whether she'd view the invitation as some sort of summons to come and see him show off but she seemed happy to accept.

They chatted for a while and when he finally hung up Eddie was surprised to find he'd been on the phone to her for almost half an hour. He smiled. She lifted his spirits and the sexual attraction he now felt for her was stronger than he could remember for any girl. Throughout that day she was never far from his mind. Saturday could not come soon enough.

Twenty-eight

In his dream Kim's mother seemed much more real than he remembered her in life, almost alive again. He wasn't sure what woke him. A noise.

And he wasn't sure either where he was or what had happened in the past weeks, but a second later everything came back to him and he realised that the voices he could hear in the house were probably those of the men from the home come to get him.

He cursed himself for sleeping so long, for staying another night at the farm. Quickly and quietly he slipped out of bed unsure whether the morning cold or the fright was causing the shivering, raising the goose bumps on his thin bare arms. He struggled to pull on his still laced-up trainers and remembered how his mother had always nagged him to undo his laces.

As he heard footsteps on the stairs he briefly considered hiding under the bed but he thought they might feel the sheets and, finding them still warm, immediately look underneath. Not an option.

There were three rooms upstairs. If they chose this one first he was caught. Holding his breath and trying not to rustle the two plastic carriers that held all his belongings he moved swiftly towards the window, praying silently as he pulled on the brass rings that served as handles. The window slid smoothly and silently up and he blessed the old rope cords that held it there as he eased a leg through to feel gingerly for the roof of the porch. His toes touched and he got the rest of his body through and onto the wet tiles. Kim thanked God for the gentle slope on the roof because the tiles were slippery and had the angle been any more than fifteen degrees or so he would have gone careering down to tumble into the yard.

The carrier bags clenched between his teeth he moved carefully, on hands and knees, to the edge of the roof to clamber down the drainpipe (another silent prayer against it pulling away from the brickwork) to the cobbled ground. Crouched low he moved quickly across the front of the house staying below window level till he reached the red shale driveway. Three long strides took him across and through a gap in the hedge into the orchard.

Hunkering low he looked back. There was a police car in the drive.

Police.

Somehow he'd thought it would have been Mr Young or one of the other adults from the home. When the police were looking for you that was serious. Had something else happened? Maybe something had gone missing from the home, been stolen, and he was getting the blame. Resting his back against a cold leafless apple tree he looked up through the bare branches at the grey sky and tried to come to terms with things, tried to figure out what to do.

If God had meant him to go back to the home He'd have left him asleep, let the police catch him. God wouldn't have let those noises wake him. And He wouldn't have sent him that good dream about his mum. She'd smiled and told him everything would be fine and for everything to be fine Kim knew he must avoid going back to that home. Maybe God didn't mean for him to find his real parents but nor did He mean for him to go back to that home. So it was best now to accept that and work the other stuff out later. Best to get further away from the farm just now till the police left. But they'd have touched the bed by now, they'd know he'd been there within the last few minutes.

No use running off wildly across the fields. They'd spot him easily. Maybe they had a helicopter in the area. And they'd probably expect him to run anyway. Hiding in the barn would be better. They wouldn't expect that. He could hide in the old grain storage unit beneath the hay bales. The police wouldn't even know that was there. Decided now. Kim moved stealthily along the border of the orchard, exiting at the top corner and sprinting lightly towards the big metal hangar of a barn.

Five minutes later a lone policeman left the farmhouse by the front door and set out to conduct a thorough search of all the outbuildings.

Twenty-nine

If it had been Eddie Malloy's intention to show off to Rebecca at Sandown then things backfired badly. In one race he mistimed his run and lost a race he should have won. In the other his horse made what looked from the stands to be only a slight mistake but it caught Eddie napping and he fell off.

When he met her by the parade ring he was proud to be seen with her. She wore a lime coloured silk jacket and trousers and matching shoes with a two-inch heel. Her large coin-shaped silver earrings bore some Chinese design and over her shoulder was a small green bag of the softest leather. Her blonde hair hung in a shining swathe. She sensed him beside her, turned and elegantly raised her head for Eddie to kiss her cheek. The smell of her perfume excited him.

For the rest of the day they were seldom more than a few feet apart. Eddie felt he'd redeemed himself slightly by tipping Rebecca two winners and her excitement at cheering them home gave him as much pleasure as anything he could remember for a long time. Although he tried to argue her out of it she insisted on paying for dinner that evening from her winnings.

They found a country house hotel with a romantic restaurant and Eddie lost track of time as he ate and talked and sipped mineral water and watched Rebecca's hazel eyes glint in the candle light and wished that he could take her upstairs to bed and make love to her for hours then hold her till she fell asleep in his arms. He wanted badly to wake up with her next morning but he knew it was too soon. This was too special, not to be rushed.

He found himself talking more to her than he could remember doing to anyone. She was an excellent listener. She in turn told him things about her family, about the heartache over her father's death.

'A car crash, wasn't it?' Eddie asked.

She nodded. 'Fifty-three, he was ... Fifty-three!'

'Young,' Eddie said.

'He was a young man, full of life. He would always have been young no matter what age he'd lived to, if you know what I mean.'

Eddie smiled. 'Most men never grow up.'

'Including you?'

'Especially me.'

He steered her off the subject of her

father, not wanting to see her look sad. They talked about Mattie and the Chinese and that night in London.

'Still got your gun?' Eddie asked.

'Tucked into my garter.'

'I wouldn't be surprised. When did you start carrying it?'

'A friend of mine gave it to me last year. I was helping her clear out her flat and she came across it, offered it to me and I thought I might have some fun with it.'

'You had some fun with it the other night.'

She laughed and sipped white wine. 'You should have seen their eyes pop wide. Suddenly they didn't look Chinese any more.'

Eddie smiled. 'Are you worried they might come back for revenge?'

'Nahhh. I think you scared the living daylights out of the boss man with that speech you gave him. You're a real tough guy, Eddie.' She smiled, teasing.

'All bluff. I'm pretty soft really.'

'I've never met a soft jockey yet. Met lots of crazy ones and a couple who were as dim as two-watt lightbulbs but I ain't met any soft ones.'

Eddie wondered how close she'd been to some of those jockeys and was surprised to feel a stab of jealousy. The longer they talked, the more she impressed him with her devil-may-care attitude to life. She was amusingly self-deprecating too which Eddie liked. The more he thought about the rescue of Mattie the more convinced he became of how brave she'd been from the outset. She'd followed the Chinese from Ascot to London, called the police, waited outside for hours then coolly went in with him to stand her ground with nothing more than a replica gun, a sense of adventure and a lot of guts.

By the end of the evening Eddie was so impressed by Rebecca that he felt somehow he should establish himself with her as something more than a brawler with a short temper and poor judgement. So he steered the conversation around again to Mattie Stuart and that race at Aintree and he told Rebecca the truth about what had been behind it all. On the face of things he played down his part in the capture of Walter and how he'd stopped Turco going any further but he knew that she was wise enough to summarise exactly what had happened and who the 'hero' had been.

She was so engrossed in his story that he was tempted to carry on and tell her about the set-up planned for Grimond next Saturday. In the end he thought better of it. He'd talked enough about himself. He didn't want to put Rebecca off. That was the very last thing he wanted.

Thirty

Kim forced himself to stay in the sickly sweet smelling dryness and pitch blackness of the old grain store for hours. When he pushed his head back up through the trapdoor he wanted to be absolutely certain his first sight wouldn't be big black boots and navy blue trousers. It was well after midday when he finally returned to the surface and he sat for a while in the gloomy barn to let his eyes adjust.

Retracing his route through the orchard he skirted the farm to make sure there was no police car waiting. He climbed a high oak in the corner of the field till he could see the land and tracks all around: no vehicles. Still, he moved carefully and quietly through the house checking every room. When he was certain he was alone in there he went to the pantry and opened a tin of beans which he microwaved along with a large potato. Adding a dollop of brown sauce to the steaming meal then pouring some flat lemonade into a red mug, he dragged a stool to the front window to eat. He wanted to have a view of the road at all times.

Once he'd eaten this he'd move into the barn, shift a few things in and make a bed in the loft among the bales. That way he could stay close to the house and keep an eye open for the police, for they'd probably be back. The first place they'd look would be the house again. Certain to. And he'd see them and shoot back into the old grain store. Maybe he should move a few things down there too in case he had to stay a while. Blankets, candles, some tinned stuff. A tin-opener, too. And a container of water. Kim knew you could survive for ages without food but for just a few days without water.

Then what?

He couldn't stay here forever. He'd have to get out and find his brother.

How?

Somehow. There had to be some way. The Citizen's Advice place or maybe the library or something would know how you go about tracing your relatives.

Wait a minute. This would be exactly where they'd be expecting him to go because they probably knew why he'd run away. And they'd know he'd have to go to places like that for help so they'd probably stake them out and just wait till he turned up or maybe warn the staff to contact them as soon as he arrived.

Anyway, what was the point? It didn't matter how smart they were or how much they knew about birth records and stuff, he didn't have the names of his real parents ... real parents ... the words rang oddly in his mind ...

So how could they even start? Where would they begin?

Kim spooned the last of the beans into his mouth, washed the plate and mug and was careful to leave the kitchen as he'd found it. Perplexed but not downcast he went upstairs to the airing cupboard his mum had kept well stocked with blankets and started preparing for his move to the barn. His mind worked constantly, throwing up different ideas, probing them, discarding them then digging for more.

Come nightfall he was as snug as he could be without being in the house. He had blankets, two pillows, a torch, a flask of hot chicken soup, some over-moist coconut biscuits, tinned fruit, the remainder of the lemonade, and a small portable radio he'd found in the rolltop desk in his dad's office. He couldn't remember even seeing it before but he knew there were some spare batteries in the pantry and when he clicked them home the radio came on loud and clear.

He kept the volume low though as he

lay on a thick bed of straw watching the waning moon through the big rectangular window. It was a clear cold night and the stars looked diamond hard and sharp. He knew that at almost thirteen and with all that had happened recently he shouldn't quite be feeling this sense of adventure, but he did. He'd never had a chance as a kid to camp out, nobody to do it with. Now he wished his brother were with him to share this. And he promised himself that one day he would be. That he'd find his brother and bring him back here. And they'd both camp out here in this exact place. And Kim set his mind hard to this and picked out the brightest star in the dark sky and promised the star that it would happen.

The next morning, 11 December, was still and very cold. So cold that noise seemed to carry much further across the empty fields of the Lake District and Kim heard the car through the window of the loft in the barn. He stood on two straw bales and, using his left eye only, peeked over the sill where it met the corner of the frame, exposing as little of his head as possible.

He watched the shiny maroon Jaguar pass the row of elms at the junction of the two tracks, noticing how its suspension effortlessly handled the potholes. A Jag.

Didn't detectives drive Jags? Confident he could be down the ladder noiselessly and into the old grain store in less than a minute he decided to wait and see.

Thirty-one

Eddie Malloy had mixed feelings about Ludlow racecourse. It lay in a beautiful setting in south Shropshire against a background of rolling hills and it was within a twenty minute drive of home. But the racecourse could be a tricky one to ride with the hurdle and 'chase courses having separate back straights. And there were four roads crossing the course. Although covered during racing by thick matting they still caught the odd horse by surprise and made him lose his action. And the ground there was often firm enough to deal out broken collarbones and limb fractures to those unlucky enough to have a fall.

Eddie wondered as he walked towards the weighing room this bright Monday morning whether he was worrying more than he used to about the disadvantages of raceriding. That was often the first sign of an ever strengthening wish to retire. Every jump jockey's clock had only so many miles on it and you never knew when yours was going to start packing up.

Never mind, maybe it was just a healthy jolt of self-preservation since he'd met Rebecca, an instinct to keep himself in good shape for her and whatever might lie ahead.

McCarthy was waiting for him by the front of the weighing room, which lay in the centre of the track. The Security man was wearing the same long thick dark coat he'd been wearing to the races in the winter ever since Eddie had met him. The man inside the coat hadn't changed much either although he was the wrong side of forty now. A line or two extra on the face maybe and a few grey hairs at the temple but his thick hair was mostly still almost black, still had that waviness of the 1950s movie stars.

McCarthy was six feet two and fought a constant battle with his weight which Eddie guessed now, looking at him leaning against the wall, was around the seventeen stone mark.

'How goes it?' Eddie called with a smile while still ten strides away.

'Okay,' McCarthy said dolefully.

'Worries of the world, episode thirty-five.'

'Pardon?'

'You always look like you've got the

proverbial worries of the world on your shoulders.'

'I have. Times ten.'

'Lots of people worse off than you, you know.'

McCarthy frowned, pushing himself away from the wall to walk with Eddie into the weighing room. He said, 'That doesn't mean I shouldn't be allowed to have worries of my own.'

Eddie smiled at Benny Vascoe, a valet, and slung his kitbag onto the slatted bench. 'Just get them into perspective, Mac, that's all I'm saying.'

McCarthy looked wounded. Eddie clasped his arm and looked up into his face. 'It's for your own good, Mac. Come on, I'll fix you a cup of tea and we'll go for a walk in the sunshine.' Eddie preferred to be away from the others any time he had to talk to McCarthy. He'd never quite felt comfortable about how everyone else might view his association with the Jockey Club Security official. It had caused Eddie some hassle in the past and he knew people talked about the fox running with the chickens.

But Mac had done him a few favours, pulled him out of some pretty deep holes. And Eddie had done the same for him. They'd never been close friends, never socialised, but they trusted and respected each other. In Eddie's eyes, Mac was still too bureaucratic and protective of his position and he wouldn't be one to rely on when things got really physical. But Eddie recognised and accepted Mac's limits and he would rather have things that way. He knew where he stood.

As far as McCarthy was concerned, Eddie was still far too headstrong, took excessive risks and didn't give a damn for officialdom. But he knew he was straight and true and that he'd physically fight for you till his last breath.

Tea swilling darkly in Styrofoarn cups, they wandered outside carrying the now steaming liquid and headed across the golf course which was laid out in the middle of the track. Eddie told McCarthy the Phil Grimond story leaving out Ben Turco. McCarthy listened, heard him through without comment.

Standing at the edge of a deep sand bunker Eddie said, 'Before you start asking questions, Mac, I'll tell you that there is someone else involved but I can't and won't tell you who it is. All I'll say is that the person will never do it again and that they are helping set up Grimond on Saturday.'

'So Grimond's the fall guy?'

'Grimond's your original nasty piece of work, I think.'

'You think?'

'He's the one that won't let it lie. Making all sorts of threats.'

'But he's not the man behind everything?'

'He's the front man, if you like.'

'Okay, but he was never the driving force?'

'That's right.'

'So what good is he to us? The way I see it he's been getting in your man's hair and ...'

'I never said it was a man.'

'Is it a woman then?'

'I'm not saying, Mac, you make what assumptions you want to.'

'My assumption is that whoever is actually masterminding the whole thing is using you.'

'You're entitled to your opinion. I don't think that's what's happening.'

Mac opened his hands to make a point and spilled the remainder of the black tea into the white sand of the bunker. 'Eddie, what are you giving me here? You're giving me the bit player without the director? You're giving me the percussionist without the conductor! You're giving me the centre-half without the manager!'

'And you're giving me a headache, Mac! I'm giving you all I can. I'm not saying don't try and catch anyone else who's involved, I'm just saying you'll have to do it without me. I gave my word. Now when I give you my word would you like to think I'm the type to keep it?'

'Of course! I know you are!'

'Well stop giving me such a bloody hard time then!'

Mac hung his head, kicked absently at some loose sand on the lip of the bunker. 'Okay, but when we catch whoever's behind it, no pleas for mercy from you.'

'There won't be, don't worry.'

'Okay, what's the plan for Saturday?'

Thirty-two

Campbell Ogilvie braked the Jaguar to a halt in the drive by the gate and got out. At last he felt he was doing something. Since he'd heard the news that Kim had absconded he had blamed himself. Ogilvie saw Kim's actions as being a result of his dereliction of duty, his complete mishandling of those interviews with the boy. He knew the police had made a cursory attempt at tracing Kim and that they thought he might still be hanging around the farm but unless he did something the boy could die in the

203

wilderness for all anyone else cared.

Kim watched the solicitor. He'd liked Mr Ogilvie from the first time they'd met. He had a friendly manner. Kim had thought he would make a good uncle. He wondered why he'd come.

Ogilvie went up the path and produced keys from his pocket, which surprised Kim. He opened the door and went in.

Kim waited. From time to time he would faintly hear his name being called.

After maybe five minutes Kim saw him come back out and walk around the side of the house towards the stables at the back, still calling his name. When he got behind the buildings up by the muckheap he was shouting something else but Kim couldn't make it out.

Eventually the solicitor came back towards the barn, still calling but beginning to clear his throat more often, his voice straining now. 'Kim! If you're here somewhere, if you can hear me, I want to help you! You don't have to go back to that home if you don't want to! We'll find a good place! You can choose it! I'll help you! I promise you that! Please just call me! I've left my card by the telephone in the house! I've written my home number and you can reach me there after six o'clock! Please call me and let me help the way your mum and dad wanted me to!'

Kim watched him turn one full circle and look at the various buildings. As his eyes swivelled towards the barn Kim ducked down and instinctively held his breath. He stayed there till he heard the car door slam and the engine start then slowly raised his head again, one eye following the Jag's elegant progress back towards civilisation.

Kim found Mr Ogilvie's card by the phone and he stared at it for a long time. He didn't know what to do. Didn't know whether to place his ultimate trust in the solicitor. He looked around him at the gloomy hallway, the stone flags leading to the foot of the narrow flight of stairs ... He couldn't think straight here.

He went back to the loft and, carrying all his stuff to the old grain store, came up, covered the trapdoor with straw bales and headed across the fields towards the hills. He strode out, swinging his arms, breathing deeply, pursing his lips to exhale silent whistles of steam in the cold air. Maybe a few hours in the open would clear his head, help him decide what to do.

Although never conscious of planning to travel in any particular direction Kim somehow found himself drawn towards Buckbarrow Crag. He didn't think about it until he found himself on the rim of the gully staring down at the spot where he'd found his parents' bodies.

Different now. Patches of brown earth showing through the crusty ageing snow like tea stains on an old crumpled tablecloth. High above, two huge rooks cawed harshly as they passed. Kim looked slowly up at them.

Then back at the hollow where his parents had died.

And he went over the rim and scrambled down to it. Only the thinnest layer of snow covered the walls of the hollow and Kim wondered how long the imprint of their bodies had remained. He wished now he'd come sooner to see it, that final mark they made on earth, before it had simply evaporated.

He sat down there, the old snow flaking and crunching like ice as he rested his back against the rock and buried his hands deep in the pockets of his mum's warm blue fleece. He looked up at the crag: at least they'd died among the hills they'd loved. He stared around him for a long time then his right hand came out of the pocket clutching Campbell Ogilvie's card. He held it almost lovingly, as though it were something precious. Then he looked again to the sky. 'Tell me what to do, Mum ... Dad,' he said quietly. 'Tell me what to do?'

Although Mr Ogilvie's office would still have been open when Kim got back to the farm he decided not to take the chance of them having taping or call-tracing equipment. He waited till after seven that evening and phoned Mr Ogilvie at home. The solicitor found it impossible to conceal his delight and excitement that Kim had called. Ogilvie had had little chance in his strait-laced rigorous profession to try and do anything outside the textbook and the success of this minor subterfuge thrilled him. He was proud too that Kim had chosen to trust him.

Kim was frightened, though he tried not to let it show. He'd felt strongly after leaving the gully that afternoon that his mum and dad wanted him to put his faith in the solicitor. Mr Ogilvie persuaded him that it would be best if they talked face to face and he volunteered to come to the farm again next day at noon. Though Ogilvie knew the boy would be too polite to demand it, Kim's silence told him he wanted his promise that he wouldn't betray him. Ogilvie said, 'Kim, I give you my solemn word that I will mention this to no one.'

Kim stared, unblinking, at the kitchen window-panes, dirty and streaked now by rain and snow. After a few seconds of hesitation he said, 'I'll wait for you in the barn, then, Mr Ogilvie. I'll probably be in the loft.'

Ogilvie smiled, realising now that Kim was placing the ultimate faith in him, telling him where his 'nest' was. He said, 'Okay, Kim, good boy. I'll see you tomorrow about twelve.' It was only when he put the receiver down that Ogilvie realised how hard he had been gripping it.

Outside the farmhouse the weather deteriorated quickly. Winds met from several different directions and ganged up, revelling in their numbers, swirling and swooping, to bully trees and rattle loose doors on their hinges, stirring wildly the dark surface of the duck pond, tearing along hedgerows and screaming through telephone wires, fighting to be first to howl down the chimneys, then rushing on to disturb slates and pummel guttering.

The rain tried to join in but heavy as it was the wind sucked and blew it in all directions, sending it where it chose so that it hammered in long bursts at the deepest windows then left them for a while to seek other ways in.

Kim sat on the stool in the warmth of the kitchen, his hands around a mug of hot soup. He smiled as he listened to the cacophony outside. It was comforting. He was no stranger to wild weather and he loved the rawness of it, the limitless power, and the protection it would give him this night, for surely no one would come looking for him in this?

He could afford the risk of spending the night in his own bed. Let the winds batter the barn and snarl through the loft; he wouldn't be there to give them any satisfaction. He'd be warm and cosy and the next day he would try his hardest to persuade Mr Ogilvie to tell him where he could find his brother.

The view from his bedroom window next morning was of a countryside bedraggled by the storm. There were slates on the ground among great green slugs of wet moss. An old tree was down in the field and part of a dry stone wall along the road had collapsed. Broken black branches lay scattered like crushed empties and a telegraph pole lurched drunkenly, its loose wires swinging slowly in the remnants of the breeze.

Kim smiled again and pulled on his jeans, white T-shirt and black jumper. He went downstairs to make tea and beans and wished he had bread to toast, thick bread. On mornings like this he loved going riding, loved the feeling of being carried safe and dry through the mud and puddles and the wreckage, but Crystal wasn't here any more. There was always his bike, which had stood unused since the summer, its scarlet and lemon frame the only brightness among the tools, bins and boxes in the cluttered back porch.

After microwaved beans and a mug of tea Kim wheeled his bike outside, mounted and set off down the drive, his tyres ploughing a deep furrow which, by the time he had reached the road junction by the big oak, had filled with seeping water.

He was gone for almost two hours, arriving back wet and muddy, face shining with health and fun, dark eyes sparkling, to hear the end of the eleven o'clock news as he switched on the radio in the kitchen. He drank a full pint of ice cold water from the tap then found a tin of fruit cocktail in the pantry. Then he remembered he had a tin of creamed rice somewhere in the loft in the barn and went to get it.

Still full of energy and tingling from the exercise, he climbed, smiling, to the loft and walked past the stacked hay bales towards the old wooden box he kept his stuff in. As he opened it and picked up the light blue tin a voice behind him said, 'So you'll be Kim, then?'

His heart almost burst through his chest and the involuntary intake of breath sounded to Kim like the loudest sound he'd ever made. He dropped the tin as he turned and his dark eyes widened in terror as he saw a policeman sitting on a hay bale, elbows on his knees.

Kim lurched desperately towards the ladder trying to escape. He knew he had never been in a bigger hurry but everything seemed to be happening in slow motion like on TV. Especially the fall. He tried to hold onto one side of the ladder as he lost his balance but something made him decide to let go completely. In the fragment of time it took him to fall fifteen feet he saw the brown stone floor come up at him, the old red tractor to his left, the lambing pens right in front, a rectangle of daylight through the main door spinning as he tumbled. Then, utter blackness.

Thirty-three

When Eddie rang his sister and said he was riding at Huntingdon on Tuesday and he thought he might drop by and see Mum, Louise seemed nervous. She told him that Mum was still recovering from her stay in hospital and was spending most of her time in bed.

All the more reason to come then, Eddie argued, but Louise eventually talked him out of it saying that their mother was spending so much time asleep he'd probably just have a wasted journey. Eddie had hesitated before finally giving up. He'd been thinking of telling Louise about Rebecca. He had no one close enough to really talk to and he felt the need to tell someone of his feelings for her. The time wasn't yet right to tell Rebecca herself and, when he thought about it, he wouldn't have felt completely comfortable telling Louise.

They'd only been reunited a year ago and had spent so little time together that he still felt he didn't know her. Maybe talking to her, trusting her with his feelings about Rebecca, would have helped build their relationship but he decided not to persevere. Louise seemed particularly on edge. He supposed it wasn't easy living with Mum full time, being the dutiful daughter when they'd been apart so many years.

Eddie wasn't too despondent. Rebecca had rung on the Monday evening and asked where he would be on Wednesday. Eddie was booked to ride at Leicester and Rebecca asked if she could come along and maybe they could go and have dinner somewhere afterwards. That had sent a wave of warmth through Eddie and in the back of his mind he was already wondering if he should ask her to come and stay that night. No ties, separate beds, no commitment.

Then he thought again. Maybe it was too soon.

He managed to ride a winner at Leicester and was especially chuffed that Rebecca had hurried from the stands to the winner's enclosure to applaud him back in. She was the first to start clapping and he smiled widely at her and stooped slightly to brush her hands with his fingertips as she reached up.

His other two rides were unplaced but again she was there waiting with words of comfort and encouragement and Eddie felt it was ceasing to matter where he finished in a race. He no longer gave a tuppeny damn so long as Rebecca's beautiful smiling face was looking up, watching for him as he walked back in.

After the last he hurried to the showers, shaved for the second time that day, then took some good-natured ribbing as he produced a bottle of expensive aftershave from his bag. On his hook in the changing room his valet, as requested, had placed a freshly laundered pale blue shirt with double cuffs and brass collar-stiffeners. Beside the shirt hung Eddie's best suit, navy blue, tailor-made. A new tie with patterns of pale green, blue and yellow was draped around the collar. On the floor by the bench gleaming black shoes reflected the round bright lights above.

Eddie dressed quickly, checked himself as best he could in the big oval mirror and left to a chorus of wolf-whistles from his friends who were in various stages of undress.

Rebecca watched him walk smiling towards her and she put her hands out, stopping him, resting them softly on his shoulders. 'You look very handsome,' she said.

'And you look very beautiful.'

'Thank you.' Rebecca wore a plain black trouser suit over a cream coloured cashmere polo neck. Her earrings were simple pearl set in gold and her thick blonde hair had the same luxuriant sheen Eddie was becoming used to. And he wondered what it would be like to gather that hair and feel the weight of it, the gloss of it, through his fingers, what it would be like to hold it suspended above her naked back before lowering it, arranging it on her skin ...

She took his arm and they walked towards the exit though they'd gone barely twenty strides when Eddie became aware of someone walking close behind him on his right. Frowning, he turned his head to see a plump, moustachioed face looking coldly at him. The man said, 'My name's Phil Grimond. I think you've heard about me. I've got something you'll want to see.'

'I doubt it,' Eddie said, still walking.

'Don't doubt it.'

'Go away.'

'Remember that odds-on chance you got stuffed on at Catterick last week?'

Eddie didn't acknowledge, kept walking.

Grimond said, 'I've got a picture of you taking a bribe from Tiny Delaware to stop it.'

Thirty-four

After a dinner during which Eddie had done his best to make light of the six by four colour picture in his inside pocket they had driven back to his flat and for the first time in a while Eddie felt he really needed the drink he held in his right hand. Rebecca had poured it, a big one over lots of ice, and Eddie was encouraged to see she'd taken an equally large one. She slipped off her shoes and folded her legs elegantly beneath her as she sat close to him on the feather cushions of the coffee coloured couch.

He'd already told her about Grimond so

he felt comfortable talking freely. He tried to hide from her how worried he was. Grimond had had no way of knowing that Eddie had already set him up for Saturday, that McCarthy's men were on standby to raid the judge's box and 'discover' the software in use. The guy had just been trying to do what he'd promised Turco he would—'deal with Eddie'.

Now Eddie was left out on the weakest of limbs. How could he call McCarthy off? Even if he could, it wouldn't be for long. The big man wouldn't wait unless there was a very good reason. But if he allowed Grimond to be arrested that picture would be the first thing the guy would produce and, allied to the video of the race and the accusations that had flown around afterwards (he recalled with dismay the doubt of the stewards at the inquiry), things would be looking very black for him.

It set him thinking about the Catterick race again too. Grimond must have stopped Keelhaul somehow. He'd heard nothing about the routine dope test on the horse and had assumed it was negative. But there were many in racing who believed that doping could be sophisticated enough to remain undetected in a horse. The horse must have been got at otherwise what was the point of Grimond setting up the scene with Tiny, photographing it?

He pulled the picture out again and cursed Tiny for conning him with that story about the autograph for the kid. He held the picture under the light of the single lamp that burned on the table by the side of the couch and Rebecca stretched across him to look down at it too. Shaking his head slowly and sighing he dropped the photo on the table and leaned back, his head resting on the cushion which continued to give under the weight.

He closed his eyes and breathed slowly through his nose. Then he felt her lips on his. Soft. Parted slightly. She rested them there. No movement. As though she were trying to still him completely. To make him peaceful. Her body too was motionless. He could not even sense her breathing.

Then she did breathe. Her lower lip moved first between his lips, probing, prising them apart till his mouth opened. Then, shifting slightly sideways she pushed both her lips between his and her hands held his head gently but firmly. And she breathed into him, kissed him. And he felt himself immediately begin to relax, as though a drug had been injected. He felt his pulse slow. He felt peace wash over him and later, when he lay awake thinking of it, he'd had no idea how much time had passed, how long they had stayed like that, kissing softly, slowly.

All he knew was that they had gone from there to deep kissing then to gentle delicate finely edged kisses that could barely be felt and from there to passion and depth again. Then to the floor. To the rug. To the light and heat from the fire. From fully clothed to naked.

Then bed.

And dreams for Eddie. Dreams of a relationship that mattered for once in his life. At last in his lonely bloody God-damned trustless, fortressed life. Even though Grimond now threatened it, threatened his livelihood. What could he do if he was finished as a jockey? How would he keep her? Somehow. Anyhow. Maybe he'd take Turco up on his SIS scam and make that million he'd been promised. Lying in the darkness he laughed as he made plans for it with Rebecca and she laughed too when he told her of Turco's outrageous scheme.

And he talked long into the night until he finally talked her to sleep. But Eddie stayed awake wanting to watch her, cherish the memory of what they'd done, of her being beside him at last. She moaned softly and rolled over to lie on her stomach, her deep even breathing telling Eddie she was still asleep.

Next morning, Thursday, after Rebecca had left for London (they had made love again just before dawn), Eddie rang Ben Turco and told him what had happened.

'Shit!' Turco said.

'Any suggestions?' Eddie asked.

'My brain don't function too well this time of the morning. You riding today?'

'Leaving for Taunton within the hour.'

'Call you back.'

Eddie got the impression Turco hadn't quite grasped the importance of what he'd told him. 'Ben, listen, this could finish me. Maybe we should cancel Saturday, I can put McCarthy off for another week or so.'

'What difference is that gonna make? If we don't go through with this on Saturday, Grimond becomes even more of a loose cannon. God knows where he'll go off next. And if you bow to this it's almost an admission of guilt. He'll be blackmailing you for something else then, asking you to fix races or something.'

Eddie hesitated. 'I know ... You're right. I'll talk to McCarthy, get it out in the open.'

'Just hold off, Ed, gimme an hour or so before you do anything. I'll call you back.'

Thirty-five

The reception on Ogilvie's mobile phone was poor and he was embarrassed at having to almost shout into the mouthpiece. His voice boomed in the long square tunnel of corridor at Carlisle Infirmary. He'd have gone outside if the rain hadn't been sheeting down. The noise of it hammering on the windows made him shout even louder.

All he wanted his secretary to do was get Kim's file out and give him the telephone number of Mrs Malloy in Newmarket. As he waited he knew he'd have to find somewhere more private than this to make the next call from. But it would have to be made soon.

The solicitor had barely moved from Kim's bedside in the past forty-eight hours. The boy had not regained consciousness and the doctor could not say if and when he would. Ogilvie felt an enormous guilt. He had become obsessed with being there when Kim opened his eyes. He was unable to bear the idea of the boy thinking for a second that he had betrayed him, as it must have seemed to Kim he had, the moment he set eyes on that stupid policeman.

Good God, how had that fool expected Kim to react? A child on the run taken utterly by surprise. How on earth had he failed to foresee the possible consequences? It was little consolation that the policeman had been suspended.

Doreen, Ogilvie's secretary, came on and gave him the number and as he scribbled it inside a thin diary Ogilvie knew he would have to travel south. He was simply not going to let Kim's mother refuse to see him. Not this time. He'd drive down there immediately, leave a letter for Kim explaining what had happened, telling him he'd gone to make a personal plea on his behalf.

Louise answered the phone. Ogilvie did not say what had happened but told her that he had to come and speak to her personally as a matter of the greatest urgency. Louise hesitated. 'If this is something to do with the boy ...'

'It is a situation which your mother must, in my professional judgement, be informed of as soon as possible. You would be very unwise to try and block that.'

That wound her up. 'I'm not trying to block anything, Mr Ogilvie! I resent ...'

'Then see me! This afternoon.'

'I'll see you on the basis that you must

let me decide whether or not my mother should be involved.'

Ogilvie felt he had no choice but to agree. Getting direct personal access to the family would be a start. He'd worry about the details later. Returning to the Intensive Care Unit he borrowed a sheet of paper and an envelope from the Sister and wrote Kim a long note almost begging the boy to believe that he hadn't broken his promise. The Sister agreed to hand Kim the sealed envelope if he regained consciousness and was fit to read. Ogilvie promised he would ring that afternoon.

Pushing the Jaguar close to a hundred on the M6 run to Scotch Corner he clicked the adapter from his electric razor into the cigar socket and even at that high speed the loudest noise in the car was that from the whirring heads as they sliced through his hard dark whiskers.

Much further south, on the M5, after numerous tries, Eddie finally got through to Peter McCarthy. When Turco had called back he'd had nothing to offer and Eddie thought it best to speak to the Security man as soon as possible. 'Mac, I don't suppose you'll be at Taunton today.'

'Sandown.'

'Homebird.'

'That's where the heart is, don't you know?'

'Not mine.'

'What?'

'Never mind. Mac, look, I need to see you on a matter, as they say, of some import.'

'To whom?'

'To meem.'

'Surprise, surprise. What's wrong? Have we got a problem with your friend on Saturday?'

'Sort of.'

'Go on.'

'Mac, it's best not discussed on a mobile. Are you going home after Sandown?'

'Yes.'

'Can I call in and see you on the way back from Taunton?'

Mac cleared his throat. Eddie knew he was uncomfortable about inviting him to his house. 'Give me a call when you're half an hour away and we'll arrange to meet somewhere.'

'Fine. See you tonight.'

Ogilvie swung the maroon Jag into the drive of the Malloy stud just outside Newmarket. Louise, who had been in black leggings and an old sweatshirt when he had rung this morning, had changed into a denim dress that buttoned from just above the two inch thick green belt around her slim waist. She'd left the top two buttons undone in an effort to look casual and relaxed but she knew the strain was showing and she saw it reflected in the solicitor's weary face as they shook hands.

Louise led him into the front room which her mother reserved for formal visitors and invited him to sit in the big easy chair by the bay window. The light from the window showed her a face about ten years younger than she'd imagined from the voice. Ogilvie looked no more than thirty-five though his tweed suit and tie and brown suede shoes were, to her mind, the dress of a man in his mid-fifties. His dark brown hair showed some grey at the temples but his brown eyes seemed open and kind and she liked his hands: long expressive fingers, well manicured. A handsome man. Wearing a wedding ring. Louise excused herself and went to re-boil the kettle, returning a minute later carrying a tray.

The solicitor stirred sugar into his tea and said, 'How is your mother?'

'Not at all well. I'm afraid that your letter last week gave her such a shock she spent two days in hospital. She's been confined to bed since coming home.'

Ogilvie stared at the cluster of tiny

bubbles spinning on the surface of the tea. This was going to be more difficult than he'd thought. He told her what had happened to Kim, watched her pretty face for change and saw none except deepening despair in her eyes. When he finished she just shook her head slowly, lowered it and said quietly, 'I'm sorry, but there's nothing we can do.'

Elbows on his knees he leaned across the coffee table and looked up into her face. 'The boy may well die. He is only twelve years of age. He is the pleasantest, bravest, most ... most dignified boy I have ever met. Dignity in the face of his whole world collapsing. He deserves to meet his mother. She deserves to know what a fine child she brought into this world.'

Ogilvie watched the lump in her throat as she swallowed before answering. 'Mr Ogilvie, before Kim was born something happened in our family, something that eventually broke the family up, something that led to Kim being adopted at birth. The pain of all that lasted most of my lifetime and it was only when my father died last year that we began to come back together again, my mother and I and Eddie. Things have been very strained since. Getting better steadily but there are still deep wounds and until those are healed there is nothing, I know, believe

me, that would persuade my mother to
see the boy.'

'Kim.'

She looked at him. 'Kim,' she said.

Ogilvie said, 'And what about *his*
wounds? What about *his* pain, *his* anguish?'

'You're trying to make me feel guilty,
Mr Ogilvie, and that's not fair!'

He saw the strain in her now, the child
in her, the sheen of tears in her blue eyes
that her dress set off so well. Even more
striking now as they glistened wet in the
bright daylight. And he wondered what
terrible thing had happened to harden her
heart so much against her own brother.

'What about your brother Eddie? Have
you told him about Kim?'

She shook her head.

'Why not?'

'Eddie wouldn't have the time, I know
he wouldn't. He's a jockey. He rides six
days a week, sometimes seven. He's never
around.'

'Kim desperately wants to find his
brother. He had always wanted a brother.
He told me that himself on the telephone
just the other night.'

Louise shook her head again slowly. 'I'm
sorry. It just wouldn't work out.'

'Why don't you let your brother decide
that?'

'Because it would affect more than my

brother. Because my mother would be the one who would suffer.'

Ogilvie lowered his voice, spoke slowly. 'Please let me speak to her. Just for a few minutes. If she becomes in the least distressed I promise I'll leave immediately.'

Louise raised her head and looked him in the eye, concentrated all the feeling she had, all the worry and despair, the fear, all in one look aimed at making him see that she meant what she said. 'No. I'm sorry but I won't change my mind.'

Ogilvie held her gaze for what seemed a long time then slowly he got up and buttoned his jacket. 'May I use your telephone before I leave?'

Silently she led him out and across the hallway to the room opposite, which they used as an office. The phone was on a long desk. She left him and went into the kitchen but Ogilvie made sure that he spoke loud enough to ensure she knew he was talking to the hospital, asking about Kim.

Louise waited till he'd hung up then walked slowly into the hallway to meet him as he stepped out of the office at the end. They stood facing each other like ill-matched gunslingers. Ogilvie said, 'No change. Still in a coma.'

Louise folded her arms and nodded.

Ogilvie said, 'If Kim dies would you like

227

me to let you know?'

She stared at him again, wondering at this cruelty. 'No,' she said softly.

He turned and opened the door. 'Goodbye,' he said.

Louise hurried towards the door and stood watching him walk to his car. 'Mr Ogilvie ...'

He turned.

'If the boy dies, please do let us know.'

Ogilvie stared at her, his face twisted by distaste and anger. 'Why the change of mind? So that you can stop worrying about him ever tracking you down? I hope he never does because he'll be sorely disappointed with what he finds.'

He got in the car and Louise watched the Jag spit exhaust smoke at her as he pulled away. The cold wind raised goose bumps on her bare arms and sorrow, misery and guilt brought tears to her eyes.

Thirty-six

Eddie had a luckless day at Taunton with four unplaced mounts and by the time he met Mac in the Chequers Hotel in Newbury he felt the need of a large whisky but thought better of it since ninety more minutes of driving lay in front of him. So they both sat in the lounge drinking mineral water. McCarthy had carried the glass bowl of nuts from the bar to their table and was plucking at them and dropping them into his mouth like some machine.

'Well, I see you're not a frequenter of bars,' Eddie said.

'Why?' asked Mac, chewing.

'You'd never see the pros nibbling from those bowls. Think how many people go to the toilet, don't wash their hands then come back and stick their fingers into the communal nuts and crisps.'

McCarthy scowled and quickly pushed the bowl away from him. Eddie smiled. Mac said, 'Never thought of that.'

'You will in future.'

The big man nodded then Eddie told him what had happened with Grimond at Leicester.

Mac said, 'And have you got this photo?'

Eddie pulled the picture from his inside pocket and handed it over. Mac looked at it and tutted, shaking his head. 'This looks bad, Eddie.'

'Tell me something I don't know.'

Mac stared at it a while in silence as if waiting for some strange metamorphosis. He shook his head again and waved the picture gently towards Eddie. 'This, my friend, whichever way you look at it, however things work out on Saturday, is going to cause you very big problems.'

On the face of it McCarthy had had little to offer. All he could do was ignore the fact that Eddie had shown him the picture. If Grimond chose to mount a campaign against him then the picture and the circumstances in which it was taken would be investigated. McCarthy said he thought it best not to discuss what his comments might be when asked to look at the case and Eddie took this to be positive.

He knew Mac well enough to realise he had his own way of doing things. Mac's overriding concern was that he should never compromise himself. He regarded red tape as an essential element which bonded the Jockey Club and its departments together and he was loath to cut through it directly. But Eddie had learned that Mac often found a method of snipping at the edges of it till it gave way. He knew Mac would give him the fairest of treatment if he had any influence on his particular case but his involvement couldn't be taken for granted.

Different Security Officers handled the North East racecourses where Catterick was situated and Mac, although a senior officer, would have to find some way of muscling in, a guarantee he couldn't give to Eddie.

It occupied Eddie's mind all the way home, along with his other obsession, Rebecca, who had never really been out of his thoughts all day. As soon as he got home he called her and went over everything McCarthy had said. She made all the right comforting noises, offered reassurances and generally made him feel much better.

But he warned her of what lay ahead. 'Mac will only carry so much clout and he'll be up against some people, stewards, who simply don't like me and never have done since they were forced to give me back my licence six years ago. Nothing would please these guys more than to see me warned off again, see me out of racing for good.'

'But surely Tiny Delaware will tell them it was a set-up?'

Eddie sighed into the mouthpiece. 'Something tells me that if this breaks Tiny will disappear until it's over.'

'Fine, then they can't try you without one of the chief witnesses.'

'Yeah, well who do you think will get the blame for Tiny suddenly not being around?'

'Then contact him now. Try tomorrow.

Tell him you know what happened and that you need him to tell the truth when Grimond starts causing trouble.'

Eddie thought about that. 'Maybe you're right. I'll try.'

'Where are you tomorrow?'

'Cheltenham.'

'Will Tiny be there?'

'He might be. We'll see. Anyway, enough of me moaning. It'll work itself out somehow.'

There was a silence which lasted longer than Eddie felt comfortable with. Rebecca said quietly, 'What if it doesn't work out, Eddie? What will you do?'

'It will. It will work out. Don't worry.' But there was no real confidence there and that showed in his voice.

After another pause Rebecca said, 'That offer, from your friend Ben, that SIS scam, would you really consider getting involved in that?'

Suddenly the disadvantages of being in love but not really knowing the person you're in love with hit home with Eddie. He simply didn't know which way she wanted him to answer. If Turco's estimate of a million pounds each had been right it would mean Eddie would never have to worry again. It would mean that come March when Rebecca got her trust fund payment he'd be on equal terms with her, at least for a while. To hell with the stewards and with racing and its petty jealousies. They could both live a bloody fine life from then on.

But was that what she wanted to hear? That Eddie would take part in a major con just to get money, to get revenge on the racing Establishment?

He said, 'It wouldn't matter much if I did want to get involved because, if I was warned off, SIS wouldn't have me back in the studio. The opportunity wouldn't be there any more.'

'But would you do it if it was there?'

She wasn't letting him off the hook. In the end, Eddie knew that no matter how desperate he was he wouldn't do it, even if it meant losing her. 'No, I wouldn't. I couldn't.'

Another pause then she said, quietly, 'Good. I'm glad.'

Eddie smiled.

One hundred and twenty miles to the north another professional was considering his future. Campbell Ogilvie was becoming further obsessed by the fate of Kim. Apart from his solitary vigil by the boy's bed Ogilvie felt he had nothing to offer, no way of trying to help bring Kim back to consciousness. He knew of stories where families had rallied round coma victims, talking constantly to them, playing tapes of familiar songs and sounds, trying to remind them of happy times, promising the return of those in the future if only they would wake up. But Ogilvie knew so little about Kim's life. His natural family knew even less but surely the blood ties there would have had deep meaning for Kim?

The sense that his real mother, his sister or brother were there would help. Somehow, surely it would help? Exhausted, Ogilvie finally left the hospital at 11.15 p.m. to drive home to his own children and his wife who was beginning to worry about his health.

One of just six critically ill patients in the small Intensive Care Unit, lit only by a softly glowing lamp by each bed, Kim lay in the corner, hooked up to monitoring equipment, his body being fed intravenously. A few minutes after Ogilvie had trudged wearily out of the room there was the tiniest flicker of movement below Kim's eyelids, then stillness again.

Late on Friday night Phil Grimond was returning to his home near Nottingham after a trip to Birmingham where he had paid a sixteen-year-old boy to have sex in a hotel bedroom. As usual, Grimond had video taped the sex session and he was looking forward to watching it when he got back. He was sure he had a half bottle of vodka left to drink during the 'show'.

Then there was tomorrow. Cheltenham. Another fifty grand or so with a bit of luck. All he needed was a tightish photo finish. He'd seen the runners in the evening paper: good competitive racing so there was every chance he'd get a couple of close finishes. And that bastard Malloy was out of the picture. Or rather, in the picture. Grimond smiled as he pulled into the long driveway of his house. Newly bought, it was in one of the posher areas. Big mortgage. That was one of the reasons he couldn't let Turco just kick sand over the campfire and roll the wagons off somewhere else. Yankee dickhead. Arsehole.

Grimond still got a kick out of aiming his little remote control gadget at the garage and seeing the door swing up automatically. He'd mastered the art of doing it now without lowering the window. He drove straight inside, switched off his lights and engine, took his bag containing the video camera from the back seat, locked the car with another remote attached to the key and went outside.

He was just pulling his jacket collar up against the cold night air when he was hit from behind, a hard blow to the kidneys. He grunted and was struck again, heavily, knocking all the air from his lungs in a long gasp. He fell to his knees. Two men pulled him back into the garage.

Fighting for air, Grimond was plunged into darkness as one of the men switched the light off. They held him, on his back, down across the warm bonnet of the car. He gasped and coughed as his lungs, working like automatic bellows, tried to refill themselves. He was aware of nothing about the men but their strength. No sight of them, no smell, no feel of their flesh. Then he felt fingers on his scalp, the heel of a hand on his face banging his head down against the bonnet, holding it hard there. He wanted to speak, to plead, but hadn't recovered sufficiently to do so.

He wasn't aware of what they used on him, didn't even feel it on his cheek at first, and all he would ever be certain about with the thing they pushed into his right eye was that it was metal. He would never be able to make up his mind whether it was searing hot or ice-crystal cold but he felt them dig his right eye out of its socket with the thing. He couldn't remember if he screamed or not. The doctors told him later that the shock of it probably brought on immediate unconsciousness. Fortunately, because it meant that he didn't feel them gouge out the other eye or slice his tongue off at the root.

The police and ambulance crew thought it particularly morbid and horrific that the removed organs were nowhere to be found.

Thirty-seven

When Eddie was legged up by Laura Gilpin into the saddle of Samson's Curls in that superb oval bowl of green that is the paddock at Cheltenham he didn't know about Grimond. Turco had been trying to reach him on his mobile for the past ninety minutes to tell him that Grimond had failed to check in and that something might be wrong. But Eddie had left the phone in his car.

So when a nervous Laura Gilpin wished him luck as she released the bridle at the bottom of the railed off canter lane in front of the stands, Eddie's mind was concentrated on bringing Samson's Curls as late as possible while still managing to win by half a length or more, a distance he considered that Grimond wouldn't attempt to alter under any circumstances.

As her horse launched into an immediate canter Laura flinched, frowned and turned slightly sideways to avoid the kickback of the deep rough sand from the hooves of Samson's Curls. She watched the muscular rear end ripple as the horse went away from her then her eyes moved upwards to Eddie's rear end in his white shiny breeches. God, it had been good to see him again, though she congratulated herself as she walked back in on having remained fairly cool with him. Quite laid back. She'd been thinking about him a lot, daydreaming. And as she made her way onto the lawn to watch the race she felt childish and ridiculous in her hope that the horse would win so she'd get to kiss him in congratulations. Laura chuckled aloud as she moved through the crowd and one or two gave her an odd look.

McCarthy had already briefed his two colleagues who were going to 'assist' him when they burst in on Grimond in the judge's box. Eddie had told him that this race was very likely to result in a close finish and that Grimond would undoubtedly have the DIM equipment primed for the finish. When McCarthy's men appeared at the meeting place by the weighing room as arranged, McCarthy wasn't there. He'd had the foresight, albeit late, to go to the racecourse office and check that it was indeed Grimond who would be on photo finish duty. That was when he was told that Grimond had not reported for work.

Eddie rode a copybook race to bring Samson's Curls to the front fifty yards from the post and win by half a length. Laura, entranced, terrified, almost suspended in time, had watched him nurse the horse so tenderly behind the leader, holding her breath for almost as long as Eddie had held the horse then letting it all out in an amazing half scream, half cheer which pierced through the crowd's roar as Eddie hit the front.

Red-faced, laughing with nerves and relief and feeling incredibly happy, Laura turned and hurried through the throng to meet them coming back in. Back on the sandy canter lane she barrelled through the incoming horses and stable lads to get to her heroes. Seeing her coming with such purpose and such obvious delight brought a wide smile to Eddie's face. By the time she reached them the tears were flowing from her shining eyes. She kissed the horse's foam flecked muzzle as his velvety nostrils sucked and blew and his sides heaved.

She reached both pudgy arms upwards towards Eddie and he crouched and put an arm round her and kissed her forehead. 'Well done!' he said. She looked up at him with deep gratitude and admiration but try as she might she could find no words. Her lip quivered, her face crumpled and she started bawling like a baby. Eddie blushed with happy embarrassment as he patted her head softly and said, 'Sshh, sshhh, Laura … you'll be fine.'

'Who was the fat woman with the horse?' Rebecca asked him later.

Eddie smiled. 'That was the owner and trainer. Nice girl. I introduced you, didn't I?'

'You did but I was too busy trying to figure out why you were kissing and hugging her so much to remember her name!'

'I only kissed her twice!'

'Come on! When she put her arms around you in the winner's enclosure I thought she was never going to let you go. I thought you'd never come out alive.'

Eddie felt a twinge of guilt and reddened slightly. 'See,' Rebecca said, 'you're blushing!'

'Only because I was so embarrassed by it!' But it was more than that. Eddie had felt something unexpected when he and Laura had hugged, something that took him completely by surprise. He'd felt peaceful and secure and, for as long as the embrace lasted, that he was exactly where he was meant to be. When they'd finally eased themselves apart they'd looked directly into each other's eyes for a few moments and they'd both known there was something there. Eddie wasn't quite sure what it was—nothing sexual, he was certain—and he didn't think that Laura knew either.

He hadn't given it that much thought and was beginning to put it down to his emotions finally being unlocked by Rebecca. Maybe the floodgates had opened now and he'd be swamping every female he met with love, or whatever this feeling was.

He continued to make a joke of it with Rebecca but she did admit to being jealous by nature. Eddie promised never to do anything to make her insecure, to bring that jealousy on, and Rebecca gripped his arm and walked with him out of the side entrance of the paddock.

Eddie had a ride in the last but he'd changed into his suit to go and look at the trade stands with Rebecca. He'd resolved to buy her the first thing she took a liking to, no matter what the price was, and, as they headed towards the trade stand area, he was enjoying the suspense of wondering exactly how much she was going to cost him.

As they passed the Arkle statue, a tall man in a long dark green woollen coat approached Eddie from just off to his right. He stopped in front of them. 'I do apologise and hope you'll excuse me. May I ask if you are Eddie Malloy? A gentleman by the paddock told me you were.'

Eddie looked at him. He didn't look like an autograph hound. 'That's right, what can I do for you?' He felt Rebecca take a tighter hold on his arm and lean on him slightly.

The man said, 'Are you the son of Mrs Jean Marie Malloy who now lives in Newmarket?'

Eddie frowned. 'Why do you ask?'

'I just need to make sure I have the right man. Forgive me. My name is Campbell Ogilvie. I'm a solicitor and I have something to tell you that you may wish to hear in private.'

Thirty-eight

Eddie left the racecourse immediately after the last race and drove home at some speed where he hurriedly picked up fresh underwear, his jeans and two casual shirts. Rebecca had been almost distressed by the fact that she couldn't travel north with him but she had promised her mother she'd visit her that night in Norfolk. Eddie promised to call her when he reached the hospital.

Within a minute of joining the M6 Eddie was doing 110 mph, confident that if he got stopped he'd have a valid reason for breaking the limit. His mind was in turmoil. When Ogilvie's story had sunk in, and that had taken some time, he'd experienced such a storm of different emotions that he simply did not know how he felt.

At first he had wondered if it was some sort of tasteless wind-up engineered by someone with a grudge but Ogilvie had shown him papers including a copy of Kim's adoptive father's will.

Eddie felt rage at his mother and at Louise for rejecting the boy. He felt anger and sorrow over his mother's abandonment of Kim as a baby although that was tempered by the influence he knew his father would have had. It would have been he who'd made his wife give up the baby because of what had happened before.

And he wished deeply that his father were still alive so he could go and shake the life out of him. March into his house, straight up to him, take him by the throat and shake and throttle the evil out of his body.

And how could they have lived so long

and not told him he had a brother? Even though they'd been estranged, they knew where Eddie was, just a brief note would have done. But no, that was a ridiculous thought, for how much more would he have hated them then?

The temptation to call his mother and Louise and rip them apart on the telephone burned so strongly that it was only his sincere promise to Ogilvie not to call them before tomorrow that stopped him. His respect for the solicitor at this time was much greater than that for his own family. Ogilvie had put his career on the line by seeking Eddie out. He could easily be disbarred from practising over all this and Eddie knew it.

Whether there would ever be a way of repaying him Eddie didn't know but for what it was worth to the man, Ogilvie had Eddie's loyalty till he drew his last breath. Ogilvie had counselled him that it would be worth waiting till his emotions had settled before speaking to his mother and sister but right now he felt that his fury would never subside. That poor kid. Deserted by everyone except Ogilvie, despite the fact that he could die tomorrow.

Eddie pressed the accelerator all the way to the floor.

The solicitor had left Cheltenham after speaking to Eddie and he was by the bed now watching the jockey come in, hurrying but trying to be silent in the small IC unit. Eddie slowed as he approached the bed then stopped and leant forward, almost peeking as a father would at his first born.

The nurse, seated by the end of the bed, nodded and smiled at Eddie.

On seeing Eddie at Cheltenham, Ogilvie had been struck by the close resemblance to Kim and it seemed more pronounced now as he watched Eddie's face, saw the frown of worry ease into a warm smile of pride. Ogilvie glanced again at Kim then back to Eddie: same dark curly hair over pale skin, deep blue eyes, same faint freckle arrangement across the nose and cheeks. (Ogilvie had noticed that in Louise too.) The only real differences were the short scar on Eddie's cheek and the few wrinkles around his eyes and Ogilvie supposed the boy might well acquire those in time.

He watched Eddie intently now as he took the final step forward and reached down to gently clasp Kim's left hand. 'You'll be all right now, Kim.' Eddie almost whispered it. 'I'll look after you.' The boy didn't stir. The only movement was the rhythm of his chest as he breathed. Eddie stared at him and Ogilvie watched the tears rise and slip silently down his cheeks, glistening in the reflection of the lamp above Kim's bed.

And the solicitor suddenly felt a sense of complete collapse. He slumped forward, head down, his shoulders fell and he could barely find the strength to bury his face in his hands. It was as though he'd been holding up a massive crumbling building full of helpless people, supporting the whole structure alone till help had come.

Eddie slowly released Kim's hand, wiped his tears on his sleeve and walked around the bed to place a hand on Campbell Ogilvie's shoulder. He squeezed. 'You okay?'

Ogilvie nodded.

Eddie hunkered down beside him. 'Go home now. I'll take care of him.' Ogilvie nodded again and Eddie helped him up and walked him to the door. Eddie looked at the haggard, exhausted face and felt deep sympathy and gratitude. He said, 'I feel ... I don't think there is any way I can thank you for what you've done. I'm just ...'

Ogilvie raised a hand very slowly to silence him. 'Just call me in the morning and let me know how he is.'

Eddie nodded. 'I will.'

Ogilvie managed a tired but happy smile and made his way towards the exit sign. Eddie glanced back to make sure his brother was okay then he went to find a convenient spot to call Rebecca from, to tell her that everything was going to be all right. But her mobile was switched off and he didn't have her mother's number. Every half-hour until 11 p.m. Eddie tried Rebecca's number but got no response. Why hadn't she called him?

Eddie told Kim's nurse there was no point in both of them staying by the bed all night. Tired, overworked and feeling slightly guilty she agreed to leave to go only as far as the end bed on the ward and relieve one of her friends.

Watching Kim's peaceful face Eddie wasn't sure whether or not to be grateful for the fact that the boy's emotional suffering, at least, was suspended. From a selfish viewpoint he wished him fully alive and conscious even for a few minutes so he could hug him and tell him everything was going to be fine.

Since he'd walked in to this ward and seen him there had never been a shred of doubt in Eddie's mind that he would take care of this boy, that he'd be brother, father, mother and sister to him if that was what was needed. If that was what Kim wanted. The pain of Eddie's own childhood had never left him and never would and he would give anything, do anything to give Kim some happiness. There was no hesitation, no wariness about what Kim may be like as a person.

Eddie looked down at that face and was transported back almost eighteen years. It was himself he saw lying there and that offered a chance he'd never expected, the chance to rewrite things, the chance to do it all again. To make things right. And by God he'd make things right. He would will this boy back to consciousness. He'd pay for whatever medical help was necessary. He didn't know how, but he would pay.

Next morning he'd call Kenneth Trevorrow, a neurosurgeon who specialised in sports injuries. Trevorrow had a special interest in jockeys and the effectiveness of skull cap protection over a sequence of falls involving concussion.

He'd persuade Trevorrow to come as soon as possible. Anyone Eddie had to see would have to come here. He wasn't leaving his brother's bed until the boy had regained consciousness. He'd better ring round and get off his rides on Monday.

What day was this? Saturday. No, the early hours of Sunday. Eddie rubbed his eyes and massaged his face, losing count of the number of times he had done that tonight.

Tiredness. Damn it. He must be getting old. There'd been times when he could stay up all night and happily ride out in the morning then go racing. He looked at

Kim again and smiled wearily. The boy still had all that in front of him. For the first time, Eddie wondered if he'd ever sat on a horse. Ogilvie had mentioned he'd been raised on a farm so there had to be every chance he could ride.

A farm in Cumbria. Same as Eddie. And Eddie wondered if his mother had known that her youngest son, her abandoned son, had been growing up so close by. How many times had she thought of him, wondered where he was, what sort of family he was with, what he looked like?

Eddie was certain Rebecca would like Kim. He smiled. They were so much alike she was bound to like him. He wondered why she hadn't rung. Maybe she was fully occupied taking care of her mother. Rebecca had told Eddie how shattering her mother had found the loss of her husband. Rebecca had said she feared she would never get over it.

But surely Rebecca would have wanted to know how Kim was? Maybe she didn't realise her mobile was switched off and she was waiting for Eddie to ring. What the hell? Why was he worried about Rebecca? Kim was the one who needed all his attention for now. He clutched the boy's hand again then sighed softly and rubbed his eyes again and tried to settle back in the hard plastic chair.

There was space alongside Kim on the cream coloured blanket and the temptation to lie and stretch on the softness, to sleep, was almost overwhelming at times. Eddie decided to stop fighting the fatigue. Straightening his legs below the bed he crossed his arms, rested his chin on his chest and closed his eyes.

When Eddie awoke Kim's position in bed had not altered and throughout the long morning nothing changed. Eddie had to fight to keep the comparison of a corpse from his mind for that was how still Kim looked. Eddie was immensely grateful when the nurse came to gently turn the boy on his side for a while to try to prevent bed sores forming. When he questioned her about seeing a doctor who could tell him more she said that it would be tomorrow before the doctor would call round again. Unless an emergency arose.

Every half-hour Eddie went out of the ward briefly to try Rebecca's number. He rang the Dorchester on the off-chance she'd returned that morning but she hadn't. At 10.30 he decided to ring his answerphone at home in case she'd lost his mobile number. He keyed in the code to play back messages. There was none from Rebecca but there were four from a frantic sounding Mattie Stuart who said he'd been trying to contact Eddie on his mobile since midnight last night. Mattie said he thought that Rebecca might be in trouble.

Thirty-nine

Eddie wondered briefly how long he could continue to tempt fate and the traffic police as he watched the speedo needle settle at 110 mph as he headed south. Mattie had told him that he'd seen Rebecca in London late last night being hustled into a casino in Park Lane by the two Chinese men she'd held at gunpoint in that nightclub.

Mattie said he'd gone in after them to try and see what was happening but that when he got there the place was packed and he'd lost them. Eddie asked why the hell he hadn't rung the police and Mattie had wriggled and sounded very uncomfortable. He'd said that after the last time when Rebecca had called them out to the nightclub and they'd found nothing he simply didn't think they would pay any attention.

Eddie knew that the truth was that Mattie was plain scared. Afraid that if he put the police onto the Triad those men would come back for him. If it hadn't been for Rebecca helping Mattie out when he needed help maybe Eddie would have understood but Rebecca had needed the favour returned and Mattie had failed her. Eddie had got so angry he'd cursed Mattie and hung up on him then found he had to call back for exact directions to the casino. Suitably penitent now, Mattie had offered to meet him there.

Eddie had been loath to leave Kim but he'd called Campbell Ogilvie and explained that another emergency had come up which would take him away for the rest of that day. Without hesitation the solicitor had volunteered to come back and sit with Kim till Eddie returned. Before Eddie left the hospital Ogilvie promised he'd ring immediately if there was any change in Kim's condition.

So unshaven and wearing the same suit and shirt he'd had on since yesterday morning Eddie jumped in the Audi and set out on the four-hour journey. What he would do when he reached the casino he just didn't know. What he would do when he caught up with those Chinese he knew exactly.

At 10.42, just as Eddie was joining the M6 motorway, Rebecca Bow walked out onto the third floor balcony of the Park

Lane casino to breathe some fresh air and try to rest her brain. It was a cold grey day as she looked out over Hyde Park. A glance to her right brought the doors of the Dorchester Hotel into view and she cringed as she recalled her meeting with the manager last night.

He'd knocked unannounced on her room door and asked if she could spare a few minutes to talk about her hotel bill which was now running at just over £12,000. Rebecca had feigned shock and surprise that he could even think to doubt her creditworthiness. Didn't he realise how much money her father, a good customer of the Dorchester for years, had left in his will? Hadn't she told him she would be getting the next million from her trust fund in just a few weeks' time? Hadn't she shown him the letter from her father's solicitor confirming this?

He accepted that and was sorry to have to raise the matter but if perhaps she could make part payment just now on her credit card or something ...?

Absolutely out of the question, Rebecca had told him. The manager left then, telling her that he would have to review the whole situation after Christmas.

Rebecca had closed the door behind him and locked it immediately as though shutting out an intruder. She'd leant on the door staring at the ceiling, her breath coming fast as the panic that was becoming so familiar closed in again.

It was out of the question to pay anything by credit card because all her accounts had been closed and she was being pursued for large debts. The flat in St John's Wood had been sold six months ago and there was no money left in any trust funds. In the twenty-two months since her father had died Rebecca Bow had gambled away more than two and a half million pounds. Some had gone on the racecourse but most had disappeared in casinos.

After last week she had negotiated another line of credit with the Chinese whose casino she'd spent the night in. And that could have been the night that changed everything, Rebecca thought, as she lit a cigarette and inhaled in the damp air. At around three o'clock in the morning she'd been over £200,000 ahead of the game. Five minutes ago she'd lost her last pile of chips and was penniless again. And creditless. Across the road in Hyde Park she watched two rollerbladers skate hand in hand laughing loud and she envied them their freedom. It was a freedom she knew she could have too as soon as her big break came. She just needed another line of credit. Just one more bite.

She knew she could do it then. She went back inside to look for Lee Sung.

Eddie had travelled less than a hundred miles, torturing himself with thoughts of what the Chinese might be doing to Rebecca. The phone rang, startling him. It was Ben Turco.

'Eddie, heard the news about Grimond?'

'No.'

'Somebody did a proper number on him on Friday night outside his house.'

'Beat him up?'

'Understatement. Almost killed him. Gouged his eyes out and cut off his tongue.'

'Jeez! Cut off his tongue?'

'Sliced it off at the root after digging his eyes out of his head.'

'Good God! Are you kidding me, Ben?'

'Come on, would I kid about a thing like that?'

'How did you find out?'

'Heard it on the radio news.'

Eddie was silent. He stood leaning on the Audi. Something in his tired confused mind suggested that this news could affect him somehow. He said, 'Ben, my brain isn't functioning too well this morning so tell me what this means.'

'Well I don't know that it means that much for you but if it was linked to what

Grimond had been doing for us on those photo finishes then I think that what it might mean for me is good old-fashioned terror. My bowels are already jogging around the track in there, warming up for the proper action.'

'Do you think it might be linked to that?'

'I haven't a scooby but it was the first thing that came to my mind, innocent and virginal as it is.'

'Seriously, Ben, do you think it could be?'

'I was never more serious, Ed. So serious that as I speak to you I'm looking towards the door at where my trusty old suitcase is packed and tapping its castors impatiently, anxious to continue its career as a receptacle for the belongings of a living person; one with all facial features and limbs intact.'

'Where are you going?'

'The good old US of A. If this is linked with the DIM stuff I'd sooner take my chances in downtown New York. At least the muggers and panhandlers leave you your eyes and tongue.'

'Usually. How long will you be gone for?'

'Till, as they say, the heat dies down.'

'Any chance of the police linking you with Grimond?'

'That depends on what Grimond kept lying around at home. I don't know if he made notes or kept a diary or something.'

'Didn't seem the type.'

'No. Anyway, fancy coming with me?'

'Other commitments, I'm afraid.'

'That girl of yours?'

'Not just her. More now.'

'Well good luck and au revoir and all that stuff. If ever you want to cream those bookies with that slice of genius I came up with—you know, with SIS—gimme a call.'

'Where?'

'I'll be in touch when I get there.'

A thought occurred to Eddie. 'Ben, before you go, did Grimond have anything to do with the Chinese at any point? The Triads maybe?'

'Not to my knowledge. Why do you ask?'

'Just a thought.'

'Don't have too many of those. Bad for you. I'll see you around.'

'Good luck.'

'Same to you, Ed, same to you.'

Eddie pressed End. Appropriate, he thought. He'd miss Turco but he'd plenty more to be getting on with. He shivered when he thought of Grimond. He didn't like the guy but, my God, that was a terrible thing to suffer. The thought of it made him more worried about Rebecca. Grimond attacked on Friday, Rebecca abducted the following night, it made him wonder if there was some connection.

He was still hours away from her. He knew he had to concentrate his mind or he'd drive himself crazy fretting. He thought of the other things he had to do, the calls he had still to make, prioritise them.

First and foremost, Kim.

Forty

Eddie had to make three calls before he managed to get Kenneth Trevorrow's home phone number. Had it been for himself, Eddie would have thought twice about disturbing the surgeon at home, especially on a Sunday, but this was for Kim and he didn't hesitate.

A woman who described herself as Mr Trevorrow's house-sitter told Eddie that the surgeon and his wife were in New South Wales and not expected back for a fortnight. Eddie had no doubt that the hospital consultant on Kim's case was more than competent but he knew it would be tomorrow before he could speak to him and he was anxious for information about Kim's injury.

The nurse had been able to tell him nothing more than the fact that Kim's scan had shown bruising to the cerebrum which could worsen. Kim was 'showing no response to external stimuli', the classic symptom of the comatose patient. There was no way of knowing how long this would continue. She'd said he could wake tomorrow or in two weeks.

Two days, two weeks, two months, whatever, as long as the boy was going to be all right in the end. If Eddie had to sit by his bed for two months then fine. He'd lose money and he'd lose rides but he was certain that Gary Rice, his main employer, the man who paid his retainer, would understand and keep his job open. He'd need to ring round the trainers who used him most. He would tell them a personal problem had come up and leave them to speculate.

Or maybe that wasn't such a good idea. He didn't know how this thing with Grimond would work out. The poor bastard wouldn't be telling any tales on him now but maybe the pictures would find their way into someone else's hands. And if Eddie suddenly disappeared from the scene citing personal problems there were plenty who'd draw the wrong conclusion.

Anyway, why burn his boats too far in advance? It was best to take things day by day. No point in calling off a full week's rides when Kim might wake up tomorrow. But he'd best ring Laura Gilpin who'd asked him to ride one at Warwick in the first race next day. He smiled as he thought about her, remembered her tearful, joyous expression at Cheltenham yesterday. God, yesterday ... seemed like a long time ago now.

And hadn't that been the damnedest thing, how they'd held on to each other in the paddock? How their eyes had met? It had caught him completely by surprise, especially when he thought of how much he was in love with Rebecca. Over-exuberance after a winner, he supposed.

Laura Gilpin was in the kitchen licking lemon flavour cake mix from her finger when the phone rang. She picked up the extension on the wall and said, 'Dial a pastry, can I take your order?'

'Oh, sorry, I thought I'd rung ...'

She recognised his voice and found herself smiling and blushing at the same time. 'Is that you, Eddie?'

'Laura?'

'Yes, sorry. Had my silly head on.'

'How was I supposed to know the difference then?'

'Very funny. You all right?'

'Well, yes, but I've got a few problems and I'm afraid I won't be able to ride that one at Warwick tomorrow, I'm sorry.'

'Standing me up, are you? Had a better offer?'

'No, of course not! I'm eh ... it's difficult.'

'Hey, I was only kidding! Don't worry, I'll be able to get someone else. Won't be as good as you but a woman can't have everything, I suppose.' Laura was disappointed and trying not to let it show.

Eddie said, 'Laura, I wouldn't normally do this and I'll make up for it. I know most of your runners are in the north and I'll be happy to travel to ride some of them if you still want me to.'

'Of course I do, I was just ...' her voice went quieter, 'looking forward to seeing you again.'

A pause then which seemed far too long and Laura could have bitten out her own tongue. She wiped her still sticky finger hard against the edge of the thick wooden chopping board and clenched her eyes closed, almost expecting to hear the click of disconnection.

Eddie said, 'It's a shame. I could have done with a shoulder to cry on.'

Laura's heart leapt. 'Mine's big enough. You could have a hysterical fit on mine.'

Eddie said, 'It might come to that yet.'

Laura was almost exhilarated now. He obviously felt something for her. She'd known that yesterday at Cheltenham but she'd needed confirmation, oh how she'd needed that. 'Well, you know where I am and you can call me any time.'

There was another pause and just as doubt was creeping back into Laura's mind, Eddie said, 'I don't suppose you've got a few minutes just now?'

Eddie wasn't sure why he'd suddenly decided to tell Laura about Kim and Rebecca although he hadn't expanded too much on the latter. He'd just said something had happened and he needed to try and find her and that he'd had to leave Kim under the care of Mr Ogilvie. Laura insisted on going straight to the hospital to sit with Kim.

Eddie said, 'That's very kind, Laura, but it wouldn't be fair to ...'

'Listen, Eddie, I don't mind, honestly I don't. My God you've done enough for me!'

'But ...'

'And I'm sure Mr Ogilvie will have a family who'd like to see him on a Sunday. I'll be there within a couple of hours. I'll introduce myself and ask Mr Ogilvie to call you.'

'But what about your farm? What about the horses?'

'Sammy and Linda can look after everything. They're well used to it. I'll just throw a few things in an overnight bag.'

'Laura, honestly ...'

'Eddie, listen, I want to help you.'

The change in her voice touched something in Eddie. The certainty in her tone, the comfort in it and suddenly he knew she'd look after Kim as though he were her own until he got back. He thanked her and said he'd hope to see her much later that night or maybe early tomorrow.

'Take what time you need, Eddie. I'll be there waiting.'

That certainty again, that calmness.

Over the last hour or so of his journey thoughts of Laura intruded frequently on those of Rebecca, adding to his confusion. Rubbing his eyes wearily he put it down to tiredness and stress and he pressed on through the outskirts of the capital into the heart of the city.

Forty-one

Back in her room in the Dorchester, Rebecca dialled Eddie's mobile number. He answered within two rings and as soon as he heard her voice he said, 'Rebecca! Jesus, are you all right?'

His anxiety threw her. 'I'm fine, Eddie.'

'Where are you? Are they still holding you?'

'Eddie, what are you talking about?'

'The Chinese. Mattie said they'd kidnapped you last night.'

'What!' She laughed, trying to give herself time to think.

'He said he saw them hustle you into a casino in Park Lane.'

'What! I've never been in a casino in my life! I just got back from Norfolk five minutes ago. My mobile's been out of service and I couldn't get calls. I've tried to ring you a few times, with no luck.'

'Mine's been switched off half the time with Kim, you know, the hospital ... Jesus, Rebecca, what a relief. Where are you now?'

'In my room at the Dorchester, safe and sound. A bit tired and smelly and ready for a hot bath but otherwise fine.'

'Can I come and see you?'

'Now?'

'Yes, I'm not far away. I'm just coming down Oxford Street.'

That threw her again. 'What are you doing in London?'

'What do you think? Coming to look for you.'

'But what about Kim?'

'He's okay. He's being looked after.'

'Brilliant then. Come and see me. You can soap my back. I'm in Room 301.'

'See you soon then.'

'Okay. Take care.'

She heard the click as Eddie pressed End and she slowly put the white phone back in its cradle and lay back against the silk padded headboard. She'd stripped off the clothes she'd been wearing all night, loser's clothes, and lay there in just her bra and pants, staring at the ceiling. That had been a close one. Bloody Mattie! What the hell was he doing around here last night? Just as well those Chinks had been so close beside her as she hurried up the steps. It must have looked like they were forcing her in there.

Never mind. She'd persevere with the mistaken identity story. Eddie had bought it okay and maybe she could turn this whole thing to her advantage. An idea was already forming as she went to run the bath.

Despite the tiredness and the heavy traffic in the city Eddie felt rejuvenated, massively relieved that she was safe, that he wouldn't have to search half of London for her. He'd better make some calls. He rang Mattie first. The trainer was in a place within striking distance of the casino and was more relieved than Eddie when he heard it had been a case of mistaken identity. Mattie had been perfectly sober when he'd seen that woman last night and he would have bet his life it was Rebecca Bow. But if she said she was in Norfolk he must have been mistaken.

Mattie apologised profusely to Eddie for giving him so much worry and dragging him down to London but Eddie told him he'd done exactly the right thing and would want him to do it again if necessary. He apologised to Mattie for losing his temper earlier and promised he'd call him in the next few days.

Mattie had been hanging around in the semi concealment of a tree in Hyde Park and he was glad to hurry away from there. He'd spent the first hour after Eddie had called in the toilet at home as the potential terror at having to consult the Triad again had scoured his bowels. He was heading home now for a very large drink.

Laura Gilpin had rung Eddie twice during his drive and he wondered whether, when she rang again, he could be bold enough to ask her to stay a while longer with Kim so he could spend some time with Rebecca. If Kim was okay that was, if there had been no change. Right at that second his phone rang and he thought Laura must have been reading his mind. But it was McCarthy. 'Easier getting an audience with the Pope than reaching you,' he said.

'Bless you,' Eddie said.

'Ha ha. I don't think you'll be making jokes when I tell you what happened to Phil Grimond.'

Eddie was just about to say he'd already heard when he realised he might be compromising Turco.

Mac told him. Eddie made suitable noises. Mac said, 'I know that's not your style, Eddie.'

'What's not my style?'

'You wouldn't have had anything to do with what happened to Grimond.'

'Then why are you asking?'

'I'm not.'

'Come on, Mac,' he said wearily.

'I'm only saying what the police might be thinking.'

'Why should they be thinking that?'

'Because of those pictures Grimond had of you at Catterick.'

'How do they know about them?'

'I'm not saying they do yet but if they pick up on them don't be surprised.'

'Have they asked you for advice or information?'

'They've spoken to my boss. He's told me we might have to do some digging.'

'Can you try and keep the spades away from me for now? I've got enough to worry about.'

'What's wrong?'

'Nothing you'd want to know about.'

Mac sighed. 'You riding tomorrow?'

'Nope.'

'When are you back?'

'Depends.'

'We need to get together and talk,' Mac said.

'Why?'

'We need to make sure nobody takes over where Grimond left off.'

'Take it from me, nobody will.'

'How do you know?'

'Mac, listen to me ...'

'Ohhh! When you say that I know you're serious!'

'Well save your breath and save your shoe leather. The main man has gone, flown the coop.'

'Afraid he'd be next on the menu after Grimond?'

'I think that's a fair assessment.'

'Will he be back?'

'Not in that line of business.'

'But in a line of business that might make me want to speak to him?'

'I couldn't say, Mac, he may never be back.'

'Sounds like you know something substantial.'

'Be a first for me, Mac, I can tell you. See you.'

'Keep in touch, Eddie.'

It was after 1 a.m. when Eddie finally left the Dorchester. He'd shared Rebecca's bath, then her bed, and their lovemaking had been as good for him as it had been the first time. And Rebecca was her usual bubbly self, laughing about 'poor Mattie' and all the hassle because he'd mistaken some other woman for her.

She'd asked him to stay the night but he wanted to get back to Kim and he felt guilty about leaving Laura there on her own. She'd been brilliant when he'd explained on the phone that Rebecca was safe and well and that he was going to see her. She'd used that line again: 'I'll be waiting here.' He liked Laura Gilpin. He liked her a lot.

Eddie cleared the city and headed through the darkness for his flat in Shropshire. He didn't know how long he would be at the hospital and wanted to pick up fresh clothes and some toiletries. He also wanted to leave an explanatory letter for Charles and Gary, his employers. He could say more in that than in a phone call. He was certain Charles and Gary would understand.

Forty-two

Laura watched the sweep hand of her gold watch move past 1.30. 'Thirteen hours,' she said quietly to herself. That was how long she'd been there, leaving the ward just three times to visit the toilet and ring Eddie.

She stared at Kim convinced that she had never been and never would be so familiar with a human face again. And such a beautiful face, so sad in its immobility. Not lifelessness, for she could see life shining in it somehow. She could see Eddie in it, a young Eddie, and more than once in the night she had fantasised that it was Eddie and that she was the one who'd nurse him back to health.

And she'd act out the Sleeping Beauty story in reverse and when he woke up he would fall in love with her and mature quickly to her age and they'd both be happy forever. And she'd smiled at the silly childishness of it all then told herself there's nothing wrong in retaining childlike dreams and wishes and she hoped she always would.

She reflected on her last conversation with Eddie that afternoon. On her reaction when he'd told her Rebecca was safe and sound. 'That's good news,' she said, feeling that it was worse news than the announcement of World War Three which it might have been when he dropped the next bombshell and asked if she'd mind staying with Kim a while longer so he could spend some time with Rebecca.

And bed her, Laura had thought. But she pushed the finer details of that from her mind and agreed almost immediately. To do anything else would be to give up hard won ground that might be impossible to regain. No, she had enough to hold on to for now. Enough hope. She'd just try and stay awake till he got back.

In the darkness of the flat the light was flashing on Eddie's answerphone. It was a message from a policeman called Blackstock who asked Eddie to ring at his earliest convenience. Eddie couldn't think what it would be about but he noted the number and resolved to ring first thing next morning.

He made tea, packed a small suitcase and, at just after 3 a.m., left again for Carlisle, arriving at the hospital two and a half hours later and creeping quietly into the ward.

Kim lay exactly as he had left him. Laura was asleep, her head resting on her forearms, sandy hair spread out covering her face. He eased himself down onto the chair beside her and reached for Kim's hand. It was only the warmth of the skin that told him the boy wasn't dead, for the hand itself felt limp, lifeless.

He looked again at Laura. Her breathing was deep and even but she was sucking in a few strands of hair with each breath. Tenderly Eddie reached out a fingertip to draw the hair away from her face. She looked contented. The lightest sheen of sweat was on her brow. He smiled and stroked her hair lightly feeling a sudden intense gratitude and affection for this big woman.

Kim's nurse came in at six o'clock and nodded silently to Eddie, checked the instruments Kim was connected to and whispered that she'd call back soon to turn him. Laura stirred at the sound, waking woozily from a pleasant dream. She turned her head to face the other way, resolved to settle again and sleep some more. She half opened her eyes and saw Eddie smiling down at her. Closing her eyes again she smiled too, thinking she was still dreaming.

Then she opened them again and looked up at him, the dreamlike smile still on her face. And she sat up slowly and leant towards him and slowly put her arms around him nestling her head onto his chest. Eddie smiled and held her, his smile growing wider as he realised she was still half asleep. Then her right arm slid down to rest between the back of the chair and the base of his spine and her left arm slipped softly across his lap.

And he sensed her happiness. And he felt contented. No guilt when Rebecca's face flashed through his mind. He had no lust for Laura. This was companionship, he imagined. He'd never known that either but he was pretty sure that this must be what it was. Companionship.

And he fell asleep too.

An hour later they both woke still semi-entwined and even in the warmth of their closeness and the heat of the ward Eddie noticed Laura's deep blush as she realised this was all real. She straightened and edged away, fixing her hair and her wrinkled blue dress.

Eddie smiled. 'Good morning.'

'Good morning.' She was still red-faced. 'Eh, when did you get back?'

'Just before six. You were asleep.'

'I'm sorry. I meant to wait up.' She rubbed her grey-blue eyes like a sleepy child.

He smiled wider. Her sense of humour was returning. 'Don't apologise. I'm very grateful to you for staying.'

'My pleasure. Best sleep I've had in ages.'

'No change in Kim then?'

'Nothing, but I know he's going to be all right. I know he is.'

'I know that too. It's just a matter of time.'

Laura nodded, glad that they shared the same certainty. Eddie said, 'I'll go and get us some breakfast. Any preferences?'

'Lots of tea and lots of toast if you can find it somewhere.'

He got up. 'See you soon.'

There was no food for patients in the hospital and Eddie had to drive around the streets till he spotted a café its bright windows welcoming, in the cold grey drizzle. He ordered toast and bought a plastic flask for five pounds with a free fill of tea. While the bread was toasting he sat at a table in the corner and rang the number of DS Blackstock, the policeman who'd left a message on his answerphone.

Blackstock said he couldn't really talk on the phone. Eddie agreed to see him if he was willing to travel to Carlisle. They made an appointment for noon.

The nurse had arranged for them both to use shower facilities and at 11.30 Eddie left Laura by the bed again and went to get changed and cleaned up before his meeting with the police. Just before twelve he walked through the rain towards the carpark. A white Rover sat close to his Audi, its windscreen misted and rain-covered.

Two cops got out. Eddie had seen enough of them in his time to recognise them before they reached for their warrant cards. Eddie did a double take on them. They looked very similar and for a few seconds he thought they were twins. But as they came closer he saw one was maybe ten years older and that he dyed his hair that reddish brown colour to keep it looking the same as his mate's. They were five nine, moustaches, dark eyes, the older's slightly more hooded, more wrinkled. They wore grey suits, white shirts, plain dark narrow ties, black shiny shoes. Close up, the older one's skin was bad, pitted. He said, 'Good morning. Mr Malloy?'

'That's right.'

He offered his hand. 'DS Blackstock. This is DS Cranfield.'

Eddie shook hands. Blackstock said, 'We'd like to talk to you about Philip Grimond.'

'Why?'

'Just routine. You knew him.'

'Met him once.'

'Recently?' Blackstock asked.

'Last week.'

'Where?'

Eddie said, 'Look, will we get in my car out of the rain?'

'Let's get in ours,' Blackstock said.

Eddie sat in the back and could smell warm bodies and tobacco smoke. The two policemen sat in the front and half turned in their seats to talk. Eddie said, 'Let me try and save you a long question and answer session.' He told them what Grimond had done and why.

They listened without interrupting, then Cranfield said, 'So you're saying he set you up?'

'Uhuh.'

'Why?'

'I told you, he was running a scam with photo finishes, I knew what he was doing and was trying to get him stopped.'

'But he wanted to carry on so he set

you up and threatened you?'

'Correct.'

'What did you tell him?'

'Nothing. I wasn't afraid of him, of the threat. I carried on with my side of things.'

'Which were what?'

'Informing Jockey Club Security.'

They spent almost half an hour probing and questioning, asking the same things numerous times till Eddie was sighing and raising his eyes in frustration. Before they left they asked for his mobile number and asked him to keep it switched on at all times.

'I can't. I'm spending most of my time just now in an Intensive Care Unit with my brother. They're not partial to ringing telephones. I'll be here if you want me and when I move I'll let you know.'

'Is it your brother who's ill?' Blackstock asked.

'He's in a coma.'

'I'm sorry.' And he looked as though he meant it. 'We'll wait to hear from you.'

'Thanks.'

Eddie turned and hurried back through the steady rain.

Twice while Eddie was out Laura had thought she'd seen Kim's eyes move under the lids but she couldn't be sure. Then his hand moved. She was certain it had moved a few inches. And she smiled widely and wished deeply that Eddie had been here with her to see it. She couldn't wait to tell him.

When he came back in he had on his jeans and brown leather jacket over a green polo shirt with the top two buttons open. He smiled at her and she marvelled at his strong white teeth. So many jockeys lost their teeth, especially the front ones, in falls. She wondered if he wore some sort of gumshield like boxers do. There was rain on him and the fresh smell of the wind. She loved the smell of him. She looked up, bright-eyed. 'He moved his hand, Eddie,' she said quietly.

He squatted quickly beside her. 'When?'

'About ten minutes ago. See where it is now?'

Eddie nodded.

'Well it was there.' With her finger she drew a line the length of his forearm.

Eddie said, 'That's brilliant news, did you tell the doctor?'

She hesitated just a second, wondering if he'd be annoyed. 'No. I wanted you to be the first to know.'

Almost unconsciously, it seemed, he reached for her hand and squeezed it then let go to do the same to Kim's. Laura said, 'And I'm sure he moved his eyes twice very late last night. That's got to be good, hasn't it?'

'Got to be!' Eddie smiled. 'We'll speak to the doctor this afternoon.'

We. Laura liked that.

She liked their closeness too when Eddie pulled a chair up beside her and they leant companionably on the bed like some happy couple by their garden fence idly contemplating the neighbours. They watched Kim and talked and Eddie didn't talk much at all about Rebecca.

They both agreed they were glad they weren't racing that day. Just Folkestone and Musselburgh on and you couldn't get two places much further apart: Kent and Scotland. No fun driving or riding in this weather.

Eddie eventually suggested to Laura that she might want to go home, that he was terribly grateful for what she'd done. She said that if he didn't mind she would stay another day or so as she felt that Kim was close to coming out of it. Eddie said he didn't mind, he didn't mind at all.

All that day they sat together, talking when they felt like it, comfortable in long silences when they didn't. Eddie went out and got sandwiches and a newspaper and sweets and a magazine for Laura. By late that evening their side of the bed was an untidy jumble which Laura attempted to hide each time Kim's nurse came in. They'd told the doctor about Kim's movements and he'd said that they were a good sign and that he'd organise another scan for the next day.

Eddie and Laura took turns dozing off, each watching the other with some curiosity when they did so. The first time Laura fell asleep Eddie stepped out into the corridor to call Rebecca. They talked for ten minutes and she sounded in good spirits. Eddie didn't tell her that Laura was there.

They sat through the afternoon into dusk. Eddie was glad that Laura had decided to wait with him, keep this vigil. He'd have to buy her a Christmas present. And Rebecca too.

Christmas was eight days away. What do you get for a twelve-year-old boy in a coma?—His mother?

Should Eddie go to Newmarket and have a crack at persuading her to see the boy? Even if it were only while he was unconscious? Like peeking at him through a one-way mirror. Damn it, why should he let her off with just that. No! Once Kim was well again he'd take him down there and make her face him, make them both face him.

The rain worsened. The King George

was just over a week away and King Simba didn't like it soft. The papers had been saying he'd go off at odds-on for the big race but Eddie knew he'd need good ground for that to happen. Still, what was the point in worrying? This was north, Kempton was much further south. The going would be fine and if it wasn't there was bugger all he could do.

He had better things to worry about.

Forty-three

Although they'd agreed a watch schedule tiredness overcame them both and the first grey light of 18 December found them asleep in their chairs, heads resting on the bed on crossed forearms, elbows touching, breathing in the same rhythm.

All Kim saw when he woke with the dawn and turned his head were the mops of hair. Where was he? Who were these people? What had happened?

He felt sore. His muscles ached, skin felt raw in places. He turned, trying to ease the ache in his back, then felt the pull of the needle in his hand as the long tube swung, in turn moving the bag it fed from.

Kim closed his eyes again.

Then opened them. Things still did not make sense. If he was alive he reckoned he must be in a hospital. Chin on his chest he raised his head; who were these others in the beds around him? Why was the ward so small and poorly lit? And who were these people asleep on his bed?

Where were Mum and Dad?

Dead.

It came back to him now with the hammer blow of that one single word in his brain. A blow that seemed to clear the jam in his memory and everything started flowing. Almost everything. Things came to a halt during the bike ride. That was the last thing he could remember. Riding his bike through the aftermath of the storm. Spraying mud and water. Laughing. Passing the still drenched sheep as he sped down the hill. Breathing hard and pedalling harder on the way back up. He couldn't remember getting back to the farm. Must have fallen off his bike and hit his head.

And who were these two? Had they found him? Or were they from the children's home waiting to take him back there as soon as he woke up. Probably. Best then if he slipped away again before they woke.

But where were his clothes and where would he go? Why send two people from the home to wait for him? From the little he could see of them he recognised neither from Mr Young's children's home. Maybe they were from a tougher one. Maybe it was like those war films and when you escaped from one they put you into an escape-proof one next.

Suddenly, one of them moved. Kim closed his eyes and lay perfectly still. A minute passed. He opened his right eyelid a millimetre; it was a woman, still asleep. He could see her face now, round and pleasant but red-cheeked and uncomfortably warm looking. He opened both eyes then closed them immediately as the door opened. He heard someone come in, sensed them moving round, felt movement as the couple at his bed stirred. Heard a whispered 'Good morning,' from the woman who'd come in. Must be a nurse.

Then the woman on the bed spoke quietly. 'Sleepyhead.'

'Mmmm?' Kim heard him stretch and yawn.

She said, 'You fell asleep on watch. The Indians could have caught us and tied us to a totem pole or boiled us alive or something.'

'I feel like they already have. It's warm in here.'

'Want some tea?'

'I'll get it. Have to go to the loo anyway.'

'Don't forget to wash your hands.'

He heard the man leaving then listened to the woman sigh and yawn. In a few minutes the man came back. As he sat down again Kim could smell coffee; as strong a smell of coffee as he'd ever experienced and he would have loved some. She said, 'Eddie, I think Kim's hand moved again through the night.'

'Which one?'

'The right one. The same one.'

The hand, which suddenly took his, caught Kim by surprise and he tensed slightly. The man said, 'Laura, I felt something then!'

Kim didn't know what to do and inadvertently found himself holding his breath. Her hand was on his forehead now and he knew he wouldn't be able to play dead much longer. She stroked his hair and her next words almost stopped his heart. 'I think you may well have your little brother back by Christmas.'

He opened his eyes.

Eddie was staring straight at him. They were both holding their breath now. Eddie saw his brother's deep blue eyes for the first time and Kim knew he could be looking at a mirror from some time in the future so closely did this man resemble him. This man.

His brother.

Smiling now, ever wider, gripping his hand tighter, holding it to his cheek. He spoke softly. 'Kim, can you hear me? My name's Eddie, I'm your brother.'

At last. At last. God must be back in heaven now. All the worry and the weight of the world lifted. Eddie was here. Eddie. His brother. A long sigh escaped from Kim and his eyes filled with fat happy tears.

Forty-four

Laura went back home that evening but they kept Kim in hospital two more days by which time Mr Ogilvie had sorted out the legal papers which Eddie signed to apply to be Kim's guardian. After much work and pleading Ogilvie managed to get an interim order from a magistrate, which allowed Eddie to take Kim home and act as his guardian until all the paperwork had been completed and approved.

They spent the two days telling each other everything each thought the other should know. Eddie held a few things back when it came to his mother, their mother, and sister and he felt angry with them again. Kim was naturally desperate to hear of them, of how he came to be put up for adoption, of why his mother had refused to meet him. Eddie settled for telling him she was quite ill and had been for some time and that he was sure that once she was better she'd want to meet Kim.

Kim settled for this but sought assurance from Eddie that he'd still be his guardian, that he could live with him and do all the things they'd talked about and of how he didn't want any Christmas presents because this was the best present he could ever have wished for.

And Eddie was overcome by a sense of responsibility that he couldn't imagine being stronger even if Kim had been his newborn son. A sense of responsibility and of a new beginning, a liberation, an almost physical striking off of the chains he felt had shackled him all his adult life. A chance to heal his own wounds, to apply this brother of his, this child, like some emotional poultice that would draw the poisonous past from his soul. And he felt no guilt at seeing Kim this way for he would make sure the boy had everything he hadn't had. Except the love of their mother. But as things were he may be none the worse for that.

They left the hospital first thing Friday morning and walked across the carpark to the Audi. Kim was impressed by it and Eddie promised he'd teach him to drive as soon as he was old enough. When they joined the southbound motorway Kim asked Eddie if he would mind taking him back to the farm one more time. 'There's one thing I want to show you.'

Kim chattered away during the drive but as they approached the rough roads leading the last mile or so he went quiet and Eddie was aware of him looking around at the hills. 'Beautiful morning to be out there among them,' Eddie said.

Kim nodded, lost in his memories. He saw the farm from a distance then just glimpses of it through the hedges. He was so proud and happy to be bringing his brother back to his home but oh how he wished his mum and dad were still alive so they could meet him. The famous jockey. Kim's very own brother.

The house was locked up now and the doors boarded and Kim guessed that Mr Ogilvie had arranged that. Probably best although he'd like to have shown Eddie his room. But he'd still get to do what he'd brought him here for.

Kim turned towards the barn. The doors had new chains and padlocks but Kim knew of a piece of tin sheeting that could be bent back. They both squeezed through and Kim thought as he watched Eddie dust down his clothes in the gloom that it seemed much more of an adventure this way.

'Come on!' he said, half whispering, and Eddie smiled as he followed his brother up the ladder to the loft. The wooden doors were closed over the window but lasers of light lanced through every crack and hole. Kim undid the latches and threw open the doors to be dazzled by the strong morning sun which haloed his body. Eddie watched as the wind blew open the boy's thick woollen shirt and ruffled his hair. He knew Kim was looking out not just at the land and the hills he'd grown up in but over his whole life, short as it had been so far. And Eddie remembered with searing clarity how he felt when he finally left his parents' farm at the age of sixteen.

He walked to Kim and put his arm around his shoulder and they both stood staring out at the panorama, the green fields and valleys, the crags and the fells that had claimed the lives of Kim's mum and dad. He looked up at Eddie. 'I wanted you to be up here with me. I used to dream about it that we'd come and camp out here some night in the summer. You know, with a little stove and some beans and chocolate and stuff.'

Eddie smiled and squeezed his shoulder. 'Let's do it as soon as summer comes.'

And Kim knew instinctively that he didn't have to make his brother promise. He knew he meant it.

There was one more place he had to take Eddie, one more thing he wanted him to see. They drove to Mr Durkan's farm where Kim proudly introduced Eddie to Crystal, his pony. 'Eddie's a jockey!' When Crystal saw Kim she whickered and neighed loudly and flicked her ears back and forth. Eddie was delighted to see the pleasure the boy took in the pony, which greatly increased when Eddie admired Crystal so much and complimented Kim on his judgement in choosing her.

He told Kim that within a week he'd arrange for a box to pick Crystal up and bring her back to the yard. 'For good?' Kim asked excitedly.

'For as long as we stay there, you and me.'

'Why, will we be moving?'

'No plans to, but you never know what life has in store. And anyway, I know how much you want to come back to the farm and some day, if things work out, we'll do that. Maybe train a few horses here. You can be the jockey then.'

'Can I? Is it hard being a jockey?'

'Dead easy. Dead easy.' He ruffled

Kim's hair and watched the smile of quiet delight, a look he was already becoming familiar with. The boy's eyes would gleam in a sort of distant way as though he were looking to the future and all the pleasures it would bring.

Forty-five

Lee Sung and his men had been considering all the information they had got from Rebecca and decided that if things did not work out at Kempton on Boxing Day then they'd go for the big one with Turco. The abduction should not prove a problem and once Eddie got an eye, or maybe the tip of a tongue, in the post then that should persuade him to co-operate.

Lee Sung's main concern was money but Eddie Malloy also had to be dealt with. The damage Malloy had inflicted on his dignity a few weeks ago had to be avenged. Once they'd made their money from Turco's SIS plan he'd have no further use for Malloy and was looking forward to removing his skin slowly and completely and leaving him to die in the greatest of pain.

Picking up the telephone he spoke

rapidly, ordering that the 'package' be prepared in good time and suitably wrapped in gift paper. It had to be delivered without fail on Monday 23rd.

On the trip from Cumbria to Shropshire, Eddie became aware of Kim's frequent glances across at him as though the boy had to confirm to himself that all this was happening. Occasionally Eddie would glance back and Kim would blush and they'd both smile.

When they got back to the flat Eddie was pleased to see that a bed and wardrobe and a chest of drawers had been put into the spare room. He'd rung Charles on Wednesday to arrange it and Kim was delighted. When the boy opened the empty wardrobe Eddie promised he'd buy him new clothes, promised they'd go out Christmas Eve on a shopping spree.

Eddie wasn't quite sure how he was going to pay for it all but he didn't care, money was no longer a priority. Anyway, if King Simba won the King George as expected there'd be ten per cent of the prize money in his bank account by the time the credit card bills came in.

While he'd been away Eddie had been emptying his answerphone remotely and the only call waiting now was from Mattie

Stuart who wanted to double check that Eddie would be there on Monday morning to ride King Simba in his final piece of work. Eddie rang him back and assured him he'd be there.

'I'll be bringing a friend,' Eddie said.

Mattie chuckled. 'Rebecca perchance?'

'Well, she might be there too but I'm bringing my brother.'

'Didn't know you had one.'

'Neither did I. It's a long story. I'll tell you on Monday.'

'See you then.'

Eddie made a few more calls to confirm he'd be back riding next day at Uttoxeter and managed to get two definites from trainers who'd been holding for him. Kim had been listening to the conversation and looked worried. Eddie put a hand on his shoulder. 'Don't worry, I won't be going anywhere without you. You're coming racing with me tomorrow and Laura's got a runner there too so we'll see her as well.'

Kim did that steadily glowing smile again and Eddie ruffled his hair and took him down to the house to meet Charles and the staff and the horses. The boy showed no apprehension as many people do when getting close to racehorses for the first time. Kim found them much different from his pony. They were sleek and muscular with smooth shiny coats and long delicate legs. They looked intelligent and noble and even standing there in their boxes he could sense the pent-up power in them. Eddie watched proudly as Kim went right up to each horse in the yard stroking necks and heads, running his hands with obvious admiration over the slabs of shoulder muscle.

'You'll make a jockey all right,' Eddie said and Kim smiled in delight at this flattery from his brother. Several times in the next few hours the boy found himself having to stop and draw deep breaths to try and calm himself, slow his mind so he could take everything in, absorb the reality. That evening Eddie cooked his first proper meal for as long as he could remember.

When finally it was time for bed Eddie went to ruffle his hair again by way of saying goodnight but Kim threw his arms around him and they hugged for what seemed a long time. And in that hug Eddie felt himself shed another layer of armour like a snake wriggles free of a dead skin.

They lay in their separate rooms, Eddie with his hands behind his head thinking of his brother and of Rebecca. She'd sounded delighted on the phone when he'd told her Kim was okay and that he couldn't wait for them both to meet. He hadn't told Kim yet but he planned to take him to London after racing tomorrow. They'd pick up Rebecca and have dinner then stay over and do some Christmas shopping on the Sunday. That would be a nice surprise for him.

Kim lay wide awake unable to contemplate sleeping again, never mind that night. Things still had not sunk in. It was as though the horrors of the past few weeks had been what had driven him into that coma and that God had decided he'd stay that way for his own protection till something better was ready to happen to him.

In the distance he heard a vixen cry out and he turned to lie on his side, facing the window. He was beginning to accept that life was a cycle of bad times and good times and that you could never be sure how long each would last. He admitted to himself that it wasn't just excitement that was keeping him awake this night, there was fear too. Fear that he might sink into a coma again and find that when he came out of it all this would be gone, and Eddie would have proved to be just a fantastic dream.

This troubled him for a long time until he finally slipped out of bed and knelt beside it to join his hands and pray that this wouldn't be taken away from him and if it was to be then let him have one year of it at least. No more pain for a while, please, God. Please.

Forty-six

Under normal circumstances Ben Turco would not have been happy to be back in New York after so many years but spending a few months in the city had become much more appealing since Grimond had had that informal surgery outside his garage.

That had scared Turco much more than he'd let on to Eddie and to Walter and Magnus. From the night that Grimond had balked so heavily at giving up the photo finish scam Turco had suspected that there was pressure on Grimond from someone else, pressure to continue. If the ultimate result had been that attack on him then there was every possibility that Turco might be somewhere on that organ butcher's list. That was why he was quite content to be 3,000 miles away across the Atlantic.

They'd taken a while to ship all his computer equipment across but it was safely installed now in a flat on Wall

Street which was costing him 3,500 dollars a month to rent. Turco thought this a good investment as the flat was located within two hundred metres of the communications network for the New York Stock Exchange and Turco thought that network could stand a little bit of investigating.

He didn't yet know what he was going to do but was looking forward to finding out. It would be his biggest challenge yet but he knew that without the worry of being stalked by Grimond's assailant he could relax and concentrate one hundred per cent on it. Rubbing his hands and smiling widely Turco sat down at his desk and switched on his screen.

About forty-five minutes' drive away, sitting in an all-night bar nervously sipping a dry martini, sat John Klemperer, an employee of the airline which had flown Turco and, later, his equipment, to New York. Before Klemperer had finished his drink the person he'd been waiting for, a small Chinese man joined him. Unsure of the protocol on these occasions, Klemperer offered the man a drink. It was politely refused as the man drew from the inside pocket of his black suit an envelope containing five hundred dollars. He gave it to Klemperer who then gave him a much smaller white envelope. Inside it was a single piece of A4 paper, which listed the New York address and telephone number of Benjamin J. Turco.

At Uttoxeter, Eddie rode Laura's horse Achilles to finish second in the novice 'chase. Laura was very pleased. Kim was disappointed that his brother hadn't won but he tried not to let it show. The excitement of the racecourse, the sights and sounds, the smells, the crowds, the roaring of them at the finish of each race, the cries of the bookies, the obvious dedication of the stable lads, the stirring sight of the horses close up, on edge, ready to race, and the wonderful sight of his brother in full jockey's gear talking to all the obviously important people—Kim again felt almost overcome at times.

Laura had looked after him while Eddie was in the changing room. She'd even let him help saddle Achilles and she'd promised that some day soon he could come and ride him at the yard. Kim liked Laura.

One person he didn't like was the huge man who came lumbering towards them in the carpark. He'd been waiting by Eddie's car, leaning on it, and as soon as he'd seen the three of them coming he'd stood up and headed straight for them. Kim had been scared watching him approach, a giant of a man wearing strange clothes and a big hat. He'd grabbed Eddie by the shoulder, almost pleading for Eddie to listen, to let him tell him what had really happened with somebody called Grimond.

Eddie had pulled him away and they'd spoken so quietly then that Kim hadn't heard anything but he did know he didn't like that man. Laura hadn't seemed to either though she didn't mention it and when Eddie came back she just kissed him goodbye and did the same to Kim, on the cheek.

When they got in the car Kim said, 'Was that man angry with you?'

Eddie smiled. 'The other way around, Kim, I was angry with him. He let me down badly and he was just apologising.'

'Are you his boss or something?'

'I'm not his boss. I'm nobody's boss and that's the best way to be if you can manage it, I can tell you. His name's Tiny Delaware, he's ...'

'Tiny!'

'That's what they call him. A sort of joke. Anyway, he's a bit of a character. You'll find a few like him if you stay in racing for a while. It's a bit like the law of the jungle, people get by on what they can, survive on their wits, dull as they might be at times ... In racing there's almost always somebody more stupid, more gullible, no matter what your level is.'

'What does gullible mean?'

'Easily taken in, easily conned. You're looking at a prime example. That's what Tiny was apologising about.'

'And did you accept his apology?'

Eddie almost told Kim that the big man had apologised out of fear. He was afraid that Eddie might have had something to do with the maiming of Grimond and he didn't want the same fate. But he immediately thought better of it. 'Yep, I accepted it. No hard feelings. Now guess where we're going?'

Kim looked up at him and just shook his head in curiosity.

'London! London Town!' Eddie shouted and tapped out a drum roll on the steering wheel.

Kim smiled, his eyes sparkling. 'What for?'

'There's somebody there I want you to meet. And I want her to meet you. You'll be impressed, Kim, guaranteed. She's very beautiful!'

Kim blushed and Eddie laughed and spun the wheel to head for the gate.

Shortly after they'd driven out of the carpark a relieved Tiny reached the exit on foot and stood with his thumb out. He never had to wait long for a lift at the races. Most of the regulars knew him and sure enough he hadn't been there more than two minutes when a lovely big Merc pulled up. Didn't recognise the blokes in it as he ducked and squeezed himself into the back. Little guys for such a big car. He smiled and said, 'Thanks, fellas!' But they just nodded ever so slightly and when Tiny saw their reflections in the rear-view mirror he just put it down to the fact that they probably didn't speak English.

Chinese they looked. Chinks. Oh, well, took all sorts.

Forty-seven

Rebecca left the club in Wardour Street running. She waved frantically at passing taxis. One stopped for her and took her to the Dorchester. She told the driver to wait. In her room, Rebecca hurriedly undressed, showered and applied make-up. The many clothes in her wardrobe had been hung with military neatness.

She chose a dark blue suit with an almost skin-tight pencil skirt and put it on over a cream coloured silk top. Checking her watch she sprayed perfume quickly behind her ears and rushed back downstairs. Her seat in the taxi was still warm. The driver passed an admiring glance then obeyed her snapped order to head for Buckingham Palace.

Eddie and Kim were already there, standing at the gates. Wanting his brother to feel he shared his sense of wonder, Eddie joined Kim in holding onto the gate bars and staring wide-eyed at the Palace. They'd been there ten minutes when the taxi pulled up and Rebecca got out, smiling widely and offering apologies.

Kim watched them kiss and blushed as Eddie introduced her. She was his height and she kissed him and made him blush even more. Then they went to see a show and had dinner at a place Rebecca had enthused about.

Afterwards Rebecca caught a taxi back to the Dorchester and Eddie and Kim went to a hotel Eddie had booked earlier. Kim had looked longingly after Rebecca's taxi as it pulled away through the busy streets, and Eddie had resisted the temptation to tease him.

They lay in the twin beds in the darkness with the sounds of London nightlife coming up from the street. Kim said, 'Did Rebecca go home because I was here?'

'Rebecca's got a busy day tomorrow.

Anyway, she knows it's the boys' night out.'

Kim was silent for a minute then said quietly, 'I wouldn't have minded, Eddie, if you'd stayed with her.'

'I know you wouldn't but I wanted to be with you tonight. Stop worrying. I'll have lots of time with Rebecca in the future and you will too.'

Silence for another minute, then, 'Are you going to marry her?'

'Do you think I should?'

'I don't know.'

'Would you marry her if you were in my position?'

'Emmm, I don't suppose I really know her.'

It was Eddie's turn to be quiet. I don't suppose I do either, he thought.

They talked some more and Kim thanked his brother for the day and for all the excitement he'd had out of it. Eddie faded off to sleep but Kim lay wide-eyed into the early hours listening to his brother snoring lightly, luxuriating in the sound.

Even if the ceiling above Kim had been open to the sky what stars he may have seen would have been faint, dulled by the pollution of light rising from the big city. But from a field of frosted stubble deep in the Staffordshire countryside the view above was heart-lifting. The stars glittered so brilliantly against the complete blackness of the sky you imagined you could see the very edges of them.

Simple fellow though he was at times it was a sight Tiny Delaware would have appreciated, especially as he was nearer to the stars than most mortals. But although Tiny lay on his back in that field close to a blackthorn hedge he could see nothing. He'd been unconscious for hours after the beating the Chinese men had given him.

The moon was in its last quarter. Silver light from it made Tiny's oozing head gleam in the wettest places. His scalp had been removed comparatively neatly considering it had been sliced off with a sword. The man had swung it by the thick heavy hair and it landed around fifty yards away from its owner.

Just as Tiny moaned and tried to turn over on the damp cold ground an old dogfox following the scent of the blood finally found the oddest of meals. He licked twice at the congealed mess on the inside of the scalp then took the whole thing in his mouth and trotted off along the line of the hedge.

Eddie and Kim went Christmas shopping

on the Sunday. Eddie gave his brother one hundred pounds to buy presents, promising the reluctant Kim it was only a loan to be repaid when he rode his first winner. He was rewarded once again with that warm smile.

Eddie told Kim that he reckoned they'd be best not going home that night. He was due to ride work fairly early next morning in Lambourn. He didn't say to Kim how important that piece of work on King Simba might be. The King George VI 'Chase at Kempton was just five days away. Victory there would put Eddie right back in the spotlight and give him a big financial boost too.

Eddie had called Mattie Stuart who'd been delighted to offer them both a bed on the Sunday night. When they got there he also offered to take them down the pub but Eddie wanted to continue setting Kim a good example. He'd been determined to be big-brotherly and do all the right things. Kim would learn soon enough about all the temptations a jockey faced.

So it was another early night, another strange bed for Kim though tiredness was catching up with him and he was asleep this time before Eddie.

Next morning Kim stood in the yard admiring and envying all the lads as they went busily about the business of looking after their horses. He watched his brother as Mattie legged him up on the big black King Simba who Kim decided was the finest creature he'd ever seen. Mattie in turn climbed aboard his chestnut hack and he and Eddie sat smiling down at Kim who wished silently he was old enough to have a horse too and go up to the gallops with them.

He wasn't aware of the clip-clop of hooves behind him till Eddie nodded at the lad who was holding the brown gelding. Kim turned slowly and the lad offered him the reins. Kim looked confused, was about to tell the lad he was mistaken when Eddie said, 'Come on, Kim, up you get or we'll be late!'

Kim said, 'Me!' pointing to his chest.

Eddie and Mattie said at the same time, 'Yes, you!' and the lad legged him up. Kim gathered up the reins and adjusted his stirrups then touched the gelding gently with his heels to follow the other two out of the yard. It was cold and they could see their breath but it was fine and bright.

As they walked the lanes and headed up towards the gallops Kim sat higher than he ever had on a horse, a racehorse, albeit retired, and saw for miles over the hedgetops. And at that moment he became certain of two things: one, that this was the best morning of his life and, two, that like his big brother, he was going to be a jockey.

King Simba worked better than either Eddie or Mattie had ever known him to and they were both convinced he would take an awful lot of beating in the King George.

Eddie had three rides at Ludlow and he and Kim talked racing all the way there. Eddie was elated at the boy's interest. He felt his chance of ever being champion again had gone but he would get almost as much satisfaction from grooming the boy to become one of the best. Kim had everything in front of him and Eddie would do all he could to help him reach the top, to give him what their mother and father should have given them both.

Eddie's mounts finished second, third and unplaced and Kim was getting anxious to see him ride his first winner. 'Don't worry,' Eddie told him, 'might as well make it the big one on Friday.'

It was dark when they got back to the flat and while Kim had a hot bath Eddie set to work making a curry. As the sauce neared boiling point Eddie thought he heard the downstairs door open. Then the sound of footsteps on the stairs and he knew it had to be Charles, his boss.

The trainer knocked lightly again on the top door and Eddie shouted, 'Come in, Charles.' He came in grinning and carrying an almost square package, gift wrapped, about fifty per cent bigger than a shoebox. 'This came this morning and I know you don't get many Christmas presents.' Charles put it down on the worktop and leant over the stainless steel pot to sniff. 'Smells nice.'

'Want some? There's plenty.'

'Maybe I will.'

'Good. Kim's in the bath. He'll be out in a minute. Pull up a chair and pour a drink.'

'Good idea. Want one?'

'Why not?'

Charles fixed whiskies while Eddie got a knife and started opening the box, which he strongly suspected would be from Rebecca. As he sliced through the broad brown tape he heard the sloshing of water next door as Kim stood up in the bath then the sound of his feet on the floor as he stepped out.

Inside the box were a fat red vacuum flask and an audio tape. Puzzled, Eddie lifted them out. The flask felt full. Each item had a card tied to it by very thin yellow twine. Eddie read the one dangling from the cup handle of the flask: 'Do what is required on Friday or you may end up without these ...' The one on the tape said, '... and with this.'

He let Charles read them then they both looked at each other as though searching for the answer. Eddie carefully unscrewed the flask lid and held it below the light to peer inside. All he could see was dark liquid.

Kim came in, barefoot, jeans on, towelling his still wet torso. Drips from his thick hair fell on the tiles. Towel moving rhythmically across his back he watched as Eddie put the plug in the stainless steel sink and slowly poured out the contents of the flask. The liquid that came out was perfectly clear and quite thick. Halfway through the stream a human tongue swam out followed by an eye and they circled in the gently swirling water.

Charles recoiled and sucked in a breath. Eddie looked at the organs. Kim stopped towelling and nudged Eddie who turned absent-mindedly, still holding the flask at an angle. Kim pointed to the flask. 'Look.' They both looked. Sitting in the mouth of the flask was another eye. Quickly turning it upside down Eddie watched the eye drop with a plop in beside its companions. He and Charles stared in awe at the organs. Kim looked quite calm.

All three looked at each other. 'Grimond's,' Eddie said.

'What?' asked Charles.

'Tell you later.'

He held the see-through tape up to the light. All it read, apart from the dangling card, was C60. Eddie pulled the card off, slotted the tape into his deck and pressed play. Four seconds later it clicked and stopped.

'Wrong side,' he said.

He turned it over.

A pop song came from the speakers. It was vaguely familiar to both Eddie and Charles but neither could name it. Eddie looked again at the card. The threat attached to the flask hadn't been hard to work out: 'you could end up without these'. But he read the card from the tape again and again as the song played and could make nothing of it: 'and with this'.

Kim had the towel around his neck now, holding the ends. Eddie said to him, 'Do you know the name of the song?' Kim nodded and told them what it was, said it had been out last year. They were no nearer solving the riddle then Kim said, 'I think it might be the group's name ...'

They waited.

Solemn-faced, Kim said, 'They're called, "Everything but the Girl".'

Forty-eight

Eddie almost ran for the phone and dialled Rebecca's number. After six rings she answered. 'Rebecca! Are you all right?'

'Yes.' She sounded subdued and Eddie knew she knew something.

'Is anyone there with you?'

'No, Eddie.'

'Tell me what's happened.'

There was a long pause then she said, 'It's best if we don't see each other again.'

Exasperated, Eddie said, 'Rebecca, tell me what's wrong?'

'I'll deal with it, Eddie. Please, it's best that way.' The sorrow in her voice seemed to deepen.

'Whatever it is we'll deal with it together. Now please tell me exactly what has happened.'

'Not over the telephone. If I come to see you and tell you, will you promise to let me deal with it? Will you promise to keep yourself out of it?'

'Can you come now?'

'Promise me, first.'

'I can't promise you that. I ... I feel

too much for you. Whatever's happened has happened to both of us, not just you, can't you see that?'

Another pause. 'Eddie, you have Kim to look after now. You must stay safe.'

Eddie looked frustratedly at Charles and Kim who stood following his every word. He said, 'Tell me where you are, I'll come to you.'

'No! No, I'll come to you.'

'Now?'

'Yes, now. I should be there in a couple of hours.'

'Okay. Please be careful.'

'I will. I'll see you soon.'

'Rebecca! Before you go tell me one thing, a one word answer. Does this have something to do with the Triad?'

Silence for what seemed a long time then Rebecca said, 'Yes.'

When Eddie put the phone down Charles said, 'Well?' and Eddie, under some pressure, told Charles and Kim what had happened with the Triads since that day they'd called on Mattie Stuart.

Charles just sat shaking his head and tugging at the thick curl that hung over his forehead. Kim, in awe throughout, asked questions, especially about the fight at the nightclub. Eddie did his best not to make himself out a hero but if he hadn't been so worried about Rebecca he'd have enjoyed

Kim's obvious admiration.

He wasn't so sure about Charles. The trainer had put up with quite a lot over the past three years or so when Eddie had been involved in other scrapes and Eddie knew that Charles quickly reached the point of washing his hands of things, of, just walking away saying, 'Don't tell me any more!'

When Eddie finished talking he could see Charles had already heard as much as he wanted. The trainer stood up. 'Eddie, as usual, I hope everything turns out okay but whatever your girlfriend has to tell you, I don't want to know about it.' Like a traffic cop he held up a hand to reinforce what he'd said.

'Fine,' Eddie said.

'I mean I know Gary gets a good giggle hearing about all this stuff but it just makes me nervous.'

Eddie smiled. 'Didn't know I was entertaining Gary too.'

Gary Rice was the stable owner who employed both Eddie and Charles. And that was the main reason Charles got nervous. So far as he was concerned, Eddie's business was riding his horses not getting into fights and shoot-outs and tracking down gangsters. He said, 'It's just as well Gary does or we might both be out of a job.'

'Tell him I'll try to keep this one up to the usual high standard.'

Turning the doorhandle to leave, Charles shook his head again. 'I'll tell him. He says you should write a book.'

'I might just do that some day.'

'If you live that long. See you in the morning. Goodnight, Kim.'

'Goodnight, Mr ...' Eddie nudged Kim who then said, 'Goodnight, Guv'nor.'

Charles smiled and left and Eddie and Kim chuckled softly. Kim persuaded Eddie to tell him of all these things Charles had mentioned, all the 'fights and shoot-outs' he'd been in. Eddie started by trying to play it down but saw Kim was enjoying it so much he moved the other way and started dramatising everything. The boy was enthralled and declared himself a definite for this racing business.

Eddie ruffled his hair. 'Take my advice and stick to the thrills you get on horseback. The rest ain't what it's cracked up to be.'

There was more drama in store for Kim when Rebecca arrived. She looked tired, worried. She wore blue jeans and a heavy black sweater, the first time Eddie had seen her dressed casually. As they hugged and kissed Kim went to put the kettle on.

While Kim was in the kitchen she whispered that it would be best if he didn't hear what she was going to say but Eddie said he had to be treated like an adult. Besides, he'd already heard some pretty hair-raising things while they'd waited for her. So Eddie and Kim sat on the couch facing Rebecca in the chair. All three held mugs of tea and Rebecca, in a resigned voice, told Eddie what had happened.

The story Rebecca told them was her own and completely true in all aspects except one—she cast her fictitious sister, Annelise, in the starring role. Eddie and Kim listened to how Annelise had inherited as much as Rebecca herself had after her father's death and how she had become addicted to gambling and not only lost every penny but now owed over two hundred thousand to the Triad.

With frequent emotional pauses and the occasional tear Rebecca skilfully portrayed herself as the dedicated sister who had paid Annelise's debts, financed expensive treatment for her addiction, sweated blood to hide the facts from her sick mother and now it had all come to nothing. Annelise was suicidal and the Triad had latched onto Rebecca now because of her association with racing, with Eddie in particular.

Eddie had been listening and trying to think at the same time, trying to figure a way out of whatever it was that was coming. He said, 'Is it the same people who lent Mattie the money? The ones who attacked him?'

Rebecca, tearful again, nodded slowly. 'And did they know you had horses with Mattie? Did they know he was badly in need of cash to keep his stable going?'

'Yes. That was my fault. I had mentioned it to Annelise just by way of telling her how I was planning to buy into the business in March to help Mattie out. But she took that information and ... and she effectively sold it to the Triad. They paid her a sort of bounty for pulling another victim into their net and I felt awful about it. That's why I called you that night when they took Mattie. That's why I enjoyed so much getting one back on the bastards!' She glanced quickly at Kim then Eddie. 'Sorry.'

Kim smiled. Eddie said, 'It's all right. Where is Annelise now?'

Rebecca sat stooped forward, elbows on knees, staring at the floor. 'She's at Mother's. I took her there earlier today. But I don't know how long she'll stay there. If she's not within striking distance of a casino she panics.' She glanced at Eddie. 'The other night when Mattie thought he saw me going into the casino on Park Lane ...'

Eddie said, 'Annelise?'

Rebecca nodded glumly then stood up. 'Anyway, I've told you the tale and that's what I promised to do. Now it's best if I get back to Mother's, see if Annelise is still there. I'll call you when all this is over, Eddie.'

He stood up and reached for her, clasping a hand at the top of each arm and holding her at arm's length, making her look straight at him. 'You're not going anywhere without me. You need to tell me exactly what the Triad want.'

Rebecca went hard-eyed. 'I don't need to tell you anything, Eddie, not a thing.'

The sudden coldness hurt him, she could see it in his eyes. She softened again, reaching to stroke his dark hair. 'I'm sorry, Eddie, but you mean a lot to me too. I know you want to protect me but I want to protect you and this is the best way to do it.'

Kim watched them both, worried about what may come next, what may come of this whole thing. It had been exciting when Eddie had told him all the things he'd done in the past but Kim realised now, could see from Rebecca's attitude, that this was serious.

Eddie held her tighter. Stared at her with complete determination. 'Rebecca, listen to me. I don't care what you say or how many times you say it. I don't care what it is you're faced with. I don't care how many we're up against or if they're Chinese, Japanese, cannibals or anything else, I am not going to let you go into it without me. I'll follow you out of here if necessary and never let you out of my sight. Now tell me what it is these people want!'

She looked at him long and hard then said, 'They want me to make you do something and I've told them no. I've told them no matter what they threaten me or Annelise with I'll never ask it.'

'Ask it. It's for me to decide.'

She stared at him and Eddie could see she was wavering. 'Tell me!' He almost shook her.

She said, 'They want you to pull King Simba in the King George on Friday.'

Involuntarily he loosed his grip on her arms. He hesitated a few seconds then said quietly, 'I can't do that.'

Now Rebecca gripped his arms. 'I know you can't! That's why I would never ask you!'

He eased himself away and sat on the couch beside Kim. Kim put a hand on his shoulder and Eddie reached to touch his fingers. Rebecca had sat down again. Eddie looked at her. 'What's the ultimatum? What happens if I don't?'

'That doesn't come into it, Eddie, because you're not going to.'

'Rebecca, tell me what they've threatened you with.'

Again she hesitated then said, 'They said they'd tell Mother about Annelise and make Mother sell the house to pay her debts.'

'And?'

'They said they'd ... they'd chop all my fingers off and scalp me.'

Kim's eyes widened as he stared at her.

'Nice men,' Eddie said. 'I think it's time we had a serious word with the police.'

'Eddie, listen, the Triads have as much fear of the police as you have of riding a seaside donkey. Try and find the name of the last Triad member to be convicted of anything. You'd go back years! Nobody will testify against them. People are too scared.'

'I'll testify,' Eddie said. 'You can testify, tell the police about the threats.'

'And what will they do? They'll interview Lee Sung and his gang who will laugh in their faces and deny it.'

'Well they won't be able to deny Mattie Stuart's missing finger, his scarred hand or his dead dog!'

Rebecca shook her head slowly as though she thought Eddie naïve. 'And you think Mattie will testify? You think he'll stand up in court and effectively admit that his business was so far down the pan he took money from Chinese moneylenders? That he tipped them a horse you had given him which got beat? Do you think he'll do all that standing up there in the dock with these guys terrifying the life out of him? Do you think he'll go home and sleep well in his bed after that? Do you think you're entitled to ask Mattie to do that just for me, because I don't.'

She'd got quite heated and Eddie admired her selflessness. He watched while she cooled down and found himself smiling slightly, hoping it would be infectious and would calm her a bit. He said, 'Okay, okay. We'll find another way. We'll find another way but as my old friend Ben Turco would say, we ain't pulling no horse.'

Rebecca leant across and reached for his hand. 'There is no way round it, Eddie.'

'We'll keep you safe, don't worry. I'll protect you if I have to watch you every minute of the day.'

She hesitated, looking at him as though he was some deluded monarch. 'Eddie, there is no beating them. There is no protection, even twenty-four hours a day. I know these people. Ever since Annelise got tied up with them I've been trying to find ways of beating them. It can't be done! Sure, we can have our little jabs at them like we did that night in Wardour

Street but that's it. You can win a round but no way can you win the match.'

Eddie just kept smiling. He'd never found an obstacle that there wasn't some way round.

Rebecca let go of his hand. 'Stop smiling so patronisingly! You think I'm over-reacting, don't you? Let me tell you a few things about the Triads. There are hundreds of them all over the world. They infest every major city. They have one single goal in life: to make money, and in doing that they operate like robots. Human feelings like sympathy and regret are unknown to them. They function twenty-four hours a day like a bloody big criminal machine.

'They're into protection rackets, control of labour, illegal bookmaking, loan-sharking, drugs, illegal immigration, counterfeit currency, replica designer products, tax evasion, money laundering, financial fraud including insurance and credit cards and Christ knows what else.

'Then there are the so-called "legitimate" front businesses: nightclubs, bars, restaurants, casinos and stuff, that's how they hooked Annelise and when they've got you they never let go!

'They're sadistic, ritualistic, cruel bastards. They use swords and meat cleavers. One of their ritual practices is the slicing of the main muscles, like your calves, thighs, forearms and biceps. Slashing of the scalp is optional but as I said, it was on the menu they offered me.

'Now if they're not picking on people like me and Annelise the Triads are fighting among themselves. They all have their own lodges, their own names. Lee Sung's little lot are known in English as The Third Degree and from what I've learnt over the past year you don't defy them. I'm not asking you to pull that horse, Eddie, all I'm saying is don't look for an alternative because there isn't one.'

Eddie watched her catch her breath, then said, 'So what did you plan to do?'

'The only thing I can, leave the country.'

'You and Annelise?'

'That's right.'

'When?'

'Tomorrow. Fly out somewhere warm. Hopefully lose ourselves in the Christmas holiday crowds.'

Eddie stood up. 'No.'

She stared at him. 'Easy to say.'

He sat on the arm of the chair and put a hand on her shoulder. 'We'll find another way.'

But what could he do? He couldn't pull King Simba. Apart from the fact that Eddie had never cheated in his life, so much depended on King Simba winning.

He badly needed the prize money it would bring, he needed that exposure back at the top level both for his career prospects and for his ego. And he needed to win, wanted to win for Kim. And that was without thinking of Mattie Stuart. Mattie's survival as a trainer depended on it.

And there was the ultimate reason he couldn't pull the horse. If he did it with this one how long before the next demand? And after that? If King Simba started odds-on, as expected, for the King George, then lost, the bookmakers stood to make an awful lot of money from it.

Rebecca had said that the Triad ran an illegal bookmaking operation. He guessed that they'd offer a better price for King Simba than anyone else and with their usual 'no betting tax' carrot they'd take hundreds of thousands, maybe more than a million pounds ... on a horse they knew was beaten before the tapes went up.

Nice work if you can get it.

'Eddie?'

He became aware of her again and of Kim who seemed to be holding his breath waiting for Eddie's decision. He looked down into her hazel eyes and smiled. 'We'll find another way,' he said. 'To hell with them. We'll find another way. King Simba wins!' He shouted and punched the air before bending to pull her close.

Kim punched the air too. 'Yes!' he cried.

Her chin on Eddie's shoulder, staring at the wall, Rebecca looked totally downcast. All three sat up late trying to work out the best thing to do. The more they talked, the more animated Eddie and Kim became, the more eager to find a solution. The brothers were each silently heartened by their reactions; it showed another way in which they were alike. But Rebecca grew increasingly dismayed and withdrawn, repeating the fact that she thought the Triads unbeatable in the long run. Eddie tried again to reassure her that they'd find a way through.

'But you're trying to do that for me when the easiest thing would be to let me ... let me and Annelise get away. Let it blow itself out.'

Eddie put an arm around her again. 'I've told you, that's not an option. We're in it together. Why don't I contact them and tell them we'll co-operate? If the horse wins at least they'll take a financial hammering, maybe enough of one to stop them operating. And if King Simba loses then it looks as though we've kept our bargain.'

Rebecca said, 'I thought he was a sure thing?'

'He'll be odds-on, and on form he should win, but there's no such thing as a certainty. He could fall. He could have an off day.'

Kim said, 'But if he did lose they'd think you'd pulled him.'

Eddie shrugged. 'Even if we said we wouldn't co-operate and he then lost they'd think the same. They'd just think we'd got cold feet at the last minute.'

Kim frowned and went quiet for a while. Eddie and Rebecca talked, almost forgetting Kim was there until he said, 'If the Triads fight a lot among themselves why don't we get one on our side?'

They both looked at him. Kim went on, 'Couldn't you contact another Triad and tell them to bet thousands with these other ones on King Simba, especially if they're going to be offering a bigger price? You'd be doing them a favour, wouldn't you? And then you could ask them to protect you from the other Triad.'

A smile grew slowly on Eddie's face and he turned to look at Rebecca. 'What do think of that then?' he asked proudly.

She didn't look much happier. 'I don't know.'

Eddie said. 'Do you know of another Triad, a rival one?'

She seemed to stare at the wall for a long time then nodded slowly. 'I know someone who does, the girl who got me all the information on The Third Degree.'

'Do you think that would be the sort of proposal she'd be willing to take to another Triad?' Eddie asked.

Rebecca hadn't counted on the kid coming up with something so smart and she was trying to think on her feet, trying to figure out where the potential benefit was for her.

'I can ask,' she said. 'But what if King Simba lost?'

Eddie shrugged. 'Luck of the draw. They'd have to be made aware of that before we started.'

'Then what are we offering them that they couldn't take advantage of anyway if they wanted?'

Eddie smiled. 'We're offering them the precious piece of knowledge that the horse will not be pulled when their rivals believe it will be.'

Rebecca put a finger on her chin, stared at the floor and looked very thoughtful.

Forty-nine

From the back of a walking horse the sight of packed stands bulging with tension and anticipation is one that even the best jockeys seldom experience. Pre-race parades on the track itself where the runners file along in front of the stands take place no more than a handful of times during the jumps season. A jockey would have to be close to champion standard and to have stayed injury-free to take part in all of them. This one, for the King George VI Steeplechase, was Eddie's first since the previous season's Gold Cup.

A jockey's usual perspective of the stands from a horse at a walk came after a race when the attention of most racegoers was on their next drink or their next bet. Even in the biggest race the excitement was over, the zeppelin of noise punctured, as soon as the winner passed the post. That left just the collective escaping murmur of moans and groans and immediate post-mortems as people made their way to the bars pulling racecards from their pockets like six-guns, arming themselves for the next attack on the bookies.

Eddie looked to his right now at the many thousands crammed into the Kempton stands. Their judgement as racing experts was on the line, their cash was down, their champion chosen. The excitement was tangible. He could feel a building wave of it as the commentator named each horse and told of its accomplishments—Gladiators entering the arena. In most cases he knew that the choice of the masses was the big black horse that walked calmly under him.

As though that were not responsibility enough he thought of Rebecca, wondering whether she secretly hoped he'd be beaten. He knew she feared what the Triad would do when their rivals made a killing on King Simba, the horse they thought was going to be pulled.

But she and Annelise had been promised protection from the rival Triad for as long as it was needed. Trouble was she did not know these others well enough to be certain they'd keep their word. She had said there wasn't a Triad existing that could be trusted completely and Eddie realised this. But he could see no other way out.

And Kim. They'd spent a wonderful Christmas at home yesterday. No snow, but the glittering newness of a sharp frost in the early morning when they'd ridden around the countryside for hours before coming back to cook an excellent lunch. A team effort. His brother was beginning to open up to him now, to give more of himself, and that had made Eddie do the same. He'd talked to Kim about his own hopes and fears and that was more than he'd ever done with anyone.

Still he held back from him the most traumatic parts of his own childhood but that was for Kim's sake as much as Eddie's. Some day soon he would tell him everything.

And as Eddie passed the winning post now in this slow parade he raised a hand as promised, waving to both Kim and Rebecca. Kim was in the stands with Mattie Stuart. Rebecca was in a small cottage on the North Devon coast watching on TV. Or so Eddie believed.

The cottage had been rented for a week in Eddie's name. Rebecca was to take her mother and Annelise there and stay put until they agreed it was safe to come out. Only Eddie knew where they were. And as the horses were finally released to break into a canter towards the start, Eddie thought that seldom if ever would a young woman have watched a horserace with such a cocktail of mixed feelings.

Rebecca was watching all right, from the Park Lane casino, flanked by Lee Sung and his henchmen.

Eddie knew that in six or seven minutes things would be resolved one way or another. Pulling his goggles down he urged King Simba into line along with the others and waited for the starter to hit the lever.

The power surge from a standing start to early race gallop can catch an inattentive rider out, and with the first jump so close, attention to actually seeing a clear yard of fence to jump was imperative for Eddie.

With the field so tightly packed the horses were pressing onto each other, spurring them on to go even faster than their natural exuberance prompted; a similar buffeting in the late stages of the race would prompt a Stewards' Inquiry but now it was just part of the dash to get a position. Horses either side of Eddie were of quite differing heights which meant Tobin's stirrup irons were clanking against Eddie's, giving off a Morse Code sound, while on his other side Bretton's stirrup pressed so hard onto Eddie's shin the pain made him shout for 'daylight'. Eddie decided that this sort of thrill, a headlong charge totally in the hands of Lady Luck, was one he could do without.

King Simba on the other hand loved every minute of it; this is what he was bred for, racing and jumping at speed. He was the type that did not merely want to get over a jump, he wanted to devour it, and that meant the moment he saw the line of black birch he instinctively quickened at it and became airborne a couple of strides earlier than his still galloping rivals.

The pair soared past four horses, landed running and within the space of seconds had gone from an uncomfortable, crowded position to a clear leader. As ever, Eddie loved the thrill of the leap and thought how lucky he was. Then his mind returned to his game plan. He knew that if he tried to pull King Simba back among the field the horse would burn himself out battling with him. Since he was in front Eddie decided to try and settle him there for a mile or so and see how things looked then.

While he was still running on a full tank King Simba attacked the fences as if they were personal enemies and in doing so stretched the gap between himself and the rest of the field to fully fifteen lengths. Eddie knew that the jockeys in the following group would think he'd gone mad and that he would run himself into the ground but he reckoned he had the pace just about right for that stage of the race.

Eddie let King Simba do his own thing in front but eased him back as he landed over each of the first ten fences, knowing that if he didn't get him in that first stride after a fence King Simba would take command.

Between the last fence first time and the first on the second circuit there is the longest stretch of turf without a fence and that gave Eddie time to think of Kim and Rebecca. Would she now be totally confused trying to work out which way the game was being played? Was Eddie trying to burn King Simba up or had he gone for broke and stolen the race?

Before he had time to consider, the next fence loomed up but this time he approached it in splendid isolation without even the sound of any pursuers let alone being squeezed up by the pack as he had been on the first circuit.

King Simba had not made a semblance of a jumping error and although now settled into the perfect stride pattern, breathing evenly and moving with ease, it crossed Eddie's mind that the challenges would soon materialise.

Three fences later as they were at the furthest point from the winning post, the last of the open ditches loomed up. As he counted the horse in to the fence a photographer suddenly stood up from a squatting position distracting King Simba.

The horse missed a stride and belted the guard rail of the ditch and his head went earthwards; Eddie let out a foot of rein and sat back in the saddle to act as ballast as his mount stretched his long neck out trying to maintain equilibrium. Eddie thought for a fleeting moment that he saw the horse's tail come into view, which normally signals the world turning upside down. But by some miracle King Simba scrambled along the grass and from deep beneath his gut found a fifth leg from somewhere to save him from turning over at thirty-eight miles per hour.

While this drama unfolded, four horses passed the sliding pair and all of a sudden the picture looked very different for many people. Eddie knew he had to give King Simba time to recover his breathing, if not his confidence, and over the next two fences he was content to let the others fight it out while he held a tight rein to give his heaving partner a chance to get back in the race.

Steadily, he and King Simba began fighting their way back into it. The leaders had burned off two of the quartet by the second last fence and there was just an outside chance that Eddie could sneak up on them unseen as the two jockeys were locked in their own personal battle, drifting towards the middle of the last fence as they threw their eager mounts at the birch obstacle as if it did not exist.

Eddie resisted the impulse to go for a medal here as his only chance lay in surprise and should he even hesitate at the last he would never raise King Simba's game in time for a late thrust at the finish as Kempton's run in is one of the shortest in the country.

As luck would have it both the leaders continued to drift across the course in the 'head down arse up' drive to the line. This gave Eddie the break he needed and he redoubled his rhythmic rowing and kicking in a final desperate effort.

He didn't hear the Boxing Day crowd's roars as he swept past to snatch a neck victory.

As he brought the horse back in to see Mattie Stuart running towards him, Eddie knew that whatever other fallout there was from this victory he'd never forget the look on Mattie's face now. After a career full of moderate horses, years of nothing but dreams and optimism, everything had finally come right for Mattie.

It was almost like one of those long-running TV sitcoms where you know that the hero, likeable as he might be, would never realise his ambitions, would always be doomed to failure.

Now Mattie had rewritten the script. His way. No longer the clownish trainer, the butt of all the Lambourn jokes. In a few minutes, in the unsaddling enclosure, they'd all be around him slapping his back now rather than laughing behind it. He reached the horse and kissed him, then grabbing at Eddie's arm pulled him downward to kiss him too.

An image of Laura Gilpin suddenly came to Eddie's mind as his own thoughts went back to Cheltenham.

And up on the wind-whipped north-east coast Laura sat watching Eddie on TV, delighted for him, proud of him, the exact same image in her mind as he had at that moment like a telepathic exchange.

On the other side of the horse was Kim. Tears in his eyes as he reached to hold the hand his brother offered and walked proudly back in beside King Simba, a mixture of joy and sadness in his heart. If only his mum and dad had still been alive. But he knew that if they had been he wouldn't be here now with his brother. And the guilt that had been crowding his mind since he woke on Christmas morning pressed harder with the same constantly repeated question: what would you choose, Kim, knowing what you know now? Would you still have your mum and dad back?

And in the hubbub and excitement, in Eddie's moment of glory, he closed his eyes and prayed to God to make the torment leave him.

Eddie's ride in the next finished un-placed, bringing him back to some reality. He wondered if he'd given the horse the best of rides because his mind had been so full of other things. How much had one Triad lost? How much had the other gained? How was Rebecca feeling? When would he see her again? Would there be trouble leaving the course this evening? Would the bad guys be waiting for him? The good ones ready to protect him as they'd promised Rebecca they would be?

He could afford to take no chances with Kim and had asked Mattie to drive him back to his place, keep him there till Eddie contacted him. As for himself, Eddie was reasonably confident he could handle things, unless they were mob handed.

He smiled. Back when he'd started getting involved with criminals, hunting them down, he'd always told himself how much he hated it, how much he just wanted to concentrate on his riding. But he was beginning to realise there was a level of addiction now. The adrenalin rush he used to get from riding had slowed to a steady stream. He knew now that from time to time he needed to hit these surprise rapids. Needed the thrill.

But just for him. He'd always be able to handle things when the danger was just his. It was different now. Rebecca and Kim made it that way.

He got changed and left the weighing room, the 'well dones' still ringing in his ears. He'd told Kim and Mattie that he wouldn't meet them again on course, just to be safe. Outside the weighing room he looked around, hoping to see potential bodyguards materialise as promised. The trouble with these Chinese was you didn't know if you were looking at a friend or enemy. He wondered if they might be persuaded to wear uniforms.

He saw no oriental face and decided to set off for the carpark. Then he felt a hand on his shoulder. Keyed up he stepped quickly back and spun round. It was McCarthy. The big Security man said, 'That's just about the quickest I've ever seen you move.'

Eddie's pulse was still high. 'Jeez, talk about the long arm of the law!'

'Believe it or not that is what's reaching out for you at this very minute. Figuratively speaking.'

Eddie looked wary. 'How figuratively?'

'They want to talk to you again. At a little more length this time, I'm afraid. And, as the saying goes, at their place, not yours.'

'When?'

'Now.'

'Why?'

'Why now or why do they want to speak to you?'

'Both.'

'Well, remember Grimond, the tongue-less and eyeless Grimond?'

'The tongueless, eyeless, bent, black-mailing Grimond?'

'The very same. The shortage of both oral and visual organs no longer troubles him as he died in hospital late last night.'

'Can't say I'll be sending flowers.'

'Well maybe you'd like to send some to your old buddy Tiny Delaware, though a wig would probably be more useful.'

'Pardon?'

'Tiny's in hospital too. They found him lying under a hedge in Staffordshire without his scalp.'

'Danged Injuns!'

'It's not funny, Eddie!'

'Sorry, but what's it got to do with me?'

'The day you were seen talking to Grimond, you were also seen talking to Tiny.'

'So?'

'So one of them's dead and the other's got pretty bad injuries.'

'And the police, as usual, have nothing to go on so they thought they'd just harass me?'

'It's a legitimate approach, Eddie. You appear to be linked to both men. *And,* they know you're protecting somebody in this photo-finish con Grimond was into. They want that man's name.'

'Well, they'll have to whistle for it.'

'Fine, you can tell them that yourself.' McCarthy turned and Eddie saw the two policemen who'd come to his flat walking determinedly towards him from the racecourse office. Well, he thought, if the Triad guys are waiting in the carpark there should be some fun and games now.

337

Fifty

They made Eddie drive north to a police station in Stafford, following him all the way. In the taped interview room they sat opposite him and went through the name and address formalities before beginning a two hour grilling about Grimond and Tiny, asking for alibis, questioning almost every answer he gave, bringing up some of his past ventures and generally trying to antagonise him.

They worked hard to try and get Turco's name out of him but he wouldn't give. Blackstock said, 'If you don't tell us then you're an accessory to serious fraud.'

'I would argue that I put a stop to serious fraud, prevented further fraud.'

The cop moved to the side of him. 'You seriously think that argument is going to stand up in court?'

Eddie nodded. 'Well put it this way, you guys are going to be in one corner and I'll be in the other. Now the question the judge is going to ask himself is, "Which of these actually traced this guy and stopped him?" So who's going to look silliest in court, you or me? I had no part whatsoever in this man's crime. How can I be prosecuted?'

Blackstock seemed slightly rattled.

Eddie stayed relatively cool throughout, getting agitated only as the time for his prearranged phone call from Rebecca came and went. Eventually they had to let him go, knowing they had no real prospect of pinning anything on him.

Eddie left cursing them. He'd missed Rebecca's call and wouldn't get a chance to speak to her again till next day. He approached his car with caution, aware that the Triad could have trailed him north. He could see no one hidden in the back seat and the muddy state of the reddish soil discouraged him from lying down to feel around the chassis for lumps of explosive. It seemed that wasn't their style anyway.

As he revved the engine he considered how much longer he could continue without telling the police everything. It was clear the Triad were involved in Grimond's death; they'd sent Eddie his tongue and eyes in a box, but how had Grimond become entangled with them?

And what about Tiny? It looked like they'd done him too. Rebecca had said scalping was one of their specialities. But why Tiny? Eddie knew the big man just wasn't smart enough to be in on a con of any sophistication or timescale.

Tiny was a hyena in the racing jungle, always loitering on the outskirts waiting to scavenge the remains. He had never been one for making a killing himself.

Pulling clear of the town centre and heading west, Eddie considered paying Tiny a visit then thought better of it. What would the cops say if they found out? Eddie's thoughts turned to Kim. Was it safe for him to be with Mattie? Although Eddie had been the one approached to pull King Simba, Mattie, as the trainer, might be held by the Triad to have some responsibility. And they knew where Mattie lived.

Eddie picked up his phone from the passenger seat then replaced it. He knew that mobile calls could easily be monitored. He'd wait for the next filling station and call Mattie from there.

The trainer was celebrating King Simba's victory and was half drunk. Eddie told him that yes, he'd love to be there but this just wasn't the best time. He spoke to Kim who sounded elated still, even more so that Eddie had rung. They talked for a while and Eddie promised he'd see him the next day at Chepstow.

'Can I come home with you then?' Kim asked.

'We'll see how things go.'

There was a silence and Eddie realised

that Kim felt suddenly insecure. 'Kim, listen, don't worry. Whatever happens over the next few days will be just temporary, just to make sure everything is okay. I want you with me all the time and I want you to know that. I'll never ever desert you.'

Again, Eddie sensed the boy's silent decision not to ask for a promise. He simply said, 'Okay, Eddie.'

'Good. Now enjoy the rest of the night and don't be letting Stuart feed you any booze. You're too young.'

'I think he's keeping it all for himself anyway.'

'Well he's got runners at Chepstow tomorrow. Let's hope they're in better condition than he'll be. Goodnight, Kim.'

'Goodnight, Eddie. And please be careful.'

'I will.'

Eddie hung up and as he reached in his suit pocket for his diary his elbow hit the side of the plastic dome over the telephone. The dull thump made the girl behind the service station counter glare at him. Eddie smiled and flicked through the diary for Laura Gilpin's number.

Fifty-one

After speaking to Laura, Eddie continued his journey reflecting on how complicated things were getting. Grimond's organs were still in Eddie's flat as was the threatening note. His main intention had been to ensure the safety of Rebecca and the victory of King Simba and if he'd called in the police then he would have been certain of neither.

All in all he convinced himself that he'd made the right decision. But where had it left him now? Backed into a corner. A suspect in the attacks on Grimond and Tiny; no alibi for the first one and the man's eyes and tongue sitting in the darkness beneath his sink at home.

Shit.

He'd just have to hope that the two Triads would at this very moment be halfway through destroying each other. As soon as he was sure they were going to leave him alone he'd give up the organs and the note. Maybe he should just tell McCarthy about them now, hedge his bets? No, that would be unfair on McCarthy, plus Eddie would then have to put up with

342

his constant nagging to come clean to the police.

Best left for now. Best left. See what tomorrow had in store.

The flat was dark but empty. No ambush. Just a few congratulatory messages and faxes. Nothing sinister. Eddie lay awake in the warm bed thinking of Rebecca, wondering if the wind was howling in off the Atlantic over the Devon coast.

And Laura Gilpin up on the opposite coast. A girl in every port.

He smiled. A port in every girl.

Hadn't even had a drink.

Won his first King George and hadn't even had a drink.

Getting old.

He turned on his side, thought of Kim. Funny how quiet the flat seemed without him. Funny how quickly he'd grown used to him being there. Sad how his mother would probably never know him. Christmas had come too soon for Eddie to do what he'd wanted and he now planned to take Kim to Newmarket on New Year's Eve. Planned to persuade his mother and Louise to bring in the New Year knowing Kim. A fresh start for everyone.

Now he'd have to wait and see what the Triad had in store over the coming week. Their New Year was still a few weeks away, time enough for them to tie up unfinished business.

It was still dark next morning when Kim got up and hurriedly dressed. Mattie had promised to let him help feed the horses. He'd told Kim just to go down to the yard at six and find Sean, the head lad. As Kim moved silently past the trainer's bedroom he heard Mattie snore deeply.

When he eventually came to, the last thing Mattie felt like was a trip to Chepstow but he'd promised to look after Kim and he did owe Eddie several favours. Also, he was still high on the success of King Simba and the thought of seeing more smiling faces hiding a secret sourness among some of his fellow trainers buoyed Mattie considerably. Those alone would be worth suffering the hangover for. Besides, a few glasses of bubbly and he'd be fine. And he could afford it now, couldn't he?

The worm had turned. Life was indeed sweet. Mattie had always known the break would come and he was confident now as he shaved shakily that nothing but good times lay ahead. The Triad had never come back for their money and now Eddie had set them fighting among themselves, so hopefully he'd never hear from the bastards again.

Mattie had mixed himself a litre of

Buck's Fizz which he carried beside him on the passenger seat. He knew he wasn't fit for driving but the others had gone on ahead and he'd just have to take his time and hope the cops didn't stop him.

He certainly wasn't confident of negotiating his way around the big black Mercedes which lay skewed across the bottom of the lane. Sober, he might have tried to squeeze through the gap but in his present state he thought it best to pull in and find out what had happened.

As he stepped from his own car two Chinese men appeared from the hawthorn bushes by the side of the road. They came at him from opposite directions confusing his intoxicated thoughts further. Mattie felt like he was in some sort of movie. He recognised these two players. The one on the left had battered his beloved Jinty against the wall. Bastard.

By the time they got to him the fear hadn't quite registered but it was on its way, travelling at some speed through his fuzzy brain. One stood behind him. The one in front said, 'Where is the boy?'

'What? What boy?' And Mattie was genuinely perplexed; he'd forgotten about Kim.

The man took Mattie's good hand and turned him roughly, forcing his hand flat on the bonnet of his red estate car. The other man moved to the front now too and raised a short sword.

Dread rose in Mattie's gut. Terror paralysed him as he remembered that night in the dark back room.

Fifty-two

Carrying a brown bag full of groceries Ben Turco cursed as he made his way through grey slush which had spilled over from the banked up walls of filthy snow thrown sideways by vehicle wheels. He'd forgotten how foul New York winters could be and could never remember it being this cold in London.

Fumbling for his swipe card he ran it through the reader on the door and gained access to his apartment house. As he made his way towards the elevator the commissionaire walked from behind the big walnut desk, his heels sending clicking echoes up through the diaphragm of the big building.

'Mr Turco, sir, this came for you 'bout a half hour ago.'

He placed a small package in Turco's left hand, which was still trying to do its share of supporting the shopping. The commissionaire hit the elevator button and whirring cables responded immediately. Turco thanked the man and rested the brown package on top of the groceries.

Travelling up to his apartment he stared at the padded bag with the typed address label; nobody knew he was here. This was the first piece of mail he'd had. Once inside he went to the kitchen and laid the bag on the long pearl coloured worktop. He opened the package. Inside was an audio tape and a typed note on good quality plain paper. It said: 'If you are not back in London by the 29th December a copy of this tape will be sent to the police. When you arrive in London call this number and say who you are. Do not go to the police. Grimond is dead.'

A central London telephone number was listed. With deepening dread Turco went to his big black music centre, put the tape in and pressed play. The first voice he heard was his own. The only other one on the tape was Grimond. The conversation was the one they'd had in that motorway service station in Northampton. Incriminating without any doubt.

Turco switched it off. Who had sent this? Where had they got it from? It had to be from Grimond who must have been taping their meeting that day. If they'd got it from him it had to be a fair bet they'd

347

been the ones who'd attacked him.

And now he was dead.

The hell with that! Turco threw the tape onto the shelf which held the amplifier and it skidded along the polished surface to ricochet off the speaker. He'd sooner take his chances with the cops than these bastards who'd got Grimond.

But wait a minute.

Supposing the British police applied for extradition?

Turco started pacing around the apartment. He had a lot invested in this place, in cracking the Stock Exchange computer. We were talking billions here, billions that would disappear down the tubes as soon as the New York cops nailed that Wanted Poster up in the saloon.

Maybe he'd better try and find out more about these jokers. He picked up the phone and dialled zero.

As the black Mercedes straightened and accelerated rapidly the back wheels added insult to Mattie's injury by kicking a spray of stones and dirt at him and his car. He stood transfixed by the shock of losing another finger, the index one from his right hand which now lay lodged in the crack between the bonnet and the wing.

The stump bled surprisingly little and Mattie could still see the white marbling of what he took to be sinew and nerve ends surrounding the knot of knuckle bone. The Chink had struck it off cleanly against the metalwork of the bonnet leaving a thin scar on the paintwork. Mattie looked from the finger to the damaged bonnet to the oozing stump in disbelief before gradually turning and sliding down, back against the side of the car, till he hunkered on the ground.

He wasn't aware how long he stayed like that, couldn't even have said if someone else had come past but eventually he realised that he must warn Eddie that they were after Kim.

Getting back into the car he found his mobile phone and scrolled through the memory keys only to find he hadn't yet fed in Eddie's number—something he'd been promising himself he'd do for weeks. And he didn't have his diary with him. He'd have to return to the yard.

Starting the car, he reversed and looked to the front in time to see his finger roll slowly off the front of the bonnet. Mattie got out, stared at the finger in the dirt then made himself pick it up. In the car again he pulled out the special built-in can holder and laid the finger in it.

Eddie got the call on his mobile at home just as he switched on his answerphone and when Mattie told him what had happened he felt, for the first time, a rising panic.

He'd never worried that much about what might happen to him, about his own life; had never valued it that much. But the thought of Kim being in real danger threw him into turmoil and when Mattie got off the phone he had to force himself to calm down and try to think rationally.

Mattie had said he thought Kim had probably left earlier in the horsebox with the lads but that he couldn't be sure and he couldn't check till they got to Chepstow. He assured Eddie he'd told the Chinese nothing, said he just didn't know where the boy was. But they'd said they knew Kim had been at Mattie's the day before so Mattie couldn't be sure they wouldn't head for Chepstow anyway.

If that was the case Eddie knew he'd have to reach Chepstow first. He'd been on his way out anyway and now he rushed downstairs, checking as he went that Laura Gilpin's telephone number was programmed into his mobile. He pressed the Send button as he pulled the car door closed behind him and by the time Laura answered he already had the Audi's speedo touching seventy.

Mattie hung up his phone, proud of the fact that he hadn't told Eddie they'd cut another finger off. He admired Eddie's nerve, his confidence and wished he could be more like him. But this was a start surely, he thought, as he gazed down at the now congealing blood around the stump.

His brain was still fuzzy though Mattie wasn't sure now if it was alcohol or shock. Anyway, he knew he'd best drive to Newbury General and see if the finger could be saved. He tried to console himself that it might have been worse. He could have been a concert pianist.

As he walked to the door he heard the engine of a powerful car and the screech of brakes outside. Before he could open the door, the Chinese had done it for him. They looked even angrier than they'd been earlier as they rushed towards him.

Fifty-three

Eddie couldn't make up his mind if he believed in God or whether fate decided most things but he had a sort of one-sided pact with whoever controlled things like speed traps that he'd never drive too fast unless he absolutely had to. This was one of those times and he flew along the twisting Shropshire roads almost forcing the screaming tyres to hold the road on tight bends.

He drove with the intensity and concentration he used to ride with in his early days when hunger for success burned in him like a furnace. No trophies in his sights now, no championships, just the safety of his brother.

The Chinese left without doing any further damage to Mattie. They had searched the house throughout and checked every box in the yard before running for the car again and screeching away in another blur of loose earth and exhaust smoke. They knew now that the horsebox that had passed them more than an hour ago was probably carrying Kim. They'd made the mistake of assuming he would travel in style with the trainer. Still, the driver was reasonably hopeful of catching the box before it reached Chepstow. He could cover the ground at twice the speed of the big wagon and he knew he'd have no problems recognising it: in common with many trainers Mattie Stuart, had his name on the back of it in three-foot-high letters.

Kim sat with his feet up in the cab of the horsebox though they didn't stretch quite as far over the dash as those of Damien, the eighteen-year-old lad who slouched alongside him. Since they'd left the yard Damien had smoked a lot and talked almost non-stop about sex, telling Kim how brilliant it was and how he'd be sure to love it whenever he got round to it.

And Kim tried to smile knowingly and prayed fervently that he wouldn't blush. He quite liked Damien but wished he would just talk about horses like old Bob the driver wanted to do. All in all Kim loved what he'd seen of this life, the independence of it, and he was determined to do his time as a stable lad before becoming a full-time jockey.

Eddie had said that was the best way; get a good grounding, learn how tough things could be at the bottom so you could appreciate it all the more when you reached the top. That's what he'd do. And he'd have girlfriends too though maybe not quite so many as Damien.

Old Bob listened only occasionally to the boys beside him. He liked to keep his mind on his driving. Too many madmen on the motorways these days. It was best to leave yourself plenty of time so you could just plug along steadily at fifty in the inside lane. Wasn't far down the M4 to Chepstow anyway. Be there well before the first race.

Less than fifty miles behind old Bob the black Merc joined the motorway, cut up a number of vehicles as it moved diagonally towards the fast lane, then, flashing headlights scything cars from its path, it moved up to 130 mph.

When Eddie hit a good stretch of wide road he flicked through his diary with his left hand till he found Ricky Galbraith's number. Ricky was travelling down from North Yorkshire to ride at Chepstow. Eddie dialled his mobile number and told Ricky he might have to ask him a big favour when he saw him at Chepstow. Ricky said he'd be glad to help.

Mattie's horsebox crossed the Severn Bridge and Kim marvelled at the sight of the water so far below. It was a clear cold day and the sea reflected the bright blue sky. Shortly afterwards the box rolled into the horsebox park at Chepstow racecourse. Old Bob had his favourite spot at each course, his lucky spot, as did many and he trundled across towards it as Kim, thrilled at being involved with unloading and taking the horses in, tried to contain his obvious excitement.

Damien was acting dead cool, and Kim didn't want him to see that to Kim this was like Christmas. They jumped out as soon as the van stopped and went towards the back to lower the ramp.

As they led the horses out Eddie

sped towards the course passing the ruins of Tintern Abbey a few miles to the north. He felt okay. Felt that Kim was okay. Something told him he would know automatically if his brother was in immediate danger. When he reached the course he drove straight to the horsebox park and braked to a halt beside Mattie's box.

Empty. Eddie could see no one around but they'd arrived quite recently because he could still feel heat from the engine. He hurried inside and when he saw Kim waiting by the gate of the stables, staring inside, he uttered a silent prayer of thanks to whoever was watching over him.

Eddie led Kim towards the weighing room, glancing around frequently, all his senses on red alert. When they got inside the jockeys' changing room Eddie finally relaxed. There were a few jocks in there already and most nodded to Eddie and smiled at Kim. It wasn't unusual for someone to bring in a friend or relative for a look round: this was the inner sanctum, visitors usually felt suitably honoured.

But Eddie had no intention of letting Kim leave the room till racing was over and Ricky Galbraith could drive the boy back north. Eddie spent a long time sitting in the corner talking to Kim, telling him what had happened at Mattie's. He warned him that they might have to be apart for a week or so till things sorted themselves out but that Kim would at least get some proper day-to-day experience with racehorses. When he heard that he was going to stay with Laura for a while, Kim smiled as he remembered Laura's promise to let him ride that big horse of hers.

Kim understood that Eddie couldn't drive him north, couldn't he seen leaving the races with him. Eddie stayed in the changing room with him, listening happily to Kim's enthusiastic description of his short career as a stable lad. The boy had forgotten all about schools and study and Eddie chose not to remind him just yet that there'd be three or four more years before he could start his racing career properly.

The only time Eddie left his side before racing was when Mikey Semple arrived. At eight and a half stone of solid muscle Mikey was a journeyman jockey caught between two stools. He rode on the flat during the summer and over jumps in the winter but he was just a shade too heavy for the former and a little too light for the latter.

Over jumps, trainers wanted jockeys who could punch their full weight rather than cart a stone and a half of unmoving lead around on the horse's back and with a minimum weight in all races (for horses with experienced jockeys like Mikey) of ten stone, Mikey was at a disadvantage.

But he kept battling away and he was much admired by his colleagues. To Eddie that day he had one priceless attribute: in height and build and hair colouring he resembled Kim closely enough to be worth using as a decoy. The Chinese would expect Kim to leave with Eddie and that was just fine by him.

Eddie didn't have to explain everything to Mikey. He just told him it was 'woman trouble', the same reason he'd give the others if they asked why Kim was being kept hidden in the changing room all day.

Come the end of racing Eddie's nerves were as taut as a starting tape. He'd spent the whole afternoon constantly looking around for Chinese faces without seeing a single one.

Just after four o'clock he showered and changed into his navy-blue suit. He talked with Kim, explaining again that things would soon be all right, but that he wouldn't be able to have any contact with him, even on the phone, till it was over.

Under the dim lights in the changing room, Kim looked up at him, many of his doubts and fears back in place. He was really scared now that he might not see

357

his brother again. Up till now everything had seemed such an adventure but as the room emptied and darkness fell outside his optimism rapidly drained away. But he knew Eddie was worried and he was determined to put a brave face on it, his eyes filling up only when Eddie hugged him and turned away quickly to stop his brother seeing just how emotional he was.

Kim watched Eddie and Mikey leave together. Ricky Galbraith came over and put a hand on the boy's shoulder. 'We'll give them ten minutes, Kim. That's what Eddie asked for.'

Kim nodded, not looking at him.

Eddie aimed the Audi south-west towards Cardiff. He wanted to pull them in the opposite direction from Ricky and Kim. He drove for twenty minutes before turning round and retracing his route to the racecourse carpark. Mikey's car was one of twenty or so still there. Despite frequent glances in his mirror throughout the journey Eddie had seen no black Mercedes, nor was there one in the carpark.

He stopped and let Mikey out, thanking him and promising a favour back any time. Scratching his head, Mikey walked away towards his old Toyota. All the trip had done for him was make him want an

Audi instead. Much more suitable for the mileage he did. Air conditioning too! He kicked the tyre of the Toyota in frustration and the car paid him back for his unfaithful thoughts by refusing to start.

Eddie was watching him till he knew Mikey would be safe and when he saw his head go back and his eyes close and his mouth form a loud curse he got out of the Audi and went to help give his friend a push start.

An hour later Eddie was back home, where he called Mattie. There was no answer at the yard or on his mobile. Eddie flopped down on the couch, stared at the half-full whisky bottle on the table then decided a drink was a bad idea. He looked at his watch: Rebecca's call wasn't due for another hour and a half.

He got up and went to the kitchen to make a sandwich. Where had those bloody Chinks got to. He'd spent all day narrowing his own eyes into what felt like a permanent slant looking for them. Not a sign. Had they given up? God, how he wished they had. All he wanted was to have Kim back home and Rebecca.

He wasn't even that bothered about his mother any more, or Louise, not where Kim was concerned. There'd be time enough for all that when this was over. But when would it be over? What would end it permanently? These Triads seemed to be like some monster from Greek mythology, multi-headed with countless grasping tentacles.

He could only hope that their pursuit of Kim was an angry reaction to being stitched up in the King George. Perhaps it would subside quickly as other things took their attention. Eddie prayed that their ruse to set two Triads against each other had worked and that they'd occupy themselves by feuding over the next century or so.

As the kettle came to the boil Eddie stretched and yawned. Maybe that was why the troops in the black Merc had disappeared. Maybe they'd been recalled to London as reinforcements.

The occupants of the black Merc wouldn't be seeing the lights of London that night. All three were locked in a cell in a police station in Bristol, their arrogant and abusive behaviour adding to the trouble they were already in for being clocked at 133 mph and eventually stopped by police on the M4 that morning.

Eddie was at the callbox ten minutes before the agreed time and had the phone off its receiver halfway through the first ring. 'Eddie?'

'Rebecca! Are you all right?'

'I'm fine, Eddie. It's so good to hear your voice again!'

'And yours. I've missed you.'

'Me too. What's been happening, anything?'

Eddie told her everything about the day. When she heard that Kim was going to be staying with Laura for a while, Rebecca gave Eddie the silent treatment.

In the darkness he smiled. 'You're jealous of Laura, aren't you?'

'For what? Are you joking? She's big and fat and goes around smiling or crying all the time. Or hugging people and kissing them!'

Eddie laughed.

'It's not funny!'

'Okay, okay. You're just going over the top, that's all. I think Laura's quite pretty.'

'Oh, do you now! Well why don't you just go and ring her up and talk to her instead of me!'

He laughed again, a little nervously this time. 'Come on, Rebecca, you know I'm kidding. Anyway, I told her I won't speak to her till all this is sorted out. We won't have any contact at all.'

She was silent again for a while then said moodily, 'Don't worry, she'll find some excuse to ring you up.'

'She won't. We've agreed that if there's

an emergency we'll contact each other through a third party. There's to be nothing direct. It's safer that way for Kim.'

'Well, we'll wait and see.'

'We will. But never mind Laura, how have you been? How is sunny Devon in the depths of winter?'

'It's a nice change from London, I suppose.'

'Does Annelise like it, and your mother?'

'Mother does but the air is a bit too clean and fresh for Annelise.'

'Are you managing to stay indoors okay while it's daylight?'

'Clod, yes! But it's really boring, we've hardly moved since we came here.'

'It won't be for long, Rebecca. And it's safest. We just can't risk you being seen, especially after today.'

They talked about how much longer they'd have to stay apart and of the likelihood of the Triads having started feuding. Rebecca said she might try and make a few discreet calls to see what was happening and that they'd talk again next day.

They discussed plans for their future together and said loving goodnights and Eddie walked home through the cold and dark with warmth in his heart and a spring back in his step. It was only as he approached the shadows thrown off by the stable buildings by the bright moon that he became cautious again and crept quietly up to his flat.

No signs of intruders.

All quiet.

Fifty-four

Mattie sat at home nursing a large whisky in what he now thought of as his good hand although it had a finger missing. It had been quite a long operation but the surgeon had managed to re-attach Mattie's finger, which Mattie had said he'd lost in an accident at the farm. Hand heavily bandaged, Mattie had declined their offer of a bed for the night and had driven home, drowsy but feeling reasonably pleased with himself for his courage. No winners for him at Chepstow, old Bob had said, but no sign either of any Chinese throughout the day. Mattie took a heavy slug of whisky. With any luck the bastards had wrapped that big black car around a tree. Christ! what a scary motor that thing was. Like a bloody hearse! Like a bloody big Nazi SS hearse!

As Ben Turco's Boeing 747 made its final approach to Heathrow it overflew Eddie Malloy's final approach along the A34 to Newbury racecourse and for the past few days Eddie hadn't been far from Turco's thoughts. He'd picked up the phone a number of times then thought better of it. But now he'd decided to get in touch as soon as he landed, if possible. Eddie might know something about these people.

Turco had been unable to find out anything in New York, which made him increasingly nervous. He knew Eddie well enough not to question his promise that he wouldn't drop him in it with the law or anyone else but the fact remained that Eddie was the only one beside Walter and Magnus who'd known what he'd been up to on the racetrack.

He'd spoken to his two ex-helpers a couple of times in the last forty-eight hours. They'd been able to tell him nothing useful.

As the big jet broke through the very low cloud cover Turco fiddled nervously with his seat belt. He didn't like flying.

As he turned into the racecourse Eddie's thoughts too were on the Triads. He'd spent a peaceful night; no unexpected visitors, no crazy phone calls. Perhaps the internal feud was well under way.

With a bit of luck Rebecca would have more news in her call this evening.

He wondered how Kim was. He'd be loving it up there, right in with the horses in all that wild wind and open space. The healthy sea air; Eddie found himself filling his lungs as he locked the car and lugged his kitbag towards the Jockeys' Entrance. Clocking on for another day's work. Three rides booked. One man and one boy to keep. And hopefully, in the not too distant future, one very pretty, very brave woman.

Although Laura wasn't to contact him direct, Eddie felt a constant inexplicable unease and kept checking the message system on his mobile phone between races just in case. After the last he was surprised to find a message from Ben Turco asking him to call a certain number.

He did. Turco answered on the second ring. 'Eddie! How the hell are you?'

'I'm all right. What brings you back from the Big Apple?'

'That's what I'd quite like to talk to you about, hence the reason I'm on my way to you at the moment.'

'I'm at Newbury races.'

'I know. I should be there in fifteen minutes. Can you wait?'

'Of course, but it's probably best if we meet in the carpark.'

Turco put on a camp voice. 'You always were ashamed of introducing me to your friends!'

Eddie smiled and headed for the carpark. Twenty minutes later he watched Turco park a red BMW and get out. Eddie went to meet him. They shook hands. Turco said, 'You look as neat as ever. Been modelling for those catalogues again?'

'Pays better than riding horses.'

'I'll bet. Wanna drink?'

Eddie looked around. Owners, trainers and other jockeys were filtering steadily into the carpark. 'Not here.'

'Fine, let's go find some place.'

Each drove his own car till they were more than five miles from the course then Eddie pulled in at a country pub. It was quiet inside where a big log fire burned. Eddie watched Turco go to the bar. The Yank was his usual tousled self with his square unshaven jaw and coconut hair. He wore jeans and sneakers and a heavy red and black check lumberjack shirt over a light grey T-shirt.

He came back carrying a bottle of Budweiser and a whisky and ice for Eddie. He sat down and Eddie watched the fire reflect on his round glasses, making his eyes look almost demonically pinpoint.

Turco told him what had happened with the tape, and that he hadn't yet called the number they'd given him.

'Are you going to call?'

Turco shrugged. 'Gonna have to.'

Eddie told him everything that had happened in the past few days. They both decided it was fair to conclude that the Triads were behind the tape. They'd almost certainly killed Grimond, because they'd been able to send his organs to Eddie, which gruesomely reminded him they were still under his sink at the flat.

'So the cops don't know about the Triads but they do know about Grimond?'

'Yes, but not about you.'

Turco leaned towards the fire, elbows on knees, hands clasped. 'Trouble is, Eddie, how long you gonna be able to not tell them?'

'I gave you my word. I'll keep it.'

'I know you will. Question is, is it fair of me to ask you to keep it much longer?'

Eddie didn't answer. He sipped some whisky. Turco said, 'I've tried to figure it out. It can't be blackmail over this photo-finish scam 'cause they could have blackmailed me just as easy in New York. They want me here to do something for them.'

'Well there's only one way you're going to find out.'

Turco dangled his bottle by the neck and nodded, then he got up and went to the telephone in the entrance hallway. Eddie watched him through the glass. Suddenly, Turco signalled him frantically to come out. Eddie joined him just as Turco was attaching a small object close to the earpiece of the receiver.

Turco said, 'Sorry, I lost you there. Could you say that again?'

Eddie could hear the angry Chinese voice very clearly. 'Las' time! I say you tell Mistah Malloy he mus' call soon! I have someone heah who he like to speak to!' Lee Sung laughed. Eddie remembered the laugh and the voice from that night in the darkened backroom.

Turco hung up. Eddie called his answerphone at home. There was a message on it from Lee Sung. It was just over an hour old and it said almost exactly the same thing he'd just overheard via Turco's little device.

Eddie's day-long unease increased when Turco put an arm around his shoulder on the walk back to their table. He said, 'Remember that SIS plan I told you about, the one you didn't think was a good idea. They want us to try and pull it off.'

'Us?'

'Me and you.'

'How do they know about it?'

They stood by the fire facing each other.

Turco said, 'Well I didn't tell 'em.'

Eddie lowered his head, shaking it slowly in despair. The only other person who knew was Rebecca. They'd caught her.

Fifty-five

Turco tipped up the bottle, draining the last of the beer. He said, 'They must have been confident of catching her to have their plans so far advanced. They want to do this in four days' time.'

Eddie pulled himself up from deep thought. 'You're kidding!'

'Nope.'

'How the hell am I supposed to arrange a studio spot in SIS with that sort of notice?'

'Well their reckoning is that you don't need to. You just need to get us access and they think that your face will be well enough known there to let us waltz right in.'

'And who are our waltzing partners going to be? They must know the SIS guys aren't just going to sit there while you push horses all over the bloody screen and dub a false commentary into almost ten thousand betting shops!'

'He said they'll send someone in with us who will look after all that.'

'Yeah, look after it with a submachine gun!'

Looking very thoughtful, Turco drummed lightly on the table and said, 'I think we better meet these guys, Eddie.'

Eddie watched him, contemplating Turco's mood. He said, 'You're excited about this, aren't you?'

Turco shrugged, still drumming. 'A little. I'd sooner it was me and you was making the killing but it should be interesting. Besides, I think I can make it *very* interesting for our little yellow friends.' He looked up with a devilish smile. It didn't make Eddie feel any better.

Turco said, 'Why don't you call them up like the man asked, fix a meeting?'

Eddie frowned and drank some more. 'I need more time to think.'

'As they say in all the best movies, Eddie, "Time is something we just ain't got".'

They went back to the payphone and Turco attached his little speaker. Eddie dialled. One of Lee Sung's henchmen answered and went to get him. Eddie held for over a minute before Lee Sung came on and sarcastically thanked him for returning the call. 'Befoah we talk business, I have someone who wanna talk to you, Mistah Malloy! Aftah that maybe you listen bettah! Hold on.'

Eddie held almost in anguish for another minute. Turco, standing close, watched his face intently. Then a very frightened voice came on the line. 'Eddie ... Eddie ...' heavy sobs now and Eddie felt himself go weak. 'Eddie ... I'm sorry!'

It was Kim.

Eddie called Laura. She sounded relieved to hear his voice. 'Eddie! Is Kim okay?'

'What happened, Laura?' He felt let down, angry at her that she could ask so casually about him.

She caught his mood immediately. 'Nothing happened! I let him go with her this morning. She said that was what you wanted.'

'Who said?'

'Your girlfriend, Rebecca.'

Eddie rang Lee Sung back to try and fix a meeting. Lee Sung said he would not see Eddie, only Turco. If Eddie turned up there would be no meeting and he would not see the boy again. For all the Chinaman's bluster this told Eddie that the damage he'd done to Lee Sung that night in London had scared the man. Much as he held the whip hand he wasn't willing to risk being in the same room with Eddie.

The jockey took the opportunity to

release some of his suppressed anger and to scare Lee Sung further. 'Okay, Turco will come and meet you but listen to me ...' he paused to let the Chinaman concentrate on what was coming next, then he spoke slowly and deliberately, 'If you hurt that boy I will kill you. If you hurt that boy I will kill you. I do not want you to be in any doubt that I will kill you if you hurt that boy. No matter what else happens I will kill you if you hurt that boy.'

Lee Sung laughed but nervousness needs no translation and Eddie realised he'd hit home. He passed the phone to Turco who made arrangements to meet Lee Sung in London in an hour.

In a daze Eddie went back to his seat. The words he'd just said replayed hypnotically in his head and he realised he had meant them. If he lost Kim now he wouldn't want to carry on life in any normal way. More than anything else he needed his brother to have a normal adolescence, to have what Eddie had never had. And he wanted Kim to be happy more than anything else he'd ever wanted. More than money, more than Jockeys' Championships, more than Rebecca.

Much more now than the treacherous Rebecca.

And he'd been around murder enough

in the last few years to realise the horror of it but he felt in his heart that at that minute he would be prepared to spend the rest of his life in prison for the murder of Lee Sung.

Turco left for London promising he'd call Eddie on his mobile as soon as he left Lee Sung. They'd discussed the plan that was hatching in Turco's head and the American had agreed to meet McCarthy later if Eddie could arrange it.

The Jockey Club Security man lived within half an hour's drive. Eddie rang him. McCarthy recognised the voice. 'Eddie, tell me this, how come you always manage to call me outside office hours?'

'Just to keep you on your toes, Mac.'

McCarthy recognised the hollowness in Eddie's voice and realised he wasn't up for his usual bit of banter before getting down to business. 'What's wrong, Eddie?'

'I need to see you, Mac.'

Waiting for McCarthy, Eddie tried to figure Rebecca out. At first he'd thought the Triad had forced her to go and get Kim. That was what he wanted to believe but Laura had said that she'd been alone this morning when she'd rolled up at the yard. Alone, smiling, confident, persuasive. She'd told Laura that information she'd gathered in London suggested the Triad were close to tracking Kim down to Laura's place.

She said she'd told Eddie, who'd asked her to come and pick the boy up.

Laura said Kim had seemed disappointed at being moved on again so quickly and had been looking forward so much to riding out again the next day. They'd had a long conversation and Eddie had had to reassure her constantly that he bore no ill will. Laura was devastated and felt guilty for letting Kim go so easily. Eddie had told her he'd been at fault for leaving the details so woolly for only contacting each other through third parties.

Although something in him clung to the hope that Rebecca would prove true, in the end too many things were stacked against it. It had been only last night he'd told her where Kim was. She was supposed to have been calling from Devon yet she turns up at Alnwick fresh and bright at 10.30 this morning.

To have been tracked down by the Triad, captured, have the information about Kim forced from her then driven so far north to turn up looking so well at Laura's was just too much to believe.

But what an actress! All that bullshit on the phone about being jealous of Laura when she didn't give a tuppenny damn about Laura or him. God, they say nothing can make a bigger fool of a man than a horse! How about a woman? What about all that stuff the other night in his flat, all that selfless stuff about not wanting to involve him?

Jeez, he couldn't believe it, how he'd been taken in. He'd check it through McCarthy or Mattie but Eddie would be willing to bet his life right now that there was no sister, no Annelise, no trust fund money due in March. No, it was all coming together now; shortly after he'd told her in bed about the potential of Turco's SIS con, Grimond had been attacked. He expressly recalled telling Rebecca that if he got warned off there'd be no SIS scam even if he'd wanted to do it because they wouldn't have had him back in the studio.

So what had she done? She'd told the Triad that Grimond was threatening to have him warned off with that falsified evidence and they'd taken Grimond out of the picture to stop him messing up their plan. Then they'd done the same to Tiny. They'd probably lost nothing on the King George because Rebecca had told them exactly what had happened. There had never been a set-up with a rival Triad.

The only person who'd been set up throughout was Eddie. Maybe Mattie too but mainly Eddie. After she'd painted such a terrifying picture of the Triads he'd wondered at her immense courage in going with him that night to rescue Mattie. Now he realised the whole thing had been a set-up. They'd rigged that just to pull him into the web.

He allowed himself a small smile. At least he'd given Lee Sung a sore face for his trouble. But now the Chinaman had his brother. Eddie dug his nails deep into the palm of his hand in anger and frustration and tried to push from his mind the terror Kim must be feeling. Hearing him on the phone had almost ripped the heart out of Eddie, almost floored him physically. And he swore again to himself that he'd take maximum revenge on these people.

And he faced the fact that if Kim didn't survive this then Rebecca would deserve punishment even more than Lee Sung. And that was something he could not yet handle.

Fifty-six

McCarthy had a good idea where the pub was where he was supposed to meet Eddie but he wasn't exactly sure. It was on this road somewhere.

He wondered what the jockey had in store this time. He'd sounded quite depressed, which wasn't like Eddie. The man had been in more scrapes than most; just couldn't resist them, and had always seemed cavalier, if not totally devil-may-care about it to McCarthy.

And some had been real bad 'uns. One of McCarthy's first judgements about Eddie when he'd got to know him was that the man had no real sense of self-preservation. That was balanced by an exaggerated sense of justice though he could perhaps be excused that after what the Jockey Club had done to him when they'd taken his licence away. Ruined his career and maybe more, McCarthy now realised.

Ever since his comeback Eddie had displayed that quiet desperation of those who kept giving life every ounce they've got even though they know deep down that they're never going to make it. For as long as he'd known him, Eddie Malloy had been trying to claw back what was gone, what was dead and buried. McCarthy had thought that it all revolved around his riding career and his warning off but when the news had broken last year about Eddie's private life, about his family problems, he'd realised that that was where the sadness, the hopelessness really lay.

And there was nothing he or anyone else could do to help the man. All McCarthy felt he could do was what he was doing now: pull on his hat and boots and go out into the night to see what trouble Eddie was in, to see how he could help.

When McCarthy got there Eddie bought him a soft drink as the barman eyed them warily, convinced that these two sharply dressed men and the little nerdy guy who'd been there earlier were cops. But he said nothing.

They sat down by the fire and Eddie told Mac everything. Now he understood the reasons for Eddie's despairing mood: anything the jockey had been up against in the past had been both tangible and beatable; individuals with limitations. This time he was up against a world-wide network of criminals as mindless and as dedicated to their task as worker ants. No matter how many Eddie could swat on his own, hundreds more would emerge to swamp him.

And Mac knew that Eddie had accepted this and that was why he had chosen to call him so quickly and to tell him everything, even the name of the guy who'd pulled the photo finish fraud. The Security man also knew that this was way out of his league. He said, 'I can tell you now, Eddie, you've got no chance unless we bring in some big guns from the London police.'

Eddie stared into his almost empty glass.

'That's what Turco says.'

McCarthy was surprised. 'Then he *is* a clever man.'

Eddie buried his face in his hands, massaged it with his fingers. 'The trouble is they've got Kim and if the slightest thing goes wrong and these people find out the police are in on it then I've lost him.'

McCarthy watched him. Never before had he seen Eddie show any real emotion other than rage over another person. This was a deep fear that was hurting him. Mac could see it in him, hear it in his voice. He leaned forward, reached out and squeezed Eddie's stooped shoulder. It was the first time either could recall any honest gesture of comfort from the rather strait-laced Security man. It did something to break through what until now had been a purely professional relationship.

Eddie raised his head and smiled wearily at Mac. And Mac smiled back, again with real warmth.

Half an hour later Turco called and said he was on his way back. He hadn't seen Kim. He'd seen nobody but Lee Sung and his two sidekicks who wouldn't tell him where Kim was being held. While they waited for him McCarthy worked on building Eddie's commitment for what was going to have to happen. He told the jockey that he had some knowledge of

Triads through a CID friend whose patch in London included Chinatown.

'You have to get these people on the spot, red-handed. You'll never find anyone to testify against them. No matter what they do to a man. They've been known to cut a man into small pieces in front of his wife and she will swear she saw nothing. Fear of the Triads is endemic in the Chinese, they're brought up with it the way you were brought up with horses. It's ingrained like a religion. It's unshiftable. It's hundreds of years old.

'The only possible way to nail them is to actually catch them in mid-crime. That's your only chance of putting them away. If we can get this Lee Sung and his men it'll be a rare coup. I know the police will appreciate it. And if you get the reputation among the Triads of someone who can get people locked in jail for a long time then you can be pretty sure you'll be left alone in future.'

Eddie looked at the big man. 'And if we don't nail them?'

'We'll give them a bloody good scare.'

'Yes, but at what point will you give them the scare and what will they give Kim?' Eddie could hear the frustration in his own voice and saw that Mac had registered it.

McCarthy finally submitted to the heat

380

from the fire and slid his big dark coat off to reveal a brown suit Eddie had seen a few times before over a fawn V-neck sweater, blue shirt and tweedy tie. Within a minute Mac had taken his jacket off too.

Quietly he broke back into the subject. 'You know we can't let this go ahead, Eddie? We've got to get them before the show goes on air as such.'

'And how do you plan to do that?'

'We'll have to decide that with the police. There's no way we can put a false result out into every betting shop, you know that. It would finish racing in this country!'

'Not if we handled it properly.'

'Come on, Eddie! Punters will accept the odd trainer pulling a fast one or a jockey stopping a horse, that's all part of the business. But do you seriously think that if the everyday punter thought a completely fabricated result could be put out into every single betting shop, he'd ever bet again?'

Eddie looked at Mac. It was the first time for a while he'd seen him so animated about something.

The big man went on. 'Would you go into a casino and risk money on roulette if you knew the wheel was fixed? Of course you wouldn't! Same goes for racing punters and if they disappear so do betting shops.

381

If the shops go there's no Levy from them to racecourses. How many racecourses do you think are a commercial success?'

Eddie shrugged, watching McCarthy's passion; at least it was taking his mind off his problems for a while.

'Go on, guess!'

'Mac, I don't know! Thirty? Forty?'

'Ten! Twelve at most! Out of fifty-nine! The rest survive on subsidies from the Levy Board and the Levy Board collects that money from punters in betting shops! See the equation now?'

'Yes, I see it. And I see the other part, the one you left out. No racecourses, no job for you.'

'Or you!'

'So what! It's been bloody good to me, racing, hasn't it!'

'You're still making a living at it.'

Eddie looked away into the fire. He realised that the real reason he wanted racing to survive was for Kim. Kim could go on and emulate him as champion but Eddie would have to keep him clear of all the pitfalls, make sure he had a long reign barring injury.

Mac detected his change of mood and tried in turn to calm himself down. Much more quietly he said, 'Eddie, you see why we can't let this even come under orders?'

'Wait and talk to Turco.'

'I'm happy to talk turkey with Turco.'

Mac smiled and Eddie found one from somewhere too.

Fifty-seven

There was a gleam in Turco's eyes when he came back and the barman thought they were using the pub as some sort of base for a stakeout as he watched the stocky figure hurry across the maroon carpet towards his friends.

Eddie got up and went to meet him asking anxiously if he'd seen Kim but Turco hadn't and Eddie, despondent, sat down again and quietly introduced Turco to Mac who eyed the American with a degree of caginess he was slightly ashamed of when he saw how open and friendly Turco was with him. Eddie left them both for a few minutes to get some more drinks though he settled this time for an orange juice. He'd need his wits about him for the next ninety-six hours.

That's when it hit home to him that they wanted to pull this stunt on New Year's Day. Shit! So much for his plans to reunite Kim with his mother and sister.

He took the drinks back to the table to find Turco, as he'd suspected, doing all the talking. And he could see McCarthy had his professional's look in his eye. God only knew what Turco had given away with his enthusiasm for gadgetry and hitting the bookies.

When Eddie settled, Turco told them about the meeting. 'They want to do this New Year's Day for several reasons: they're obsessed with some other Triad stealing their idea so they want it over with before anyone gets the chance. They want it done at Cheltenham as they reckon the market will be strong enough there to stop the bookies realising too much is being placed on one horse. Also, there are seven meetings planned that day so they reckon the staff in the shops will be under too much pressure to pick up on their bets and warn head office in advance.

'And, they want it done in the big long distance 'chase because their illegal bookmaking operation will lay the odds-on favourite at odds against.'

Eddie said, 'Well what good will that do them? The horse might win anyway and the proper result would be known within a few minutes once the people in the on-course shops at Cheltenham saw the result didn't tie in with what had actually happened on the racecourse.'

'Ah, but they've thought of that. And this shows they have done their homework. They must have been planning this for a while. They're going to have someone cut all telecommunications to Cheltenham just before the off and that includes slicing the satellite cables at the course.'

'So—it might take a couple of hours to fix but at the latest next day their punters are going to know the true result.'

Turco shrugged. 'So what? They'll be long gone with the cash by then!'

Mac spoke for the first time. 'Why did they tell you all this?'

'I dunno. I got the impression they were showing off a bit. And maybe they wanted me to know they'd gone into it in depth so we'd be put off pulling any tricks.'

Eddie said, 'What about Kim, didn't they say anything about where they were holding him?'

Turco shook his head. 'They said they'd hand him over at a pre-agreed point once the result was in and confirmed.'

'Which pre-agreed point?'

'To be confirmed.'

Eddie and Turco looked at each other as if in silent conspiracy. McCarthy said, 'Listen, you cannot go ahead with this. I don't care what your plans are to try and retrieve the situation afterwards but you cannot put out a completely false result!'

Eddie looked at Mac and the Security man saw the rekindling of a twinkle there. Eddie said, 'Wait till you hear the retrieval plans first. Tell him, Ben.'

Now it was Turco's turn for the twinkle in the eye.

When he finished Mac looked at him for a while, wondering at his brain and his imagination. Mac said, 'And you've got all the kit you need here in London to do this?'

'Everything. It's still in my flat.'

McCarthy shook his head in wonder. He didn't know how he was going to keep Turco out of trouble with Jockey Club officials or indeed the police and he respected the American for not even asking him to. But he knew he'd have to try and do something if Turco could pull this off.

Mac told them he'd have to go home and that he'd contact his man at Scotland Yard and set up a meeting for tomorrow. He'd call Eddie in the morning.

When he'd gone Turco said to Eddie, 'If you need a bed for the night you're welcome to come and stay at my place.'

Eddie shook his head. 'I want you to show me where your meeting with Lee Sung was. That's where I'll be staying the night.'

'I doubt it,' said Turco, 'We met in a carpark.'

Turco could see that Eddie wasn't sure if he was joking. 'No kidding, Eddie. Come home with me. We'll be close to McCarthy's man then if he can set a meeting up tomorrow.'

Eddie nodded, too weary to argue and disinclined anyway to go back home without Kim. As he got up to follow Turco out he promised himself that he wouldn't go back home at all until Kim was with him. Until he was safe.

If Laura Gilpin had known about that promise she'd have dialled Eddie's mobile much sooner than she did. She left it until after eleven that night by which time Eddie was having a cup of tea and watching Turco do marvellous things with his spacewars game on the penthouse window high above the London traffic.

Eddie recognised her voice and realised he was glad to hear it. 'Are you all right?' she asked, obvious worry in her voice.

'I'm okay. I'm sorry, I should have called you back, Laura.'

She liked it when he used her name. 'Any word?'

'Yes, but no good news. Something's been arranged but it's best not to talk about it on mobiles. Where are you?'

There was a slight hesitation, then she said, 'Outside your place.'

Eddie was surprised. He didn't speak.

'I felt terrible, Eddie. I had to see you. I wanted to see you.'

She knew there was a longing in her voice and she didn't want to disguise it, couldn't disguise it. It wasn't just that she felt she'd let him down so badly, it was that she was in love with him and she wanted just to be with him, especially when he was so troubled. 'I need to see you,' she said quietly and Eddie felt a reassurance, a return of at least a little peace to his soul, and he remembered how he'd felt when they'd hugged at Cheltenham.

'Can you drive to London?'

'I can drive to hell and back.'

He smiled. 'That's corny, Laura.'

'It was, wasn't it? I promise never to be corny again.'

'I'll hold you to it.'

Her heart lifted and her stomach turned over. Eddie gave her directions. Before saying goodbye she said, 'Eddie, listen, Kim's going to be all right, I can sense it. I know he will be.'

'I hope so.'

'He will. Keep your chin up. I'll see you soon.'

It was almost one o'clock when she found the place. Eddie was waiting outside as he'd promised and they both felt better for being together again, travelling up in the lift in companionable silence.

Turco went to bed soon after Laura arrived but she and Eddie sat up till after three talking. Laura listened to how Rebecca had deceived them both and she felt genuine sympathy for Eddie, for his hurt and disappointment over her as well as his fears for Kim.

But the news about Rebecca was the best she had ever heard in her almost thirty years of life. It made her feel like a girl again. It made her understand the truth of the saying about someone's heart singing because hers was blasting out a bloody great aria and she knew it would be up all night doing encores.

They say that the show ain't over till the fat lady sings. Does that apply to fat ladies' hearts? she wondered, as she watched him, looked at every pore in his face, counted the ghosts of the summer freckles across his nose, admired the scar on his cheek, the whiteness of his teeth, his mouth moving as he talked, the pulse on his neck, the turn of his earlobe, the expressiveness of his long fingers, the depth and intensity of his wonderful blue eyes ...

And she knew that even if she had to fight a whole colony full of Triads to get Kim back for him, to make him happy again, she would do it. She would gladly do it. When finally she went to her room and lay down she spent long periods holding her breath so she could listen for the sounds of his breathing in the next room. The breath, the living breath of her man.

Fifty-eight

All three of them left the flat at 9.45 next morning, Sunday, 29 December. The weather was mild and there was no forecast danger to racing over the next few days so it looked like the seven New Year's Day meetings would go ahead.

They took a cab across to Scotland Yard to meet McCarthy and his man. McCarthy introduced him: Chief Inspector Mills. He was a big man, early fifties maybe, with a salt and pepper moustache and an upright bearing. Eddie had noticed that about a number of senior policemen he'd met over the years; they carried themselves well, had a definite presence, though in Mills's case his six foot three, fifteen stone frame, undoubtedly contributed to this.

Eddie introduced Laura to McCarthy as well as to Mills. The Chief Inspector had a room set aside for their meeting and as they went in the strong smell of brewing coffee brought a smile to Turco's face which, for once, was clean shaven.

They talked for almost two hours. Mills made Turco go over his plan again and again and by the end they were pretty sure they'd covered most eventualities. Next stop was a hotel near Marble Arch for a meeting with the MD of SIS. Turco had wanted to have it at the SIS studio but the others thought that wouldn't be such a good idea in case Lee Sung's men were watching the place.

The only other meeting planned for that day was one Turco was supposed to attend that evening at an address to be advised by Lee Sung. The Chinaman was taking no chances whatever that his money would be lost. One of his demands had been that Turco give him a live demonstration of how he was actually going to do this image manipulation.

But one of Chief Inspector Mills's suggestions had been that Turco put Lee Sung off till the night before, New Year's Eve. None of them knew how Lee Sung would react and while a postponement wasn't crucial to their plans they all agreed it would give them a greater chance of success.

With some trepidation but a thrill of excitement Turco called the number Lee Sung had given him which Mills had already had identified as being a callbox in a hotel near Wardour Street. The area around there seemed to be Lee Sung's patch. That was where Eddie had first come upon him when he'd rescued Mattie and it was in a carpark close to there that Turco had met him last night.

They were all reassured. This factor would be crucial to their plans.

Lee Sung did seem suspicious when Turco told him he couldn't make it but the American played his part brilliantly. 'Hey, listen, I can bring the stuff, no problem, but I'm telling you it won't work properly yet. You want to see a demo on video and on live TV and it's got to be adjusted for that. If you're happy seeing it not working properly then I'll bring it right along tonight. Just say the word.'

But Lee Sung finally conceded that Tuesday 31st would be okay, warning him that if the equipment didn't work to his satisfaction the whole thing was off and the boy would be killed. Turco did not tell anyone about this final threat.

Turco spent the remainder of that day and most of the next playing his games. McCarthy went home. Eddie and Laura went walking in London. Laura watched him with a feeling of helplessness as they walked the streets; he was looking everywhere for his brother. Eddie couldn't pass a house without slowing and gazing through the window. When he saw a man with a boy, no matter how far away, he'd hurry in that direction, apologising to Laura each time for dashing off and leaving her.

Laura thought it pitiful to see and she longed to hold him, to comfort him, but she knew that the time wasn't yet right. To Eddie that Monday seemed the longest day. At least on Tuesday they'd have the tension of waiting for Turco to come back from his demo to the Chinks. That was where the first part of the plan would be put in place. If that failed they'd be right up against it.

When Turco made the call late on Tuesday afternoon he was given the address and warned to travel alone. Eddie and Laura helped plot his route with the A to Z then gave him a hand to pack his gear into the hired BMW They stood close together watching his tail lights disappear.

The house was in East London, well outside Lee Sung's normal area, but that didn't bother Turco or the others too much. They knew it would probably be a one-off visit for the Chinaman too.

It was on a sprawling estate, a bungalow, and it took Turco a while to find it. The rain was falling gently as he walked up the path. One of Lee Sung's sidekicks opened the door then his friend joined him and they both helped Turco bring in his gear.

Lee Sung was waiting inside. He grunted at the American and pointed to the big TV set, which had been wheeled into the middle of the room. Turco could clearly see the castor indentations in the carpet in the corner. He walked around the set as though assessing an accident victim, looked suitably pensive and was well aware that the three men were watching him closely. He signalled the two younger men to bring his three leather bags over beside the set.

Turco knelt down behind the TV and opened his bags taking out three separate cream-coloured units plus a keyboard, cabling and two remote control pads. A smaller bag contained a toolkit and Turco opened it. From the other bag he took an electrical extension and held it up towards one of the men without speaking or looking. The man hurried to plug it in a socket on the longest wall.

Turco said to him, 'I need you to stay there by that switch and turn it on and off as I tell you.' The man nodded. Turco took a screwdriver and removed the panel at the back of the TV and started unrolling his cables. Lee Sung moved closer, which was exactly what Turco wanted.

He worked silently for five minutes rigging up various things, telling the man by the socket to switch on and off now and again. All the time Lee Sung was inching closer.

Turco was kneeling. He straightened his back and turned towards the other young man. 'I need more light. Find me a flashlight or something.'

The man looked baffled. Turco held out his arm as though he had a flashlight in his hand, clicking his thumb back and forward. 'Flashlight, you know? Torch?'

Lee Sung looked at the man and barked something and the man went through the door into what appeared to be a kitchen. Right then Turco made to look at his watch and saw he hadn't one. 'Shit!' He looked up at Lee Sung who was quite close to him now. 'You got a watch on?' Lee Sung nodded quickly. Turco held his hand out. 'Gimme it a minute.'

Lee Sung, happy to be useful too, slid what looked like a silver Rolex off his wrist and handed it to Turco. Turco raised it and looked closely at the dial, screwing up his eyes. Then he leant forward to make a tiny adjustment to one of the units. Again he leant back, again he narrowed his eyes. 'Where's that goddamn light!' He looked impatiently at Lee Sung. 'Go see where he's got to with that light, will ya? How the hell's a man supposed to work without light?'

Lee Sung hurried obediently off.

Turco was singing when he got back to the flat. His voice was less than tuneful but as Laura and Eddie heard it carry along the hallway they felt a surge of relief because they knew the first part of the plan was safely in place. They talked for a long time. Turco high because of what he'd done, the others too tense to sleep. They even tried Turco's spacewars game but nothing could take their minds off the fact that tomorrow was D-Day. Make or break.

Fifty-nine

The Cheltenham race was timed at 2.10. The horse Turco had to make the winner was called Grasshopper Green which would start at a minimum price of 20-1 according to the papers. Some forecast 33-1.

Lee Sung had more than a thousand men in place all over the capital. He'd thought of trying to cover much more of the country but in London a strange face in a betting shop was far from unusual and fairly big bets were often accepted without so much as a raised eyebrow.

Of the 3,000 or so shops in the London area, Lee Sung had done his homework. He knew which were frequented by Chinese, who were known in the betting world to be fearless punters anyway. Even without a planned coup, a Chinese placing a £200 bet on a 33-1 chance would cause little consternation.

Each of these men had £250 to place on the horse which, even if it started at the minimum forecast odds, would return over £5 million for Lee Sung. It would cost him a million of that in expenses but the profit would still be healthy. Especially when he added his take on the 'beaten' odds-on favourite. And none of the agents could screw things up in advance because none would find out which horse they were betting on until five minutes before the race.

Lee Sung had rightly concluded that if Turco's equipment was so sophisticated he could easily arrange to have the second hand of the on-screen clock stop at 2.05 07 signifying the number 7 to the agents. Each agent's eyes would be glued to that screen waiting to see which second number that clock would stop at. Then the bets would be placed just a few minutes before the off. Too late to alert anyone or shorten the price at the track even if the communications to Cheltenham were not sabotaged as Lee Sung had arranged that they would be.

At exactly 2.10 Rebecca would have Eddie's young brother on the centre of Tower Bridge. Eddie was sending a woman to pick him up but he had been warned that the boy would not be handed over until the result was called and confirmed. If anything went wrong then Lee Sung had warned Turco to tell Eddie that the drop into the Thames from Tower Bridge was a long one.

Turco had confirmed to the Chinaman that Eddie had arranged an SIS studio visit for three people and it was scheduled for 1.15. He told Lee Sung that would give him more than ample time to set things up, reassuring him that that was exactly what the equipment had been built for. It wouldn't need all the tweaking he'd had to do for the demo.

Lee Sung told him to pick up his man outside Moorfields Eye Hospital at exactly one o'clock.

And they did. Eddie and Turco looking suitably tense as the black-suited Chinaman in the white shirt and black tie got in the back. It was a trip of only a few hundred yards to Corsham Street and SIS headquarters.

Eddie got them in and downstairs to

the basement studio where he introduced
Turco and the Chinaman as friends. The
studio manager and his three staff had
been fully briefed and had thought they
might find it tough shamming flight and
surprise when the Chinaman pulled the
gun. But they found they had no difficulty
whatsoever.

The reality of a Smith & Wesson pistol
was pretty damn solid whether they'd
known it was going to happen or not.
Turco had the real acting job now, trying
to reassure everyone that all would be well
if nobody did anything silly. Eddie took
a back seat as the American, loving the
limelight, the drama, moved hurriedly but
calmly around running his cables, tinkering
with the edit suite, all the time making
comforting noises.

'Now, just take it easy, guys. We didn't
want to do this. We're just victims of
these crazy people same as you are. Bigger
victims. But don't worry. Stay cool. This
guy will be outta here by 2.20. Just a little
matter of a horserace to fix first. In the
meantime you'd best just go about your
business of providing a normal service to
all them friendly bookmakers out there.'

And the SIS team did just that, cueing
video tape, mixing in text shows, giving
commentaries and watching the clock as
it moved towards 2.10.

At 1.50 Laura Gilpin was sitting in Eddie's Audi in the carpark of the Tower Hotel right on the north bank of the Thames at Tower Bridge. She could see most of the bridge. The day was clear with a stiff breeze coming down the river. There was no sign of Rebecca and Kim.

At four minutes past two the blonde woman appeared, walking towards the centre of the bridge from the south bank. That looked like Kim with her. He had on a long coat he hadn't had with him when he'd left Alnwick. Rebecca's coat was wide with long baggy sleeves and although the boy appeared to be holding her hand Laura thought he might be tied to her wrist somehow.

She locked the car and moved towards the bridge.

At 2.05 and 07 seconds the clock on SIS screens stopped for almost thirty seconds and 1,017 Chinese agents, each in a different shop, filled in the name Grasshopper Green on betting slips which already had the £250 stake written on. They moved towards the counters.

In the darkened SIS studio the man showing most tension was the black-suited Triad man in the corner. He was holding the gun almost constantly at eye-level and his arms ached. He'd been sweating heavily for the past ten minutes and his acrid smell now permeated the room.

The mischievous Turco kept screwing up his nose and staring at the man. Turco was in place at the controls of the big edit suite and the studio commentator was set to take over from the man on course at Cheltenham whose connection, everyone knew, was about to be cut anyway.

The horses moved into line at the start. Turco was cool. This wouldn't be hard for him. All he had to control was one horse; it didn't matter a damn where the others ran, he just had to move Grasshopper Green forward at the right time.

On Tower Bridge, Rebecca watched the fat woman walk towards her and she gripped Kim's hand tighter. In her other hand was a phone which she held to her ear. On the other end of it in a London betting shop Lee Sung was watching the field for the 2.10 to come under starter's orders.

As agreed Laura stayed at least a hundred yards away from them though she could see tears rising in Kim's eyes as he looked pleadingly at her. That bitch! Laura too pulled out a mobile as it rang.

'Is Kim there?'

'He's here, Eddie. He looks fine.'

'Is it Rebecca who's with him?'

'Yes.'

'Is she holding him?'

'Yes.'

'Is he close to the parapet? Is he in danger?'

'He's close but his feet are firmly planted on the ground. He'll be okay. I won't let her do anything to him.' Laura's eyes hadn't left Rebecca's since she'd looked at Kim.

'Don't go closer till the race is over,' Eddie said.

'I won't, Eddie, don't worry.'

At Cheltenham the starter dropped the flag and the field set off over four miles on good ground, a journey that would take around nine minutes. Suddenly the service to the on-course betting shops went down and all landline telephones went dead. People hurried out of the shops to watch the race live.

Lee Sung stood at the rear of the big betting shop watching Grasshopper Green's steady progress with an ever widening smile showing brownish chipped teeth. Turco played the dramatist all the way to the end, manipulating the image to come late on the run in and win by a length.

Back live at Cheltenham the real Grass-hopper Green struggled over the last in fifth place.

Lee Sung's grin was at its widest as he watched an SP of 33-1 flash up on the screen. If all 1,017 agents had placed their bets as planned the bookies would be paying out more than eight and a half million pounds. He had to ask Rebecca to repeat herself because he hadn't really been listening.

'Is everything all right? Can I let the boy go?'

Lee Sung nodded, still smiling. 'Everything fine. Let him go.'

In the SIS studio the gunman was backing towards the door when he realised he was supposed to have got the key from the studio manager so he could lock them in. Rushing towards the man he demanded the key and was given it. He backed away again through the door and as he was locking it behind him he heard a voice warning him to keep completely still. Turning his head very slowly to the right he saw four armed policemen in bullet-proof clothing aiming guns at him.

Lee Sung stood almost dazed by his success. He would be recognised by his contemporaries now as a great man, a brilliant Triad leader. Pulling the betting slip from his pocket he walked towards the pay-out counter and presented it for payment. The manager asked him if he would mind waiting until the jockeys had weighed in and would he also accept a cheque for £5,000 and the balance in cash.

'No cheque! Cash!' he shouted loudly.

'But ...'

'No cheque! Cash!'

The manager said, 'All right, sir. Hold on a minute, I'll see if someone can help us out.' He went through a door in the rear of the shop and returned almost immediately followed by two smiling plain-clothes policemen.

Confusion replaced anger on Lee Sung's face and he turned quickly trying to leave, only to find the two punters 'queuing' behind him smiling and gripping him firmly, one on each arm. Followed by their colleagues they led him out of the shop.

In 1,017 other London betting shops the Chinese agents stood staring in dismay at losing betting slips. They couldn't understand why this great horse had run such a bad race when they'd been promised a certain percentage. He'd barely managed to finish the course, never mind win.

On Tower Bridge, Rebecca watched warily as the big woman came towards her. Slipping the mobile phone back into her pocket she carefully unlocked the handcuffs from Kim's wrist.

She looked around. There were few people on the bridge, none close by. Except Laura. She stopped in front of them now and Kim finally wriggled free and threw his arms around her. Laura pulled him to her bosom and held his head. She said softly, 'Everything's going to be fine now.'

Over Rebecca's shoulder she could see the two plain-clothes men approaching as arranged and if things were working out Rebecca would be looking at two more coming from the north bank. But Rebecca was staring up at Laura, almost haughtily. Then her look suddenly softened and for a moment Laura thought she was going to say sorry. But she didn't, she just turned to walk away.

Laura said quietly, 'Rebecca ...' and as she turned her blonde head Laura hit her square on the chin with a straight-armed fist. As Rebecca collapsed Laura smiled and said, 'Kung Fu to you, Baby!' Then she laughed out loud and Kim turned to see Rebecca unconscious on the pavement and he smiled too and marvelled at Laura's outrageous laugh as they walked past the two policemen who now ran to crouch over the prostrate woman.

Sixty

Turco hosted the party that night and the high tech SIS boys just loved his spacewars game. McCarthy and Chief Inspector Mills were in good form, with Mac the most relaxed Eddie had ever seen him.

Since he'd got Kim back Eddie had never let him outside of touching distance. Laura had stayed just as close to both of them and all three now sat on the big couch while Eddie told Kim how they'd pulled it off.

'It was mostly down to the Yank, really. When he was doing the demo for Lee Sung he planted a tiny microchip in his watch which not only told us exactly where the guy was at every minute of the day, it also recorded all his conversations so the tape alone should be enough to put him away for about twenty years never mind Grimond's murder, your kidnapping and the attempted fraud.

'As soon as we knew which betting shop

Lee Sung was in it only took minutes for the SIS decoder in that shop alone to be identified and isolated so it was only that one shop that got the false race. All the others were kept live for a prearranged stopping of the clock which would indicate which horse they should be putting Lee Sung's cash on. Then they were switched back to the proper service. So all the Triad stake money went down the drain. McCarthy and Mr Mills set up the police operation and for once everything went sweet as a nut.'

He ruffled Kim's hair. 'Remember it this way. You'll find as you go through life that few things will work out so well.'

Laura said to him, 'You sound just like a very serious big brother!'

Eddie smiled. 'I am, aren't I, Kim?'

Kim just smiled. He'd been through so much he wasn't going to let his guard down. Wasn't going to let himself believe that all the trouble was over. Not for quite a while yet. But Eddie and Laura had promised to take him back up to Alnwick tomorrow. He'd loved it there. And Eddie had said he'd take a few days off now to spend it with him, riding on the beach and through the sandhills. Kim felt a filling warmth at the thought of it and edged himself even closer towards his brother who was close enough on the other side to Laura.

He'd best watch out. Eddie hadn't seen the mean punch she packed.

Before the party broke up, Inspector Mills took a call telling him that Rebecca had confessed and told the full story anyway so there was no doubt now that Lee Sung and his men would go down. Rebecca said she'd co-operated with Lee Sung out of fear. She admitted setting Mattie and Eddie up.

Just before midnight the four who remained in the flat, Turco, Eddie, Laura and Kim, linked hands and, twenty-four hours late, sang Auld Lang Syne and wished each other a Happy New Year.

Eddie and Laura went hand in hand onto the balcony to look at the stars in the clear sky but few were visible. 'Light pollution,' Eddie said.

'I know,' Laura said, still staring upwards. 'Imagine what they'll look like from the beach at Alnwick.'

'Brilliant,' Eddie said quietly, pulling her closer.

They stood for a few minutes then Eddie turned her slowly and kissed her. Warm and soft and long. Their foreheads met gently and they stared into each other's eyes.

Eddie said, 'Shall we go to bed?'

Laura shook her head. 'Not here. There's a special place where I want us to make love for the first time. At dawn.'

'Where?'

'Pack your bags and come with me. I'll show you.'

'Now?'

'Now.'

It was an order. Eddie smiled and they kissed again then turned hand in hand. Laura said, 'Let's get Kim.'

All three travelled in Eddie's car. Turco said he'd arrange for Laura's car to be delivered to her home. Kim slept almost all the way back north while Eddie and Laura talked quietly.

She pressed him to hurry so they'd be there before dawn and in the darkness Eddie smiled at her craziness and wondered why he hadn't seen what was there much sooner.

Kim was still asleep when they reached Alnwick and between them they carried him carefully into the house and put him to bed. Eddie stretched and yawned and put his arm around Laura. She put one around his waist.

'Take me to this special place,' he said, yawning and loosening his tie.

'Okay but I wouldn't start getting

undressed. Not just yet.'

She smiled wickedly. Eddie looked puzzled. Laura opened a huge airing cupboard at the top of the stairs and started pulling out heaps of blankets, piling them into Eddie's arms.

'What the hell are we doing, sleeping on the floor or something?'

'Worse than that.' She kept dragging them out till she too held a pile.

'Come on,' she said and Eddie followed her downstairs shaking his head.

She led him outside then locked the door. 'We'll be gone a while. Kim'll be safe.'

'*Laura!* Where are we going?'

'To that special place.'

'It's bloody freezing! If you think I'm making love in a barn or something ...!'

'Worse than that.' She was walking away from the house now.

'Laura, for God's sake!'

'Oh stop moaning! You big cry baby. Come on, it'll soon be light.'

'Where are we going, you crazy woman?'

'The beach.'

'You're kidding. Tell me you're kidding!'

'No kidding. Hurry up or we'll be late.'

Eddie smiled through his shivers and plodded on with his armful of blankets.

He refused to undress until he was under

every single blanket and the weight of them made undressing almost impossible. But they managed it and they lay in each other's arms on the beach listening to the wind and the sea and watching the diamond sharp stars.

Eddie said, 'How long have you been planning this?'

'Since the last time we were on the beach, walking the horses in the sea, remember?'

He nodded, smiling. 'A lot of water under the bridge since then.'

'A lot of water under the britches too.'

He smiled again then kissed her and as dawn broke over the sea they made love. And if Eddie thought it had been good with Rebecca he realised all it had been was sex. Good sex but sex just the same. With Laura, for the first time in his life he understood the saying, making love. It was wonderful, completely different from sex.

They lay still in each other's arms again as the sky grew ever brighter. Warm now, Laura said, 'Lovemaking always makes me hungry. Couldn't you just murder a Chinese?'

'Is this as good as the jokes get? Who writes your stuff?'

'All my own work. Wanna hear some more?'

'Later. Let's go and have breakfast.'

'We need to swim first.'

'No chance!'

'You mean fat chance. Freeze there or freeze here!' and Laura rolled away from him dragging the blankets. Grabbing as many as she could she set off running towards the sea swirling them behind her.

'Laura! Jeez, I'm freezing!'

Her whoops came back to him on the cold wind and, naked, he raced after her following her deep footprints in the sand. She let the blankets go and one flew either side of him as he caught her knee-deep in the icy surf. They fell screaming in shock and joy and revelation as the ocean opened and with it, for Eddie and Laura, the whole world.

Author's Note

If you are unaware of Eddie Malloy's family history I apologise for not tying things up in this book. To have done so would have been to spoil the enjoyment of new readers who may now like to read the others in the Eddie Malloy series. Those who do may wish to consider reading them in the order they were written: *Warned Off*, *Hunted*, *Running Scared* and *Blood Ties*.

Anyway, thanks for reading this one. I hope you enjoyed it.

This Large Print Book for the Partially sighted, who cannot read normal print, is published under the auspices of

THE ULVERSCROFT FOUNDATION